SERVANTS OF SATAN—OR
WARRIORS OF WIND AND SUN?

Bettylou had not even struggled when the raiding party kidnapped her from the Adobe of the Righteous. Sentenced to death, did it matter who her destroyers were? But now, held prisoner in the midst of this enemy camp, she was beginning to remember the stories her people told—stories of fierce, murderous tribes of sinful thieves. They were said to be true Servants of Satan, headhunters, cannibals, drinkers of blood. . . .

Could her captors be these terrible fiends? Had she been taken to provide these warriors with a cannibal feast?

Great Science Fiction by Robert Adams from SIGNET

A WOMAN OF THE HORSECLANS

—◦•◦—

A HORSECLANS NOVEL

by
ROBERT ADAMS

A SIGNET BOOK
NEW AMERICAN LIBRARY
TIMES MIRROR

Copyright © 1983 by Robert Adams

All rights reserved

 SIGNET TRADEMARK REG. U.S. PAT. OFF. AND FOREIGN COUNTRIES
REGISTERED TRADEMARK—MARCA REGISTRADA
HECHO EN CHICAGO, U.S.A.

SIGNET, SIGNET CLASSIC, MENTOR, PLUME, MERIDIAN and NAL BOOKS
are published by The New American Library, Inc.,
1633 Broadway, New York, New York 10019

First Printing, November, 1983

1 2 3 4 5 6 7 8 9

PRINTED IN THE UNITED STATES OF AMERICA

This twelfth book of HORSECLANS
is dedicated to:

The First Lady of Pern, Anne McCaffrey, esteemed colleague;
the littlest princess, Tracy Weiner;
the second-littlest princess, my niece Cherie;
Rhoda Katerinsky and all my other friends at *MS* magazine;
Alfie Bester, one of the finest living talents in our field;
Lydia and A. E. Van Vogt;
Laurence Janifer;
Roy Torgeson; and all the folk of the Horseclans Societies.

CHAPTER I

Bettylou Hanson set down the heavy, smelly slop bucket and paused for a moment on the upper porch of the Building of the Son to gaze through the deepening dusk across the neat acres of gardens immediately surrounding the Abode of the Chosen. Beyond the gardens lay the broad ring of rippling grain fields and, beyond them, the fenced and always guarded pastures from whence the herdsmen were even now driving the sleek, lowing cattle. The herd guard dogs—big, prick-eared and long-haired beasts, bred up over many generations from the packs of wild dogs that once had roamed the plains—nipped at the heels of the cattle, easily dodging retaliatory hooves and horn swipes.

The girl strained for a moment to see if her blue eyes could pick out the tall, broad-shouldered form of Harod Norman. Then she shook her shaven head and, sighing, picked up the odoriferous bucket again, reflecting that that part of her life was forever gone, had died on the winter night on which the Elder Claxton, full of the Passion of God, had taken her maidenhead, died when her secret sinfulness had caused God to see to her quickening by the Elder's seed.

She realized that for her life of any sort could be measured in mere months of time. Immediately the babe she bore was weaned, she would be scourged one last time, then would be driven out beyond the farthest pastures, onto the open prairie itself, to die of hunger or thirst or wild beasts. Through His Holy Servant, the Elder Claxton, God had made clear to all the world her secret and most heinous Sin. And so would her final disposition be that of all the other Sinful since first His Chosen folk had survived God's fearful Time of the Judg-

1

ments and banded themselves together in the First Abode under the Holy guidance of the very first Elder.

For as long as she could remember, Bettylou Hanson had heard over and over the story of how, long, long ago, the land had supported a vast multitude of folk, most of them dwelling in huge concentrations called "cities."

These "cities" were very hotbeds of Sin, Elder Claxton attested, and all of the inhabitants of them spent their entire lives in the worship of Evil in all of its dreadful attributes. Therefore, it was only fitting and proper that these Sinful Ones—who had viciously mocked and savagely persecuted the few, widely scattered Holy Ones since time out of mind—should have been the first to suffer pain and death in the Time of the Judgment.

Some few of these Sinful Ones—the luckier, possibly less sinful, could the real facts ever be known—died quickly of the rain of cleansing fire visited upon them; but the vast majority were not so blessed with a quick, clean death. The Sinful died in their millions over a period of weeks and months of a few new, terrifying diseases, a diversity of older diseases, starvation or simple fear—fear, Elder Claxton had always pointed out, of the just and terrible punishment of God foreordained and earned many times over by their sinfulness and their unremitting persecution of their spiritual betters who had of course been the ancestors of the Claxtons, the Hansons and all the other families of the Chosen People of the Lord God.

But even though the land had been long ago cleansed of those millions of Sinful Ones, Sin itself was not dead. Even among the Chosen People, the seed was sometimes tainted with traces of the ancient wickednesses. And, as Woman had been the very first evil temptress of godly Man (of which great and eternally unforgivable Sin Woman was reminded for the most of her life once each moon by discomfort and shameful, unclean, milk-curdling bloodiness), so too was Woman the carrier of the tainted seed of Sin and Wickedness.

And so, in every succeeding generation of the Chosen since the awful Time of the Divine Judgments and the Cleansing of the Land, had the Holy Seed of the Blessed Elders sought and found and rooted out those women who hid, harbored and were contaminated by the Seed of Sin.

Bettylou, however, was the very first Hanson in whom the

foul taint had ever surfaced, so she could feel no true anger at her family's recent mistreatment of her, for she was the living mark of their disgrace—her shaven head, crimson-dyed scalp and swelling belly ever-present reminders of their now-sullied name, their scandal and dishonor.

Why, she had asked herself over and over again in the last half-year, why her, Bettylou Hanson? Elder Claxton came unto every girl of the Chosen sometime in the first year after her initial moon-blood; so had his father done and his father's sire and likewise for all the generations back to the gathering of the Chosen and the building of the first Abode of the Righteous. The injection into their maturing bodies of the Elder's Holy Seed was simply another part of growing up in the Abode; every adult woman had experienced the like from the present Elder or his father, yet not one in a score suffered more than momentarily.

Only in those rare cases where Sin had its foul lair within her flesh did a girl conceive of the Elder. A year and a half ago it had been Sydell Manchester; now, it was Bettylou Hanson.

The last edge of the sun-disk sank below the hazy western horizon, but Bettylou's labors never ceased. Through the length of the dusk and even into the full dark of the night, the pregnant girl stumbled down the long flight of wooden steps to the ground with full buckets of garbage or sewage, dumped their noisome contents into the long trench wherein the waste would all be fermented into fertilizer for fields and gardens, then rinsed the emptied containers with water from the stock well before trudging her long, weary way back up the twenty cubits or more of steep stairs to the residence levels for another slop bucket.

When the herdsmen had byred their cattle safe from night-prowling predators, had—with the indispensable aid of their dogs—chivied the blatting sheep into the strong-walled, roofed-over fold, dropped the massive bars that secured the livestock from easy access, then fed and kenneled the dogs, they gathered about the well troughs, laughing, splashing at each other and joking while they washed.

Bettylou set down her just-emptied wooden bucket and stood silently in a patch of near-darkness near the foot of the stairs, waiting for the men to finish their evening ablutions before she made use of the water troughs to rinse the bucket of its fecal foulness.

While she stood, she thought. Why had God created her so? With a pretty face and well-formed body? She had not conceived of the Elder the first time he took her, and had she been as ugly and misshapen as flat-chested Lizzie Scriber or a mountain of fat like Gail Collier, that once would have been the only time that Elder Claxton would have come to her.

But, of course, feminine beauty was well known to be a probable symptom of a creature that harbored Sin, and so the Elders always revisited such girls at least once each year following the initial visitation until those so seductively endowed were safely wed. Elder Claxton's seventh visit to Bettylou had proved her downfall.

"Oh, why, Lord God, did You not see me born without that taint of the ancient Evil?" The girl mourned silently, to herself. She would not have thought of praying for any deliverance from her present travails and her approaching doom, for she believed all that she had been taught and so felt herself to be no less than deserving of all the cruelties that had been and would be heaped upon her Sin-harboring body. Evil must always suffer and then die, and that meant that Evil Bettylou Hanson must suffer and die, for such had always been the course of events in the Abodes of the Holy Ones, the People Chosen of God.

Their washing done, the men trooped past the silent girl, feet squishing in hide brogans, water dripping from beards and hair onto already-soaked shirts. The older men pointedly ignored Bettylou, the younger ones—Short Isaac and Amos and Esau, Fat Gabriel and Caleb and Aaron, boys with whom she had played as toddler and child—carefully avoided her eyes, and one and all fell silent until they were well past her and on the steep stairs.

But not big, tall Harod Norman, he who was to have been the husband of Bettylou Hanson . . . once. His brown eyes met her hazel eyes, briefly, and she thought she saw pain in their depths. But then the pain—if pain it truly had been— was replaced with an utter and unmistakable disgust and the massive young man just stomped past her, pausing only long enough to spit on her upraised face before setting his big feet to the steps.

Harod, her Harod, her irredeemably lost Harod. Bettylou

continued to watch his big-boned form, rising head and thick-muscled shoulders above both older and younger herdsmen, up the full height of the staircase. There at the top waited Sarah Tuttle, with the flames of the just-lit torches glinting on her long, thick black braids. Harod easily lifted Sarah from off her feet, high enough that he might soundly buss both her cheeks and her dark-red lips as well before they two went off arm in arm with several other couples.

Watching, dumbly, from below, in her shorn shame, with the slop bucket stinking at her bare feet, Bettylou's burning tears mingled with Harod's scornful spittle on her cheek.

For the half of an hour more, through the deepening dusk, the gravid girl labored up and down the stairs, bearing heavy buckets of garbage down and empty, rinsed buckets up, proceeding now mostly by feel of fingers and bare toes and familiarity, for little of the torchlight from above reached stairs or ground, and torches were not normally burned at ground level.

The last bucketload was of assorted bones, mostly. A handful at the time, she picked them all out and threw them over the high fence into the kennel run, her actions precipitating an immediate noise of snarlings and snappings and growlings from within. Then, stepping gingerly lest her still-tender feet encounter the chance sharp stone, she crossed to the trench and dumped the residue of the bone bucket atop the rest of the waste. It was while she was plodding back toward the water troughs to rinse the bucket that she smelled that first, strange smell.

It was not an unpleasant or noxious smell, but it was most unfamiliar, being compounded as it was of smoke and cured hides, horse sweat and man sweat, with a strong hint of crushed herbs and sour milk, all commingled.

Then, beside the narrow, high-silled door that pierced one of the larger doors of the horse stable, she dimly perceived the shape of what she at first took to be a stripling. The figure beckoned to her, wordlessly, and she set down the bucket and paced over to him, assuming that he had been sent from above to set her to shoveling up and hauling out manure or some such similar task, before she would be allowed to finally wolf her nightly bowl of scraps and seek her hovel near the sheepfold.

But as she neared the figure, it became clear to her wondering eyes that it was no boy, but rather a short, slender, wiry man. He appeared to be no more than one or two fingers taller than was Bettylou herself. Shorter he was than even Short Isaac, a full span—possibly even two spans—under the four cubits which was the average height of adult men of the Chosen. Nor did the short man own the big bones and thick, rolling muscles which were the heritage of men of the Abodes of the Righteous.

But he lacked not for strength, as she found when he reached out and clasped a callused hand about her wrist to draw her insistently toward the barely ajar door.

The girl neither struggled nor screamed, but allowed herself to be drawn to and through the doorway and into the stable. Since God had turned His Holy Face from her, had caused to be quickened the cursed Sinfulness within her body, there was nothing worse that could possibly befall her. The thought passed briefly through her mind that the man might well kill her with the long, broad knife cased at his belt, but she knew that she would be set out on the prairie soon enough to starve or be mauled to death by wild beasts, so she could only consider a quicker death to be a mercy.

Upon the highest of the three tiers of porches, more than thirty-five cubits above the ground, Solomon Claxton, youngest son of the Elder of this Abode, had just seen to the proper placements of the first shift of night guards. Now, in the guardroom, alone save for the snoring second shift, he had just seated himself at the table by the lamp and opened his ancient, well-worn bible when the dogs set up a ferocious clamor from the kennel.

Solomon was reading this night from the Book of Judges, his thick lips shaping out each word painfully as his horny finger drew his eyes to it. But the prematurely gray farmer had barely commenced when one of the section leaders of the first shift, Ehud Manchester, strode hurriedly into the long, narrow room. They two were about of an age and were friends of long years standing.

"Sol," said Ehud without preamble, "it's suthin goldurned funny goin on downstairs. Hear them dogs, don'tcha? Reckon I oughta take fellers with guns down to see 'bout it?"

The thought flitted through Solomon Claxton's mind that for all that a man could not have a better man beside him when he chanced to be fighting off godless, heathen nomad raiders or a pack of starveling winter wolves, Patriarch Manchester's son, Ehud, was at times somewhat slow of wits.

But he smiled and reassured his old friend. "Ehud, as I came upstairs, I saw the Scarlet Woman lugging a bucket of bones down. You know how the dogs always snarl and fight for a while over bones. Besides, you might recall what my father, the Elder, had for to say about sending armed parties down at night."

Ehud did recollect those words and what had precipitated them, and, if his memory had needed prodding, he had certain personal touchstones to awaken recall. In the dead of the hard winter just past, a guard had claimed to have seen a horde of fur-clad nomad raiders creeping across the snowy fields toward the barns and storehouses. A cranklight had been set up, and when its beam had swept over the nearer fields, several other men had definitely seen *something* moving.

However, when a hastily assembled and armed party had reached the ground, nothing was visible amid the swirling, drifting snow, whereupon the ninny commanding them had split them into three parties and sent them off into differing directions, hunting they knew not what, well armed, in visibility that ranged from poor to nil.

Two men had been killed—one of them Ehud's younger brother—and two more wounded—one of these being Ehud himself—before one ill-advised party discovered that they were battling the other two parties in the deep snow of the pitch-black stableyard.

The next day, spoor and droppings of a bear had been found in a sheltered spot close by to where the something had been seen on the tragic preceding night, and Elder Claxton had then ordered that no more parties would set out from the Abode of nights lacking his personal order to do so.

Solomon closed his bible, pushed back from the table and stood up, saying, "But we ain't none of us up here for to take no chances, Ehud. We'll git us out a cranklight and do 'er right, heah?"

The six cranklights were the most ancient things in the Abode, far and away older than the Abode itself. They had been brought, long, long ago, from the First Abode, somewhere far away to the north and east, to be installed for a few generations in the new Abodes built by colonists from the original. Then, when these newer Abodes had prospered and multiplied to the point of overcrowding, more colonists had gone out to build yet newer Abodes and had had shared out to them cranklights and rifles and such other needful items.

All adult men and even a few of the women knew how to set the devices up and properly operate them, but no one now alive knew aught of constructing new ones—a talent which had been lost long ago, along with the skills for making new barrels for the rifles. Repairs were sometimes effected by replacing the worn part with an identical part from the dwindling supply of spares or from one of the ever-increasing number of worn-out cranklights.

Solomon Claxton himself supervised the careful removal of the closest cranklight from out the special closet that housed it. He saw to its setting up in the carved wooden swivel socket in the rail of the porch, personally connected the power box to the light, then set a husky young farmer to cranking the handles on each side of the box.

First, a coal-red spot commenced to glow from somewhere deep beneath the thick, polished glass lens. As the crank man maintained the steady, rhythmic cranking, the spot became red-gold, then yellow-gold, then silver-gold, then silver, silver-white, and soon was become so bright that no man could look directly into it without a degree of pain and a long period of near-blindness.

Taking the handles of the lamp, Solomon swept the far-reaching beam out across gardens and the fields beyond. Expecting to see nothing, he was deeply surprised when the beam picked up a clear movement. His scalp prickled and his mouth took on a touch of dryness.

"Cat!" Ehud almost shouted in Solomon's ear. "Long-tooth cat, Sol, a dang *big* 'un too, moving th'ough the wheat, yonder. See 'im?"

Solomon had good eyesight, he saw the beast too, and it surely was a big cat, even for a specimen of its Devil-spawned ilk—a good two cubits at the shoulder, in fine flesh, with a fawn-colored pelt and the white fangs that extended well below the lower jaw. Had it been coming toward the buildings of the Abode, he most certainly would have awakened his father, the Elder, and then led a party out against the huge predator—one of the most dangerous of all the wild beasts that plagued man here on the verge of the vast, grassy wilderness.

But the monstrous feline clearly was not bound for the Abode and presently harbored no designs upon the beasts below or their owners above; rather was it pacing slowly, deliberately across the expanse of the rippling wheat field at a right angle to the buildings. He had done much hunting in his lifetime, had Solomon Claxton, and he knew well that the big beast would not be moving so slowly and calmly were it not carrying a good bellyful of meat.

He let go the handle of the cranklight and turned just in time to see Ehud settle his shoulder firmly against the buttplate of a long swivel-rifle, shake a bit of priming powder into the pan, position the frizzen, then start to draw back the flint.

Moving fast, Solomon threw open the just-primed pan and brushed out more of the fine powder, then slammed down the hinged wooden breech cover over the action of the piece.

"No, Ehud," he told his friend gently, not in a tone of reprimand. "Not tonight. A gunshot would awaken every soul in the Abode. You'd rob them all of their sleep to no real account, and the Elder would assuredly wax wroth.

"Come sunup, the hunters will track that cat, kill him if he's denning dangerously near to the Abode. Never fear, you saw him first, so you'll get the pelt if the Elder doesn't want it. You know I'll look out for my oldest friend, don't you?

"Now, I'll see to the putting up of the light, and you grab a man to reshroud the rifle."

CHAPTER II

In the close darkness of the horse barn, with straw under her bare feet and the short, wiry, odd-smelling man beside her, poor Bettylou Hanson felt no fear, only a numb, dumb acceptance that what would here befall her would surely befall her. The man still held her arm clasped firmly in one hand, but he did not grasp so tightly as to hurt her. Then she felt his other hand rove lingeringly over her swelling breasts, then move downward, stopping and resting upon the distension of her abdomen.

"Hairless woman," he hissed into her ear, his warm breath laden with an odor of milk and curds, "how many moons before you foal?"

"Four moons, maybe part of another," Bettylou answered dully.

Abruptly, there were two more men close beside Bettylou and her captor. One of them, no taller or stockier than he who held her, jammed some kind of rag into her mouth, using his other hand to force and hold open her jaws in order to effect his purpose, then a strip of cloth was knotted tightly behind her head to hold the gag in place, while at the same time another man was behind her lashing her wrists together with a cord or thong of some description.

She was led, bound and gagged, among a group of horses and mules, and strong arms raised her easily to the withers of one of the beasts before a mounted man. Though this rider grasped her tightly with his right arm and hand, she somehow sensed that he meant her no slightest harm, that his grasp was as much intended to steady her as for any more sinister purpose.

The ponderous bar came up with a shrill, protesting squeal,

10

and then the high, broad door swung wide agape, opening the way for the dozen or so raiders to ride out on the choicer of the horses and mules they were lifting this night while leading the rest, these others hurriedly packed with such gear and hardware as had been easy to hand in the stable and adjoining areas. Those equines they were rejecting for one reason or another they drove out before them.

The last raider, before he left the stable, used flint and steel to light a torch, whirled it about his head until it was blazing brightly, then rode up and down the length of the now-empty stable igniting piles of straw, bales of hay and the like before trotting out to join his comrades.

The barking, howling, yelping and snarling of the kenneled dogs had never ceased; and now, as the riders kneed their mounts over to cluster about the man bearing the blazing torch, the shouts and curses of men were added to the canine clamor.

Bettylou Hanson heard the deep-throated *thrrruum* of bow-strings all around her and saw half a score of fiery red-yellow streaks mount upward from the stableyard to sink into and commence to lick avidly at as many sections of the residence levels of the two nearer buildings. Seemingly directly over her head, a swivel-rifle boomed, throwing a lance of fire for a good five cubits beyond its muzzle. Far back, from the highest porch of the Building of the Father, there were two more reports, and the girl heard close by her ear a humming like that of some monstrous bee.

The raider archers followed the fire arrows with a couple of volleys of shafts aimed at the black silhouettes outlined by the lamps, the torches and the leaping, crackling flames now throwing yellow-white sheets of destruction across whole lengths of wooden wall and nibbling here and there at roofings. Some hideous shrieks and several thuds of fallen bodies testified to the skilled accuracy of these raiders, and Bettylou could not but marvel at how such deadly aim was maintained by men loosing from the backs of nervous and restive horses.

The Hanson girl's last, departing glimpse of the Abode, wherein she had been born and had lived all of her young life to date, was of smoke billowing out of the emptied stable which was the ground floor of the Building of the Son, while the upper levels of both it and the adjoining Building of the Holy Ghost looked to be completely wreathed in leaping flames. A few more swivel-rifles boomed to no effect as the raiders galloped through the gardens and across the grain fields, but all these were from well above ground level.

They rode on at a steady, easy pace for about a mile as the moon emerged from her cloudy shroud to light their way through the last of the farthest pastures and thence into the flat and brushy wilderness toward the line of copses that marked the verge of the prairie.

On the far side of a low hill in the sheep pasture, some score of small, big-headed horses stood about cropping the moon-silvered grass, while a brace of men who looked akin to and were dressed and accoutered like her captors squatted, grinning, one of them holding a sheep, a young ram, by a tether.

Bettylou was amazed at the silence of the raiders. Not a single word was exchanged among any of the men, while the grazing horses ceased to feed almost as one and rapidly ambled over to stand still as girths were tightened and the men mounted them, ready now to lead all of the beasts stolen from the Abode of the Righteous. The ram blatted piteously just before a sharp raider knife slashed open his throat; the blood was carefully caught and shared out equally between all of the men. Bettylou was offered a horn cup, but she paled and gagged; she knew that she would certainly have spewed had there been aught save pure emptiness in her stomach.

Still without a word spoken, the raider drank the hot blood himself and turned away just as another approached bearing a greased hide bag from which he took a lump of whitish-gray and very strong-smelling cheese. This lump he held at the bound girl's mouth until she finally took a bite of it then a larger bite, then all of the remainder of the lump.

Tied into the saddle of one of the captured horses—Solomon Claxton's hunting horse, God-sent, she noted—chewing at her mouthful of the delicious cheese, Bettylou saw the pair who had captured the stray ram flop the still-quivering carcass onto its back, open it and rough-dress it, helping themselves while they worked to the raw liver, heart and kidneys of the sheep as well as to the blood that collected in the body cavity. The gutted ram was lashed onto another of the stolen horses, and leading it and all the others, the raiders set out at the same slow, easy pace toward the western prairie.

As dawn began to streak the eastern skyline with muted

reds and oranges and yellows, the raiding party and their loot—equine and inanimate and human—had advanced well out onto the endless expanse of grasses. Exhausted by the long ride, Bettylou Hanson drooped, her chin sunk upon her chest, no longer even trying to really ride and letting the hide thongs knotted about her legs and body keep her in the saddle of the big, powerful gelding, God-sent. But tired as she was, she could not sleep for the ache of her bruised, abused bottom and the discomfort of inner thighs rubbed raw and incessantly stung by salt sweat.

She was dimly aware that someone was riding now beside her, did not really take notice of the fact until a rough, callused hand lifted her chin to better view her face, then began to untie the thongs securing her numb hands.

They had been moving steadily southwestward, but then, as soon as her hands were freed, the entire party turned almost due north, coming presently to a trickling watercourse and following this to its confluence with another, larger one some few hundred yards from the marshy shore of a small lake.

In a sizable clearing carpeted in short grass—rare, this far out on the prairie, and of a bright, intense green—and surrounded by a dense stand of trees—cottonwood, elm, elder, basswood, walnut and, nearing the lakeshore, huge, droop-branched willows—the raiding party reined up, dismounted and began to unpack and unsaddle. Their own small horses they left unfettered, free to roam where they would, but those recently lifted from the Abode they made haste to hobble firmly, lest they essay a return from whence they had just been brought at such a cost of long, careful planning and deadly danger.

Bettylou was untied and lifted down from the saddle of the gelding with a rough gentleness, allowed to drink her fill from a skin of fresh, bitingly cold brook water. Then one of the raiders led her over to the shade of an elm, tied her ankle to its trunk with a long rawhide riata, indicated that she should sit there upon the sward, then left her to her own devices along with the waterskin and a leather bag of the strong, tasty, whitish cheese.

Munching at the cheese and sipping from the waterskin, the girl stretched muscles stiff and sore from the long hours in the saddle and watched the smoothly efficient activities of these

strange, silent little men. Thus far, the only words she had
heard any of them speak had been addressed to her; they
never exchanged a single utterance between themselves or to
horse or mule, yet they went about the communal-effort tasks
of setting up camp without pause or miscue.

After unsaddling but before picketing, all of the captive
horses and mules were led in groups down to the brookside
and there watered, then briskly rubbed down with handfuls of
the bigger, coarser grasses brought in from the encroaching
verge of the tall-grass prairie.

This accomplished, the raiders posted guards, gathered
wood, built a fire and finished dressing the sheep carcass for
cooking. Bettylou noted how carefully the inedible portions
of the sheep were retained—the stomach bags and the large
intestines emptied of contents, turned inside out and washed
in the brook, thicker, longer sinews painstakingly separated
from bones and muscles, scraped and washed, then hung up
on branches to air-dry; the small, pointed, black hooves were
put aside and the inner surface of the hide was scraped clean
of clinging bits of fat and flesh.

They set the legs of the sheep aside to roast, but the rest of
the carcass was reduced by flashing knives to a pile of meat
and fat and gristle which was heaped atop the offal— lung,
small intestines, various glands and larger veins and arteries.
The defleshed bones were all cracked and placed in a water-
filled caldron along with the sheep's head and the contents of
three or four pouches produced by as many of the raiders,
plus the partially digested herbiage that had been removed
from the stomachs of the beast.

When she watched this penultimate addition, it was all that
Bettylou could do to repress the urge to vomit up the fine
cheese, and she vowed to herself then and there that come
what might, she would never, could never partake of so
barbaric, so nauseous a mess.

And, in her eyes, it got worse. While most of the raiders
lay snoring or lazed or sat working sporadically at sundry
small tasks, and the stew-pot began to send the first tendrils
of steam aloft, hunters came strolling in from individual
forays in the morning coolness. One bore a small, straight-
horned antelope; two others had killed large hares; and these
were dressed, skinned, butchered and added to the pot; and so
too was a large fish one of the men had caught barehanded at

the mouth of the brook. But meaty portions of each slain creature were always added to the pile of mutton and sheep scraps. Bettylou wondered why. Were these for a burnt offering to their false gods? (After all, the gods of these raiders were most assuredly false, for of all living folk, only the Chosen worshiped God Almighty.) But she dared not draw their attention to her by asking.

Once she had been tied to the tree and provided with water and cheese, she had been afforded all the attention and obvious scrutiny they had afforded the hobbled four-legged captives. Very soon after the man who had tied her and brought the food had left her, Bettylou had repaired behind the thick trunk of the ancient elm and lifted her worn, torn, filthy scarlet smock—the only garment that such as she were allowed by the Elder and the Patriarchs of the families—and squatted long enough to empty her painfully full bladder. But if her brief absence was noted by her captors, such was not apparent upon her return to view.

Of a sudden, Bettylou recalled that rare visitors from other Abodes of the Righteous had been said to have spoken of fierce, murderous tribes of sinful thieves, who called themselves the Folk of the Horse or some such name. Saturated with Sin, they were said to be true Servants of Satan, headhunters, cannibals, drinkers of blood rather than water, filthy, stinking folk who never washed and who wore their clothing until it rotted off. These same visitors had averred, she had been told, that the Satanic savages lacked the ability of speech and made no other sounds save screams and roars and screeches like any other wild beasts. Could her captors be . . .? Had she, Bettylou Hanson, been taken to provide a cannibal feast? Was this horror the final punishment of God for her Sin?

Briefly, she quivered in newfound terror, but then her keen mind took charge. Yes, the raiders did drink fresh, hot blood, but they drank water, as well; they might be headhunters, cannibals or both, these facts remained to be proved or disproved, but up to now, they had offered no violence or any real ill treatment to Bettylou. Indeed, they one and all had treated her far more kindly than had her own folk of late, at least since she had been proved one of the Accursed of God.

As regarded those other disgusting attributes of the legendary barbarians, Bettylou could not call any she had been near

filthy. Yes indeed, they did smell very different from the
boys and men around whom she had grown up, but they
looked no grubbier and smelled no worse than any farmer or
herder or hunter of the Abode might look or smell between
his monthly baths.

And as she watched, this particular matter was resolved, as
by twos and threes, raiders trooped down to the brook bank,
stripped to bare skin and dived in to swim and frolic like
boys, shouting and splashing for a while, then squatting in the
shallows to wash their dusty, sweat-tacky trousers and shirts.

When the raiders stripped to swim and wash, Bettylou
noted that although their faces, hands and other regularly
exposed skin was nut-brown from sun and weather, the bodies of most were as fair as was her own, all save one man
who was so different in so many ways as to make her think
him sprung of a different race than the others.

Where they were fair, he was of a light-olive skin tone.
Few of the other raiders were much taller than was she, but
this man towered to better than four cubits, she reckoned. His
bones, too, were heavier than those of the other raiders,
though not quite so heavy as those of the men of the Chosen.
And where men of the Chosen all developed thick, round,
rolling musculature, this tall man and most of the smaller
ones were equipped with flat muscles. Moreover, the tall
man's hair was as black as a crow's wing, though streaked at
the temples with strands of gray. He had not yet come close
enough for her to see the color of his eyes.

Bettylou had decided finally that the pile of meat and
innards was really and truly a sacrifice of some kind, when
those for whom it was intended slipped silently out of the
woods behind her to claim it from the heaving, crawling,
buzzing carpet of metallic-hued flies.

The girl sprang to her feet, shrieked but the once before an
excess of terror froze her throat. Then her eyes rolled upward
in their sockets and she slumped bonelessly to the ground.

The bigger, dark man, he who had fired the stable, paced
over to where Tim Krooguh crouched over the Dirtman girl,
concern writ plainly upon his face. Laying a hand on the
shoulder of the wiry clansman, he spoke aloud.

"I'm sorry, Tim. I should either have mindspoken the cats
to come into camp slowly so that she could come to see that
they were not dangerous to anyone here, or beamed assurance

into her mind beforehand, as I did on the first part of the ride, last night. But I'm tired and . . . Oh, well, what's done is now done. Let's just hope the poor child hasn't been shocked into premature labor.''

Two huge felines strolled over to stand flanking the taller man, communicating silently, mind to mind, even while licking broad tongues absently at bits of meat and spots of blood on their furry muzzles.

''We, too, are sorry, Uncle Milo. We did not mean to so frighten cat brother Tim Krooguh's captured female.''

The tall man just shrugged. ''As I just told Tim, what's now done is done, irrevocable. But it was all my fault, really, not any misdeed of yours. What news from our cat-sister? Do the Dirtmen make to follow us?''

The average prairiecat could send its thoughts ranging over far more distance than any human telepath could expect to either send or receive; this was but one of the talents that had made the human-feline alliance of the prairiecats and the Horseclans a very valuable one.

Since first this unique breed of great cats had come to live among the clans some fourscore years agone, they had helped their two-leg ''brothers'' to either exterminate or absorb the vast majority of other tribes of nomads upon the prairies, plains and high plains, so that now young warriors could be blooded only through means of raiding the permanent settlements of Dirtmen—the despised, alien farmers who had begun several generations ago to encroach upon the prairie here and there, coming from older settlements in the east, the southeast and the northeast to plant colonies, fell trees, erect permanent buildings, burn off the tall grasses, dam or divert streams and bring the dark soil under the merciless sway of their ox-drawn, iron-bladed plows.

The larger of the two cats—a mature, red-brown male, with a pair of upper canines between three and four inches in length—had seated himself close beside the tall man's leg. With his long, thick tail curled about to rest upon his widespread forepaws, he commenced to lick his chest fur, mindspeaking the while in answer.

''No, Uncle Milo, Mother-of-killers says that most of the craven Dirtmen are fighting the fires in their great yurts of wood and stone, they and their females and even their cubs. Some few are trying to round up the stock you two-legs drove out and this cat and Flopears scattered so thoroughly last night.

"She wishes to know how much longer she should watch the silly Dirtmen. She says that the noises they constantly make hurt her ears and that the unholy stink of them sickens her."

The tall man scratched his scalp, beaming his thoughts. "Even if the bastards find our trail quickly, the distance we covered last night will take the likes of them close to two full days to traverse, and by tomorrow's dawn, we'll be back safe in the clan camps. Tell our cat-sister that she can now forget the Dirtmen."

Flopears—an immature male of lighter color than Elkbane, the older male, but with big bones and the outsize paws and head which presaged the growth looming just ahead in time— did not have ears that were at all floppy. But the name was an old and most honorable name, and he had been granted it to replace his cub name of Steakbone. It was most unusual to grant a warrior-cat name to a less than mature feline, but Flopears had earned it in full measure the previous year when, barely more than a big, gangly cub, on night herd guard, he had slain three full-grown wolves.

This youngest cat was the first to notice the signs of returning consciousness in the female Dirtman captive and without order began to beam soothing, formless thoughts into her awakening mind. While so doing, he noted with mild surprise that her mind was that of an incipient mindspeaker, an inexperienced and completely untrained telepath.

Bettylou Hanson opened her eyes to see the freckled face— even more freckled than her own—of the man who had tied her to the elm tree hovering over her, concern and worry evident upon it and shining from the blue-green eyes under the thick auburn brows.

Glancing to her left, she could see the bigger, darker, black-haired man squatting between two monstrous long-fanged cats. Although she clearly recalled screaming and then losing consciousness when those two cats had so suddenly leaped into the midst of the camp from out of the woods behind her, she could not now imagine just why she had then been so in fear of them.

It was like last night; in her mind she once more felt that

sense of an utter rightness, of comfort, freedom from any danger, total absence of fear of those men and their cats.

The bigger man spoke, his words understandable Mehrikan, but with slight differences in accent and pronunciation of words. "What is your name, child?"

"Bettylou, Honored Elder, Bettylou Hanson," she replied, rendering him the title automatically, for although he did not appear to be so old as was Elder Claxton, he too radiated that same, silent, unexpressed and inexpressible air of natural leadership. Then she calmly questioned him.

"Honored Elder, are you all of the heathen rovers? Do you cut off folks' heads and then eat the bodies?"

The tall man smiled fleetingly. "We all are Horseclansmen, Bettylou. I am called Milo Morai. While some few of the more southerly clans do take the heads of and mutilate the dead bodies of their foemen—which practices they learned from an even more southerly people, the Mexicans—Clans Krooguh and Skaht do not, and it is their young men who make up this raiding party of mine.

"Despite all of the half-truths, exaggerations and outright lies that your folk tell of our folk, no one of the clans is yet sunk to cannibalism."

He jokingly mindspoke, "Unless members of the Clan of Cats are taking to munching manflesh on the sly . . .?"

Elkbane beamed aggrievedly, "Please, Uncle Milo, don't think things so unpleasant, so sickening, so soon after I've eaten that cold mutton. If you could only imagine just how foul is the taste of two-leg blood, you could not then be so cruel to your cat-brothers."

"But how . . .?" Bettylou half-whispered to herself in consternation. Then, aloud, she asked, "Please, Elder Morai, did . . . could I have struck my head when I fell? Though your lips never moved, I could have . . . I . . . I thought I heard you talking somehow to that biggest cat . . . and him *answering* you!"

"She is a mindspeaker, Uncle Milo," put in Flopears, "though I doubt she ever has used that ability before today."

Bettylou saw broad smiles appear both on the face of Elder Morai and on that freckled one of the auburn-haired younger man. Then, although his lips were unmoving still, the Elder was once more speaking . . . no, not really speaking. But she could hear . . . no, not really hear, but she knew exactly what he was saying . . . no, *thinking*.

"Just so, my child," came the Elder's beaming. "Thoughts are transmitted far faster and much more accurately by this way, that we Horseclansfolk call 'mindspeak,' than by oral means. Also, it is the only really effective way of communicating with prairiecats or horses, and there are a few other animals, wild animals, with whom a strong mindspeaker can converse, as well. I sense that you possess powerful but presently quiescent mindspeak abilities, child. Therefore, after we all have eaten, Tim and I and a few others will begin to show you how to bring them to the surface, to properly make use of them."

By sunup of the next morning, when the returning raiders came in sight of the grazing herds surrounding the two-clan camp, Bettylou Hanson had been mindspoken by all of the raiders, all three of the cats and several of the horses, as well. Moreover, she had discovered to her bubbling delight that she could answer just as silently, so she was feeling safe and comfortable and very much at home among her erstwhile captors even without the reassuring beams of Milo and the cats.

She still wore her red dress. It was somewhat more faded now from a thorough washing in the brook, but one of the raiders had skillfully mended all of the rips and tears. However, that was no longer her only item of attire; her feet and her lower legs were now protected by a gifted spare pair of Horseclans boots, into which were tucked the legs of a pair of baggy homespun trousers. They were the first breeches of any sort that Bettylou had ever worn, and she was not certain that she liked them, although they were, she easily admitted to herself, invaluable protection from the cutting blades of the tall grasses through which they had had to ride for much of the journey from the daylight camp.

By way of the lessons in mindspeak, she had learned many things. She had learned that the freckle-faced, auburn-haired man who had captured her and who now claimed her was called Tim, that he was the third-eldest living son of the Tanist of Clan Krooguh. The title had been strange to Bettylou and the explanation of it had been even more singular.

Tim's father was the husband of the eldest sister of the present chief of Clan Krooguh, and therefore Tim's eldest brother would be, by Krooguh Clan custom, the next chief upon the demise of his maternal uncle. Tim's clan and some others reckoned legal descent through the mother, therefore he was a Krooguh, rather than a Staiklee, his sire's name.

She had learned that this was Tim's second raid, Though he had slain two foemen on his first raid—proven, well-witnessed kills, both of them, one with an arrow, one close on, with the saber—he personally had seized no notable loot, although he had of course shared in that loot apportioned to his clan from the proceeds of the raid. He now was immensely pleased at the good fortune he had enjoyed in capturing her, a comely, young and obviously fertile woman.

She had learned that Tim Krooguh was only four years her senior, he being not quite of eighteen winters. She had learned that this was about the average age for most of the men of this particular raiding party. When the general friendliness after they had ridden out at sundown had overcome to some extent her awe of Elder Morai, she had asked him his age. With a tinge of dry humor, he had beamed, "Old as the hills, child." She had not presumed to press him for a more specific answer, just then.

She was beginning to truly like these strange men, all of them, but especially Tim Krooguh and Elder Morai. Being of an honest nature, therefore, she had tried to make them aware of her Sinful status, of the unholy Evil she harbored, the Sin-tainted seed which had caused her to conceive of Elder Claxton last winter.

Tim had seemed to not understand or really care, while Elder Morai had just shaken his helmeted head and beamed, "Bettylou, you must understand that you are no longer among the Dirtmen. Horseclansfolk do not adhere to that savage perversion of a religion or make claim to worship so cruel and capricious a god.

"Tim will wed you by clan rites, if his chief approves of you. And approve of you Dik Krooguh assuredly will, if only because I approve of you. That babe in your belly will be born one of the freest of men and women, a Horseclanner. Although life may be a bit difficult for you at first among us, I can see that you are made of the proper stuff; you'll rapidly adapt. Soon you'll be a full-fledged woman of the Horseclans, and you'll come to really pity those poor creatures among whom you were born and reared.

"When once your babe is born and is old enough to no longer require constant attendance, Tim will take you out to the Clan Krooguh horse herd to introduce you to the senior stallion, who then will conduct you about until you meet a filly you like who likes you. You'll also be given weapons and taught how to use them properly—saber, spear, dirk, saddle-axe, sling, but especially the Horseclans bow.

"You will abide in the yurt of Tim's father, Djahn, sharing the communal chores with your sisters-in-law, such other wives as Tim may take unto himself, any concubines the men of the yurt own or may come to own, and all supervised by Tim's mother, Lainah."

"I will not then be Tim's only wife, Elder Morai?" she asked. "How many others will there be?"

Elder Morai had shrugged, beaming, "No more than two or three at the time, including you, Bettylou, unless he should become the chief of Clan Krooguh. In that case he might take more wives or a few female slave-concubines. A chief has need of a large household, you see."

She wrinkled her brow in puzzlement. "But, Elder Morai, Tim says that he never will be chief, rather that his eldest brother will be."

Morai frowned. "You must understand, Bettylou, we of the Horseclans lead a life that is most often hard, though more often rewarding. And though we live freer than any other race of folk, our lives are fraught with daily dangers, some of them deadly. Men of the Horseclans do the bulk of the fighting, almost all of the raiding and the larger part of the hunting of bigger, more dangerous animals. Therefore, the attrition of male warriors had always been high, and that is the major reason why men take as many wives as they can support or abide and get on them as many babes as Sun and Wind will give them."

"Tim has already lost two brothers. One of them drowned as a child while the clan was crossing a river, the other— who was Djahn Staiklee's firstborn—was slain three years ago while riding a raid. It is easily possible that both of Tim's remaining brothers will die before their uncle, old Dik Krooguh, in which case Tim would be his successor."

"But fear you no loss of status in any future. You will be Tim's first wife and will always be paramount in his yurt no matter what may befall or however many wives and concubines he may take. And that child now in your belly, if it be a boy and live so long, will be the progenitor of a new sept of Clan Krooguh."

Bettylou shook her head and almost spoke aloud before she remembered and caught herself, then beamed, "But Elder Morai, I still find it hard to credit that this Tim Staiklee will so readily accept, father, give his honorable name to the get of another man."

"You still don't understand the Law of Clan Krooguh, child," Milo replied. "It is a bit complicated if one is not accustomed to the Krooguh variety of matrilineal succession. You see, the first Horseclans all were patrilineal, but a few generations ago, one of the high-plains clans—Clan Danyuhlz, I think it was—lost all of their adult men in some manner or other, including all who possessed direct claim to the chieftainship, and so, rather than see the name of an old and noted clan lost forever, irredeemably, the next tribal council decided that the eldest living son of the late chief's eldest sister should be chief, taking his mother's rather than his father's surname.

"This emergency measure worked very well for that one clan—so well did it work, in fact, that other clans have adopted variations of it over the years, for many and sundry reasons. The majority of the Horseclans remain patrilineal, but these two clans—Krooguh and Skaht—happen to be of the matrilineal minority; but even in these two clans, only the families of the chief and the tanist are compelled to live under the strictures of matrilineal succession; other septs and families are free to choose between matrilineal and patrilineal, and most choose the latter.

"But Tim is of the line of chiefs, Bettylou, and as such will not pass on his name to any of his children. This babe you now carry and all others he may get upon you will bear your surname, Hanson; rather, they and you will be called Hanson of Krooguh, that is, the sept of Hanson of the Clan Krooguh. That will be your name, too, child; for the rest of your life you will be known as Behtiloo Hansuhn of Krooguh."

Feeling it to be imperative that Bettylou make the best possible initial impression on Chief Dik of Krooguh and the other Horseclansfolk, Milo and Tim Krooguh conferred in mindspeak and came to the agreement that until the night of the feast that would mark the successful return of the raiders, Tim's captive woman should be lodged in the home of Milo. Milo was to continue to coach her in mindspeak, educate her in the mores of her new folk—the Horseclans—have her suitably arrayed and clothed for her presentation at the feast and instruct her in the proper responses and bearing for the simple Horseclans marriage rites.

Before the circular dwelling that he called home in the Krooguh-Skaht camp, Milo lifted Bettylou down from the saddle of that gelding which once had been the prized hunter of Solomon Claxton. When he had off-saddled both equines and removed the bridle from the gelding, he mindspoke his own warhorse, telling him to return to the horse herd, taking the new animal with him and introducing him to the king horse.

Through the latticework of laths that made up the sides of the circular dwelling, Bettylou could see that there were three women—two younger, one older—already inside and working at various tasks, though just now all were looking up and calling a welcome to Milo.

CHAPTER III

———•◦•━━◈━━•◦•———

While the two younger women bustled out, scooped up the two saddles and the other gear and bore them inside the single round room of the dwelling, the older woman, smiling, mindspoke Milo.

"Stole a Dirtwoman, did you, Uncle Milo? Well, she's not bad-looking, big-boned, of course, most of that ilk are, many of them run to fat, too, as they get longer in the tooth. But they run to strength, as well, which is a valuable asset in a slave . . . or is she to be a wife, eh, when once she's dropped her foal?"

The woman's grin broadened. "I doubt me not that she'll be a pleasant ride. But, wait, are you certain you're not bringing disease into your household and the camp? What happened to her hair? Why is her scalp so red?"

Milo returned the grin, beaming, "Ehstrah, my dear, between you and Gahbee and Ilsah, I have all the female household that I can properly service of nights, and well you know that fact, so don't think to get me into another marriage at any time soon. Besides, Bettylou Hanson here is not my captive, but rather that of young Tim Krooguh. He means to wed her properly, and it's up to you and me and the others to take her in hand and see her suitably arrayed and the like to impress old Dik Krooguh and see him approve her as a first wife for his nephew."

The older woman wrinkled up her brow and beamed, "But is it wise, Uncle, to allow obvious disease to be bred into one of the Kindred clans?"

Milo snorted and beamed, "Ehstrah, this poor girl is not diseased. According to their peculiar customs, they shaved off all her hair and stained her scalp red.

25

"Now, are we going to just stand here mindspeaking for the rest of the day? I, for one, could do with some food and milk and a bath and some sleep, and I don't think Behtiloo would be averse to the same."

Stiff and sore from the long hours in the saddle, Bettylou Hanson tripped on the foot-high wooden doorsill of the shelter and would surely have fallen had the older woman not grasped her arm in a strong, hard-palmed hand. Retaining her hold, the woman guided the girl to a piece of gaudy carpet partially covered by a tanned wolfpelt and sat her down upon it.

One of the younger women removed the lid from a hanging bucket of stiff waxed leather and dipped up a bowl of warm, frothy milk, then handed it to Bettylou, with a broad smile. As soon as the milk had been avidly drained, the same young woman took back the bowl and refilled it from the bucket.

The meal that she and Milo were shortly served was, to her, filling, but distinctly different from most of the foods of the Abode of the Righteous. There were several varieties of cheeses, a stew of at least two kinds of meats and a profusion of unfamiliar greens and root vegetables. The bread was flat, oval loaves about as large as her plam; it was coarse, heavy, and she was certain that neither wheat nor rye nor corn had been any one of the constituents of its dough. Some of the fruits in the bowl bore a resemblance to and tasted somewhat like the fruits of the Abode—apples, cherries, plums—but no one of them looked to be as large or well formed as those carefully nurtured fruits. She assumed, correctly, that they were wild-grown.

But the copious quantities of food proved to be a powerful soporific for Bettylou, and when she began to nod, Milo simply pushed her into a supine position and the older woman had one of the younger throw an old cloak over the pregnant girl.

"If ever before ye hast doubted my preachments, my people, never, ever will ye again so doubt me. Ye have seen—verily hast ye seen—that the servants of the Evil One still do walk this world and visit death and destruction upon us Righteous, upon this people Beloved of the Lord of Hosts. Upon us and our works did they wreak the full measure of punishments for the many and most foul transgressions against God's Law, the heinous Sins of the spirit as well as of the flesh of which each of you errant sinners knows yourself to be guilty.

"Only by true repentance and firm cleavage to God and His Holy Law by each and every one of you and in all ways will God allow us to rebuild the Abode of the Righteous and prosper. . . ."

Solomon Claxton, his hands and arms from wrists to shoulders still swathed in greasy bandages, eased his battered body into a position that was at least marginally less uncomfortable in his armchair of carven oak. Once again he silently thanked God that this House of the Holy Spirit had been spared, for with it had been spared this meeting hall with all of its appurtenances.

Elder Claxton, Solomon's father, had been at it for about two hours now, and was just getting warmed up to his subject, his eyes blazing from beneath his bushy brows, blazing as brightly as had the fires which had been conquered only bare days agone.

Worn out with days and nights of unremitting toil, sapped by the pain of his burns and injuries, Solomon allowed the chairback to keep him upright, while he tried to ignore the stifling heat, the sweat bathing his body, the flies and the stink of the rancid fat with which his burns had been dressed.

But if he suffered, he knew that the sufferings of those not so privileged as to occupy the chairs in the Row of the Patriarchs must be near to the limits of physical endurance. Many of those men and women were afflicted as badly as or worse than was he, and their hard, narrow benches had no backs, no arms. In just these last two hours, seven men and women had slumped from off their benches, unconscious, and had had to be borne out of the meeting hall; Solomon was of the opinion that many more would do likewise of this hot, muggy Wednesday night. Had he been in their places, he would have "fainted" long since, but, alas, the Patriarchs had to, were expected to, set an example, and Solomon Claxton took his status in the Abode of the Righteous very seriously, as befitted the Elder's chosen successor.

"Not that Pa is right all of the time," Solomon thought to himself, trying hard to get his mind off the aches and pains and itches just now tormenting him. "Pa's dead wrong right often. More wrong about things in recent years than when I was a boy and a young man. If he comes to keep getting worse at making important decisions, I suppose me and the Patriarchs will just have to send him home to God, one night, like he and them as was the Patriarchs back then did to Grandpa, his pa.''

''. . . Minions of Satan came and bore her off, bore off the Scarlet Woman, who had been known to us as Bettylou Hanson ere my Holy Seed rooted out and exposed to all the world her true, hellish Evil. Many men still living, men who sit now amongst you, saw with their own two eyes how she was borne off, sitting before a mounted demon, his arm most lovingly enfolding her, and her smiling up at him! Can ye then doubt that Satan walketh still across this once-cleansed world? Canst doubt that full many a girl who dwelleth amongst us, the Holy, Chosen flock of the Lord, harboreth the pure essence of ancient Evil, that . . .''

''Pa can call them demons if he wants to,'' mused Solomon Claxton, ''but they were nothing but another batch of those savage, murdering, thieving horse-nomads come in from the plains out there to do whatall they have allus done best— kill, steal, burn, lift stock—that's all it was.

''Can't imagine why they stole the Hanson girl, though. Far gone as she was, a good raping would likely of kilt her. But, knowing how them bastards are, they probably kilt her anyway and dumped her body out there somewhere in the wilderness, God pity her. Funny, she was allus a sweet, biddable chit. Sometimes I wonder about all of this Holy Seed and Scarlet Woman business. I wonder just how and when and why it all got started. I've read my Bible end to end and never found nothing relating directly to any of this Holy Seed stuff.''

Uttering a weak groan, one of the older Patriarchs slid out of his armchair onto the floor, but Elder Claxton ranted on, as if unaware that yet another of his battered flock had succumbed to the effects of oppressive heat and fresh wounds.

''If Pa don't wind down soon,'' thought Solomon Claxton, ''I'll just have to do somethin about thishere mess. Tomorrow's coming, and until we get us some more horses and mules, us men who are sound enough to work is going to be hard put to it doing all that has to be done in the fields and all. Pa just don't realize, it being so long since he done any farming, or work of any kind for that matter, but what with all the men and boys was kilt or hurt so bad they can't work and with nothing but a few span of oxen for draft, we're all going to play pure hell getting all the crops in on time, this year; so Lord's Day or no Lord's Day, Gospel Night or no Gospel Night, we should all be working or resting, not sitting here just listening to Pa rehash the raid and the fires and all and trying to lay them all at the door of that pore Hanson girl, just because she had the bad luck for to get grabbed and carried off and kilt by them black-hearted bastards.''

The big man sighed and cautiously shook his head at that thought. ''God rest her pore little soul. And if we done her the wrongs I reckon we might've, I hope she asks God to forgive us.''

Bettylou Hanson slept for almost thirty hours, there on her pallet of hide and carpets.

''Let the child sleep, Ehstrah,'' said Milo, upon himself awakening. ''She had a long, hard ride for one so ill accustomed to a nightlong of rump-pounding in a saddle. Nor do I think that she'd been used well by her own folk before young Tim stole her.''

Estrah sniffed. ''Not fed adequately, either, Uncle dear, by the look of her. She's lean as a winter wolf. You're dead certain she's not diseased . . .? You do recall what happened to Clan Guhntuh, years back, when they took in that girl they found wandering on the southern plains?''

Milo sighed a little exasperatedly. ''Yes and no, Ehstrah. Yes, I well remember how Clan Guhntuh was extirpated by some form of viral plague. No, I tell you this girl is suffering from no more than exhaustion, plus the effects of the abuse and deprivation to which her own folk subjected her this last few moons.''

''They must be a singular folk, those from whom Tim Krooguh stole this Behtiloo Hahnsuhn, Milo,'' Ehstrah remarked with a single shake of her graying head. ''Don't they know the danger to the child she carries that starving her portends?''

'' 'Singular' is a very mild term for those religious fanatics, Ehstrah,'' Milo stated baldly. ''I don't think you've ever been this far east before, have you?''

She again shook her head, and he went on, ''But I have, long before we married, you and I. I think it was Clan Grai I was then riding with, and we found a girl a bit older than this one. Stark naked, she was, her back covered from neck to knees with a single mass of festering sores from a brutal flogging, all her scalp shaven and painted red as sumac.''

"She, that girl, was pregnant, too, like this one?" asked Ehstrah.

"No," he replied, "but her breasts still were heavy with milk, so we looked about for a babe, backtracked her, but we found nothing, and when she had been nursed back to health, I found out why. Fetch some tea and dry curds and I'll tell you that grim tale."

Ehstrah smiled and bowed as low as any slave woman. "And what kind of tea does my master desire?"

With the new-risen Sacred Sun warming his right side and Ehstrah's left, Milo squatted comfortably across from her with an ancient metal drinking cup in his left hand, making forays upon the bowl of cow's-milk curds with the right. Close beside the bowl, the copper pot of tea steamed gently upon its brazier, lacing the cool morning air with the pungent odor of fresh spearmint.

"The ancestors of the Sacred Ancestors, Ehstrah, although they owned a high degree of civilization and labor-saving devices beyond the counting which gave many of them creature comforts such as folk today could not even imagine, never achieved a really homogeneous culture. Up to the very moment when that legendary folk died as a nation, still were there tiny groups that—for reasons of religion or philosophy, mostly—chose to band together and live lives that were generally harder and much more primitive, usually deriving sustenance from farming."

"What has this history lesson to do with that Hansuhn girl, in the yurt there, Milo?" Ehstrah asked impatiently. "Gahbee and Ilsah and I can always make good use of an extra pair of hands, and if she is to become a woman of the Horseclans shortly, it is none too early for her to start learning just what will be expected of her."

Milo shrugged and poured himself another cup of the spearmint tea. "You're right, of course, Ehstrah . . . but only partially. Yes, it is important that Bettylou Hanson learn of us and our ways, but it is equally important that you, who will be her mentor, learn of her people, their customs and her background.

"As for you poor, poor overworked and underappreciated

women—the three of you—you have only yourselves, one man and his gear and an average-sized yurt to care for. Do you seriously expect me to feel sorry for you three racks of lazybones? Just look around you and consider how many clanswomen make out alone or with only a slave woman in doing the work necessary for a husband and a gaggle of children. Be happy, woman, with the good things you have!''

Setting down his cup, Milo drew from out his belt pouch an ancient and battered meerschaum pipe and a bladder of dark shreds of tobacco. Careful to not drop a crumb of the infinitely precious stuff (it was available only from those rare, intrepid traders who occasionally ventured out onto the prairie from the east or by being traded from clan to clan up from the southeast), he packed the pipe, then lit a splinter in the coals beneath the brazier and puffed the filled pipe into life.

Ehstrah had never developed a taste for tobacco. She filled her own carven wooden pipe with dried basil leaves, lit it and dutifully listened as Milo went on with his recountal.

''I stated that the folk who came before never had a really homogeneous society, Ehstrah. One of the reasons that they did not have such was the matter of religions.''

''They did not reverence Sun and Wind, then, Milo?'' She wrinkled her forehead in puzzlement.

''No, they were none of them so wise, my dear. They were saddled from birth to death with a great greedy horde of priests or those who claimed to serve and speak for a god— the best of these were deluded fools, the worst were liars, hypocrites or charlatans of the basest sort, serving nothing and no one save their own acquisitive natures and endlessly clawing toward wealth and power over the lives and purses of those who foolishly put faith in them and the fables they spun.

''The majority of these precursors called themselves by the name of 'Christians.' Their religion was called 'Christianity,' but even it was not a single entity, rather was it divided and redivided into a good dozen major and many scores of minor sects, most of them claiming to be the only true sect. Moreover, most of these sects were constantly denigrating all other sects, nor were they at all averse to beating, maiming, torturing, burning, raping or killing in the vain attempt to prove the absurd claims that they mouthed. And these were the older, larger, better-organized and better-led sects, mind you.

"There were a host of other, smaller, even more fanatic sects. Certain of these were groups of out-and-out lunatics—in the cases of their leaders if not in the cases of the followers. Most of these smaller sects, though eccentric in speech and deed, hurt no one save their own members, but a few were blatantly sociopathic, practicing exceedingly perverted versions of the religion they claimed to honor.

"In self-defense, the folk among whom these smaller sects dwelt sometimes found it necessary to drive these antisocial groups out of their land entirely, or at the least away from the larger centers of population. It is from such a group that the folk of the Hanson girl are descended.

"Due to this fact, Ehstrah, because of the maniacal mores her people practice and pass on, you and the others must be very patient with Bettylou. She has been taught to believe that she is nothing less than the very wellspring of evil."

"Evil? That girl?" snapped Ehstrah. "Tell me that you're joking, Milo. Lunatics they must indeed be, and malicious to boot, to teach such arrant nonsense to a pretty girl."

Milo shrugged. "They only pass on what they themselves were taught. The legends of the very beginning of their religion are very misogynistic, placing the blame for all the miseries of mankind on the supposed first woman and her sexuality."

Ehstrah rocked back on her heels, laughing gustily. "And what of the sexuality of the first man, eh? A woman can't do it alone, you know! Had it not been for that first randy bastard, there'd have been no second man or woman or generation. I never heard of adult men and women believing, living by, such utter rubbish. They sound so stupid as to need to have someone lead them in out of the rain. Can't any of them think for themselves, reason for themselves? Men are men and women are women, male is male and female is female, there are good and bad of both sexes, but no babe is born bad, not of either sex, and no legend no matter how hoary or hallowed is going to make such a supposition so!"

"Nonetheless, Ehstrah, this is just what Bettylou firmly believes. It is all she ever has known. She further believes that were she not basically evil, she would not have conceived of the old goat of a priest—'Elder' is his title—who has been swiving her periodically since her puberty."

Ehstrah nodded, her mouth now a firm line of resolution.

"Well, it's high time that this Hansuhn girl began to learn some hard truths, began to learn to think for herself."

Milo smiled. "You're definitely the one for that job, my dear. Just pass on enough of all I've told you to Gahbee and Ilsah that they'll not deem Bettylou a half-wit, eh."

Bettylou Hanson awakened to find a rythmically breathing little bundle of russet fur pressed tightly against her breasts and upper belly. For a brief moment, she was frightened, then, when she had risen sufficiently to prop up on an elbow, she could discern that the bundle was but a soundly sleeping cat of some sort.

Her movement awakened the cat, and it first sat up and yawned cavernously, curling a long, wide, red-pink tongue from out a mouth well equipped with a full set of sparkling-white teeth and needle-pointed fangs. Although the creature was every bit as large as a smallish adult bobcat, the fact that its paws and head were oversized for its sturdy (verging on chubby) body led Bettylou to assume that it was possibly a cub of one of the huge felines such as had accompanied the clansmen on their raid.

After stretching thoroughly, forward and backward, the cat plumped down and began to wash its face, now and then taking a lick at its thick chest fur.

Bettylou had always been intensely fond of small animals— puppies, the kittens of barn cats, baby rabbits, kids, lambs and the like—so it was a natural, unconscious act to reach out a hand and stroke the soft, dense fur along the cat's spine.

The deep, audible purr was expected, the strong mindspeak beam was not, and Bettylou started until her memory of the last few days assured her that she was not hallucinating.

"Killer-of-all likes you, two-leg female, so he will not kill you. Besides, you are nice to sleep with; you do not roll and thrash about as do so many of your kind. Give this cat some of those wet curds from the bucket, up there, *now*."

There were no other humans about and the feline beamed a gnawing hunger equal to Bettylou's own, so she arose, picked up a brace of bowls and, using one for a scoop, filled the other with the fresh curds and set it down before the cat, who set to with purpose. She filled the second for herself, found a wooden spoon and began to eat.

Then she almost dropped both bowl and spoon when one of

the two younger of Milo's wives stepped over the high sill of the door and entered . . . stark naked, save only for her low, felt boots.

"So, you finally woke up, did you?" said the nude woman, with a warm, infectious smile. "Gahbee and I were wondering whether or not we should start to build a pyre for your body." Then she caught sight of the cat crouched growling softly before the bowl of curds.

"Oh, no, not him again. Behtiloo, Furball there is the most unashamed glutton in the camp. As a nursing kitten, he almost sucked his poor mother dry, going after her dugs whenever the poor cat made to sleep or rest, and as a cub he is half again the size of the rest of his littermates. He will eat anything that he can get his teeth into, and he ranges far out in search of prey, which is good; but what is bad is that he never is sated, and here in camp he will steal food from those too wise for him to cozen out of it."

She had been mindspeaking, and, still eating, still growling, the young cat replied threateningly, "Beware, two-leg female, do not so slander Killer-of-all-things, lest he tear out your ugly, furless throat! This cat never steals, he only takes that which he needs, as is the right of any clansman."

Ilsah trilled a laugh. "Call it what you wish, Furball, but you were wise to get out of here before Ehstrah gets back from the sweatbath, else she'll lay her strap on your fat carcass again, drive you squalling out of the yurt as she did the day she found you hanging by the teeth from that dried brisket."

"Ugly and vicious as is that abominable two-leg female, she does not frighten this cat!" was the cub's quick response, but then, of a sudden, he grabbed one more mouthful of the curds, crossed the width of the yurt in two leaps and was out the door.

A few moments after Furball's abrupt departure, the older woman, Ehstrah, crossed the threshold, every bit as bare as was Ilsah, her unbraided hair dripping water down her back and her buttocks.

"Make certain everything edible is hung high or shut away," she instructed Ilsah. "I'm certain I spotted that roguish cat, Furball, skulking about our yurt as I approached it. I'm going to have to have Milo converse with the cat chief about Furball again, I fear me.

"Well, so you're among the living again, Behtiloo Hansuhn. Had no trouble finding food, did you? Good, but don't limit yourself to a bowl of curds, child. You're welcome to anything in the yurt—milk, meat, tea, berries, honey, whatever we have. No one goes hungry in the Horseclans camp . . . unless all go hungry."

Despite her protestations that the curds were sufficient to her hunger, the older and the younger there and then sat the girl down and fed her to repletion and beyond—a handful of tiny hard-boiled birds' eggs, several joints of a cold roasted wild rabbit, chunks of some sort of a cold gruel, fried to crispness and topped with honey, all washed down with fresh, warm milk.

The two women had not only cooked for Bettylou, but had avidly joined her in eating the meal. With all the bones well gnawed, skillfully cracked and sucked free of marrow, with the last crumbs of the fried gruel and the remaining smears of honey devoured, the older woman addressed Bettylou, saying, "All right, child, you can start stripping off those clothes. After riding for days in them and then sleeping in them for a day and a half, I'd guess they could stand a good soaking and a day of wind and sunlight. Gahbee will be back soon, then you can go with her to the sweat yurt, and when you've bathed, you and Gahbee can wash your clothes and Milo's. It just never ceases to amaze me how incredibly filthy he can get them riding a raid.

"Well, what are you waiting for, child? Undress."

Then, belatedly recalling Milo's admonitions and that this new Horseclanswoman-to-be was a scioness of an entirely different, an alien, Dirtman culture, she sent her mind probing into that of Bettylou, who had not yet learned how to shield her innermost thoughts from a telepath.

Ehstrah squatted and, taking the girl's hand, drew her down beside her on the floor. "Behtiloo, please recall that you are no longer amongst the folk who spawned you and would have cast you out soon. We Horseclansfolk find nothing evil or shameful in the flesh and skin that houses our spirits, no more than do the cats and horses. We wear clothing simply for protection against the elements, for warmth or to prevent chafing by armor or weapons belts. So purge your mind and your heart of these old and most peculiar Dirtman ways. You now are—or, rather, soon will be—one of the freest, most favored of all women under the domain of Sacred Sun, a woman of the Horseclans. You must set yourself to the task of thinking and behaving like one, child.''

With such trepidation, Bettylou first kicked off the felt boots, then lifted the faded, much-stained and now-filthy scarlet dress over her head. Turning to face the wall, red with shame despite the older woman's words, the girl untied the waist thong and allowed the dirty, sweat-tacky trousers to fall about her ankles.

Ehstrah hissed softly between her teeth at the sight of the new scars furrowing Bettylou's back from neck to knees. At that moment she came to feel real hatred for the particular brand of Dirtmen who would do such to a pretty young girl for the ''crime'' of being quickened. So it was that, not waiting for Gahbee, she gathered up the clothes herself and, after having Bettylou step back into her boots, led her by the hand out of the yurt and toward the sweat yurt. She felt very protective of this young woman who had suffered so much and must now be feeling so alone here. Besides, a second bath this morning could do no harm.

CHAPTER IV

The hunters had returned with a full bag of assorted game, and parties of young boys and girls under the leadership of certain of their elders had ridden far out into the stretches of prairie beyond the camp environs and brought back travois after heaped-high travois of roots and tubers and herbs and wild grains and berries and other fruits. Children fanned out into the nearer grasslands with slings and snake sticks, baskets to hold eggs and bags to carry snake carcasses or whatever other small game they were able to down. The planned celebratory feast was becoming a reality.

A long pit was dug straight through the dusty middle of the encampment, piled high with wood and dried dung and twisted bundles of dried grasses, then set ablaze, while a horde of the women and slaves readied the various viands to cook as soon as a suitable bed of coals was available. Precious metal racks and tripods were brought from the various yurts and laid by ready for use in preparing the food.

Bettylou Hanson was set to grinding a mixture of wild grain and seeds into a coarse meal in a stone quern. Each time she filled a waiting bowl, Ilsah took it away and replaced it with an empty one, then made dough, kneaded it and fashioned small, flat cakes, setting them beside the door. Periodically, Gahbee collected them and took them to the verge of the blazing firepit, where they and others prepared in other yurts were being baked in a reflector oven.

At one end of the camp, those adult men not engaged in tending the firepit worked at skinning and butchering the field-dressed game. Most of them were completely nude and blood-splashed and -streaked from head to boottops. Older or infirm men sat or squatted close by keeping the knives and cleavers sharp, framing the hides on wooden racks while they still were fresh and pliable, swatting at flies, smoking their pipes and chatting endlessly.

No sooner was the bulk of the large-game butchering done than the children came trooping in with their bags of headless, writhing snakes, some dozens of rabbits and hares, a silver dog-fox, a brace of fat groundhogs, a porcupine, a large spotted skunk and a rare prize which brought all the men gathering about it and the tiny girl who had downed it with a single, shrewdly cast slingstone, then manhandled it back to where bigger children could take over.

Most of the men—all of those under forty winters—had never seen an antelope so small. The little beast weighed about twenty pounds and might have been the young of a larger species, save for fully developed scrotum and the pair of short, slender, needle-pointed black horns that adorned its now-cracked skull.

"Well, I'll be dipped in dung!" exclaimed Milo. "A dagger-horn, it is, or I'm the king stallion. I've seen a dozen bowmen loose a cloud of arrows at a herd of these without hitting a one, and here's a prime buck downed by a girl of six with a damned sling! Will wonders never cease?"

Big Djahn Staiklee of Krooguh, whose clan of birth usually ranged farther south, where the minuscule dart-horns were more common than this far north on the prairie, grinned through a sticky, blood-crusty light-brown beard. "I'm no mean bowman, as any here can attest, but I'm here to say that I've missed more than one of those lightning-sprung little antelopes. If the girl has the kind of eye-hand coordination that such a feat required, think what a maiden-archer she'll make in a few more winters' time."

One after the other, the more important of the men solemnly praised the hunting prowess of Teenah Skaht. Then the animal was hung up, and opened, and the liver and heart given to the little girl to either eat on the spot or bear back to her family's yurt. When she trotted out of sight, she was munching happily while dribbling blood down her chin and onto the bare chest of her nut-brown body.

The other children received such praise as their accomplishments merited, then were invited to watch the cleaning and skinning and butchering of the varied assortment of small game they had killed and fetched into camp, with the older ones being urged to help and thus learn more of the necessary skills of survival on the prairie.

While her body moved rhythmically at milling the wild grains, Bettylou Hanson thought of all the things she had learned in this last seven-day. She had always heard that the horse-nomads were a filthy people who never bathed deliberately and wore their clothes until they rotted off. What she had learned here was that they were all of them more cleanly than were most of her own people; where folk at the Abode of the Righteous washed face, hands and arms several times each day, they washed the rest of their bodies once or twice a month in good weather, far less frequently in cold weather. Horseclansfolk, on the other hand, seemed to make almost daily use of their commodious sweat yurt—steaming in the damp darkness, then emerging to rinse with sun-warmed water and going about their various tasks nude until sun and the ever-constant wind had dried their hair and skin, since they did not consider sight of a naked human body offensive or sinful as had the Righteous. Bettylou was beginning to become accustomed to the sight of naked women or girls, but she still could not help blushing and turning her gaze away at the naked boys or men.

Her mindspeak abilities—both in reception and sending—were manifesting themselves by veritable leaps and bounds through dint of practice and the patient tutelage of her mentors, Chief Milo Morai, Ehstrah, Gahbee, Ilsah and most of the other men, women and prairiecats with whom she came into contact. Everyone seemed to be more than happy to take or make the time to help a newly discovered mindspeaker to develop her inborn ability.

In addition to folks, cats and horses, Milo had told her that a really adept mindspeaker could enter the minds of and converse after a fashion with such diverse creatures as wolves, bears, members of the weasel clans, treecats and other wild felines, dogs, swine and even the occasional wild ruminant—domestic cattle and sheep being basically too unintelligent to do much real thinking, being ruled by instinct, mostly.

Milo had also averred that mindspeak ability ran in families, and, thinking on that, she thought she could puzzle out now a riddle that had perplexed her all her life, since first she had heard it—the tale of her mother's granduncle, Zebediah the Pig Man.

They had said that Zeb Alfredson had been little older than Bettylou now was when the present Elder Claxton's father had assigned him the task of herding the score or so adult and juvenile pigs that the Abode then owned. Sometime during the first year that he headed the detail of pigboys, a sow died in farrowing, and the only piglet that survived her did so because Zeb took him up and nursed him with pig milk he somehow obtained from other sows. This piglet grew into a vastly oversized boar, and Zeb announced that his name was Nimrod.

Zeb persuaded the Elder and the Patriarchs not to butcher Nimrod but to retain him as a stud boar. He also persuaded them to allow the swine to run free in the woods and outer pastures and fallow fields, rather than keeping them cooped up in the filthy, malodorous pens so much of the time, demonstrating his ability to ride out on a small mule and bring them all in at the end of each day. Since his method of handling the swine freed a half-dozen boys for more of the endless tasks of farming and stock-raising, Zeb quickly became a very popular young man with the Elder and the Patriarchs and there was even speculation that he might someday be a Patriarch himself.

Then, of a crisp autumn day, he rode out to fetch in the swine, but he did not ride alone, for bear tracks had been seen at several spots in the hinterlands. He rode along with one of his younger brothers, each of them armed with a rifle, a bear spear and a long, heavy-bladed knife. They rode not the familiar mules, but a brace of fine, tall hunting horses, less likely to become hysterically unmanageable at the sound or smell of a bear or other predator.

What happened after the two rode out of sight of the Abode of the Righteous, that long-ago day, no man knew for certain. The reports of two rifles were heard and some thought to hear human screams and bestial roarings, all muted with distance. The son and heir of the then Elder led a party of mounted men out at the gallop, but the woods were then more extensive and by the time they came across the proper clearing, it was all over.

Zeb Alfredson's younger brother lay dead, throat torn out and lower face bitten off. Zeb himself had been terribly savaged by the bear and survived only bare minutes past his rescuers' arrival. Both rifles had been fired, and Zeb's spear was covered in blood from point to crossbar.

Of the huge silvertip bear, precious little remained other than a gashed and bloody hide full of torn flesh and splintered bones. Nor was the bear's nemesis difficult to guess, for the clearing was full of agitated pigs, pigs of all ages and sexes and sizes, a few of them with hides scored by long, sharp claws, but all with bloody snouts and two of the boars with tatters of gory bearskin hanging from their tushes.

The men had gotten nothing meaningful out of Zeb; he was just too far gone in pain and loss of blood to make any sense. But it was said that just moments before the life left his battered body, Nimrod shouldered his four hundred pounds through the gathered group of men, stood looking down on Zeb's torn, blood-streaked face, and, as the single, remaining eye began to glaze over, raised his snout and fearsome tushes skyward and voiced what could only have been called a howl, a sound such as none of the farmers had ever heard any swine make before or since.

The two bodies were borne back to the Abode of the Righteous, and it was not until morning that anyone thought to go out and bring in the herd of swine, and by then they all were gone. The hunters tracked the herd with hounds and did catch a few, but found that the only way to bring them back was to kill them. Nimrod was sighted on two occasions, but no one ever was able to get a clear shot at him—he seemed to know just what the rifles were and the capabilities and limitations of them. On another occasion, the hounds cornered him, but by the time the hunters arrived, the monstrous boar was long departed and the ground was littered with dead and dying hounds. At that point, the hunters gave up the pursuit.

"Could he have been a mindspeaker with the pigs, Chief Milo?" Bettylou asked after recounting the old tale. "He was my mother's father's brother, after all."

Milo nodded. "He almost certainly was, Bettylou, judging on the basis of your tale. Swine are very intelligent, you know, much more so than dogs, for instance, and the boar Nimrod must have truly loved your ancestor to have been willing to lead his herd against a full-grown bear to protect him. You clearly come of good stock, girl. It pleases me that you'll bear Horseclans children."

Bettylou had heard in the Abode that the prairie was virtually swarming with hordes of horse-nomads, that their gigantic camps covered square miles of grasslands, but such assertions could never be proved by what she had seen to date.

In addition to the sweat yurt, there were thirty-four other yurts in the camp—eighteen for Clan Krooguh, fifteen for Clan Skaht and one for Clan Morai. Among these dwelt forty-eight males of an age older than thirteen, which added up to nothing near a horde, in Bettylou's mind. Of course, both men and women could and did fight if attacked, and both sexes hunted even the most dangerous game animals. Also, Chief Milo assured her that there existed Kindred clans much larger—perhaps as many as threescore adult males in a clan—and there were more than fourscore Kindred clans on the prairies, deserts and high plains, all drifting hither and yon, following the grass and the water.

Chief Milo opined that if the Abode-spawned tales were more than whole-cloth exaggerations, the square-miles-covering camp might be the recollections at third or fourth or fifth hand of someone who had seen or heard of one of the rare tribal camps—conclaves of scores of clans planned for years in advance and at which there might be as many as ten thousand, briefly, until the graze became insufficient to maintain the herds of cattle, sheep and horses.

"*All* of the clans assemble at such times, then, Eld . . . uhh, Chief Milo?" Bettylou inquired.

Flashing his white teeth in a brief smile, he shook his head. "No, child, at most perhaps half of the Kindred clans at any one time and place."

"But why not get all of the clans together at once, Chief Milo?" Bettylou probed.

Patiently, he answered, "For one thing, it is a really impossible thing. Yes, there are some fourscore or more of the Kindred clans, but those clans are spread over something like four million square miles or more of territory—ranging generally farther north in spring and summer, farther south in autumn and winter, and seldom in one place for more than a moon. Nor can I think of any area that could support such a vast number of folks and herds and cats for any meaningful length of time; the camp would needs have to be moved before many of the clans could reach the predetermined location, for although a party of picked raiders can move very fast, cover fantastic numbers of miles in a few nights' ride, you will soon learn that a clan on the march proceeds no faster than the slowest of its members or wagons or cattle . . . and that can be snail-slow at times."

"Where do you usually meet, Chief Milo?" she asked. "When? I mean, what time of year?"

"Usually in late spring or early summer, Bettylou. Once we met on the high plains, but mostly we meet at some spot—some marked or easily found spot—on the prairie. At the last such, five . . . no, six years ago, we met in and around the ruins of a town that used to be called Hutchinson in an area that once was the State of Kansas. It was decided there by the council of clan chiefs that the next one would be met at a spot farther north and west, but no firm site was selected for it, so it could take place, whenever it does, in any location, and those chiefs who for whatever reason or none don't like the time of the conclave or the location just will not bother to make the journey. Kindred Horseclansfolk are a freedom-loving lot and refuse to be bound by anything other than the Couplets of Horseclans Law, that and the inborn obligation to defend other Kindred against non-Kindred folk."

"But, Chief Milo," she said puzzledly, "if the Kindred clans are truly spread so far, how do any of them *ever* hear of these meetings and learn where to go for them?"

He shrugged. "Tribe bards, for the most part, who travel widely and almost constantly. Also, from messages left here and there in traditional places, cryptic signs that only a Kindred clansman can interpret. Then too there are the roving smiths who glean metals from ruins either use themselves or barter to the clans they happen across in their travels. They pass the notices of meetings on to the Kindred clans, for all that some of them are not by birth Kindred."

"If these men are not Kindred, Chief Milo, then what are they?"

He replied, "Vagabonds with a flair for metalworking or trading from the more settled areas to the east and west and north and south of the plains and prairie, Bettylou, a good many of them. Some most likely malefactors of one stripe or another who found or made the farming areas too hot for themselves to endure and still live. That or non-Kindred nomads."

"Then all of the horse-nomads are not Kindred, Chief Milo?"

"No, child, though there are now far fewer non-Kindred folk roving about than there were a hundred years ago, the plains and the prairie are still not yet the uncontested stamping grounds of us Kindred. But that day will yet come, child. Perhaps you'll live to see it."

He had spoken the last sentence with so grim an intensity that she felt compelled to probe more deeply. "Are the Kindred clans not on good terms with these other nomads, then, Chief Milo?"

"Not hardly!" he snorted. "Oh, one would think that with so many hundreds of thousands of square miles of open country to roam, there would exist, could exist, damned little possibility of friction between relatively small groups of folk leading very similar nomadic existences. But it simply has not worked out so peacefully as that over the years.

"Understand me, Bettylou, we Horseclansfolk were a feisty lot from the very beginning, about two hundred and fifty winters back, but we were none of us basically savage, random killers. We fought for and still do fight for survival—the elements, beasts and men, when necessary. But we would much prefer to bring non-Kindred nomads into the tribe by marriage or adoption than to kill them for their women and their herds. Quite a few of your present 'Kindred' clans became such in just those ways.

"Your father-in-law-to-be, for instance, Bettylou. The Clan Staiklee were once bitter enemies of the Horseclans, back some three or four generations. Their tribe was not large, but their warriors were every one as tough, as skilled and as resourceful as any Horseclansman, and they made it most difficult for us in the northeastern reaches of that area that long ago was called Texas. They fought us unstintingly for nearly a generation, and they might have done so for much longer had they not owned a wise chief who came to realize that his tribe was much outnumbered by the warriors of Kindred clans and vastly outnumbered by the incredibly bestial and savage tribes of utter barbarians who were just then making to push up from the southwest.

"Because he would not see his tribe ground to powder between barbarians and Kindred, he negotiated an initial meeting with four Kindred clans, and, shortly, those four became five. That done, the five summoned other Kindred clans from the north and the west and, all united, were able to extirpate or turn back all of the southwestern barbarians.

"Numerous Kindred clans were originally non-Kindred, from the Texas area—Ohlsuhn, Morguhn, Maklaruhn and Hwilkee are perhaps the foremost of them, aside from Clan Staiklee."

As the time to begin the feast neared, clansfolk of both sexes and all ages packed into the sweat yurt, but not Bettylou Hanson; the knowledgeable Ehstrah had seen to it that she, Ilsah and Gahbee had completed their ablutions well in advance of the rest. And when the three returned to the Morai yurt, Bettylou had been given back her red dress.

She could only stare and stutter, barely recognizing the garment, for what had been back at the Abode of the Righteous a badge of Sin and Shame and a portent of certain Doom had lost every last iota of that identity and become a purely and a thoroughly Horseclans garment.

The faded-red dress had been redyed a deep crimson, and the floppy, open-cuffed sleeves had been somehow made fuller and fitted with drawstrings at the wrists. Head hole and sleeves and a large expanse of the rest of the reborn garment were now rich and heavy with Ehstrah's fine, meticulous embroidery; she also had used embroidery to conceal the stitches with which each tear and rent had been closed. Bettylou had never before been in receipt of anything so lovely, not in all her short life, for the garb of all of the Righteous was unremittingly drab—unbleached wool and linen and a mixture of the two, unadorned leather or rawhide. Unable to contain herself, she felt tears rolling down her cheeks still damp from the bath and irresistible sobs welling up from deep within her.

Ehstrah—with grown children older than Bettylou by her now-deceased first husband, and just then feeling very motherly—hunkered down beside the sobbing girl and took her into her arms. Bettylou tried, between sobs, to thank Ehstrah and the others for all their many kindnesses to her since her arrival in the camp.

"No, no, child," soothed Ehstrah silently, "at such times as this mindspeak is far better, easier."

She slipped into the girl's mind, briefly . . . and started as if she had been stabbed suddenly. *"Milo!"* Her mindcall lanced out. "Uncle Milo! Come to your lodge at once! Urgent!"

"Whew!" exclaimed Milo. "I'm very glad this happened when it did, glad that we could show the poor child's mind how to purge itself thoroughly, once and for all, of all the filth and perverted religion her kinfolk had shoveled into it. Such a load of mental and emotional sewage would have ended in driving her mad. It will be at least two hours more until everyone is gathered out there, so let her sleep until the last minute, eh? It will do her good."

Ehstrah nodded, fingering one of her small arm-daggers and musing darkly, aloud, "If only I could have ten minutes, even five, alone with that priest, that Elder Claxton, the randy old goat, the child-raping bastard, he'd forever after lack the parts to do to another the evil he wrought upon this helpless girl. Milo . . .? Do you think . . ."

Skimming her surface thoughts, he shook his head. "Put it out of your mind, Ehstrah. There are not enough of us— warriors, maiden-archers *and* matrons, included—to attack that place with a bare hope of success. They have weapons and artifacts from the time before this with which they could kill at great distances, at much farther away than even the heaviest bow can cast. To succeed against those Dirtmen would take at least a dozen clans and would result in many, many dead Horseclansfolk for little loot that would be of use to us in the type of life we lead. The best thing we can do is avoid the Abode of the Righteous and pass on the word that other Kindred clans should follow suit."

Ehstrah sighed and grudgingly sheathed her dagger. "Of course you are right, Uncle Milo—you must be, for you have seen far more of war than have I . . . or any man or woman in this camp, for that matter. But . . . but it galls me that a despicable man like that should go on, year in, year out, causing untold sufferings, and go forever unpunished."

"No," replied Milo. "I agree that it doesn't seem right or proper, Ehstrah, but most likely this priest is as much a victim as are his prey. Both he and they were probably reared into the same perverted religious beliefs. They don't know that what they are doing, that the way they are living, is wrong. They call themselves the Righteous, and I'm sure they firmly believe that, all of them, else—being human—they'd long since have deposed these Elders and Patriarchs."

He rose to his feet. "Now, I think I should complete my sweat and my wash."

Ehstrah looked up at him from beneath her thick brows, grinning provocatively. "Don't go overeating or -drinking at the feast, Honored Chief. Gahbee and Ilsah and I, we have firm plans for you tonight."

CHAPTER V

Bettylou's first sight of Chief Dik Krooguh repelled her. He was short—shorter even than his nephew, short even by the standards of his race of short men—bandy-legged and physically incomplete. He lacked an eye, and part of both ears and was otherwise hideously scarred by his lifetime of warring, raiding and hunting dangerous beasts. But he was jolly, warm of manner, and his ready laughter had boomed right often over the length and the breadth of the feasting ground throughout the most of the celebration.

With the feasting generally done—warriors, women, children, even slaves stuffed to repletion and far beyond with food—the little chief arose from his place and approached Bettylou where she sat between Milo and Ehstrah. He moved with a rolling gait, and that, combined with his somewhat garish clothing and personal adornments, might have served to give him a comic appearance save for the unmistakable air of calm dignity which he effortlessly bore about him like a cloak of state.

The wrinkled hand with which he took her arm and assisted her to arise was lacking all of one finger and parts of two others, but still was possessed of a crushing though well-controlled strength. He led her slowly, wordlessly, to a spot where the maximum numbers of the assembled folk could see her, then mindcalled Tim Staiklee of Krooguh, who carefully wiped off greasy lips and chin, arose from his place and strode to his uncle's side, trying hard not to grin.

Chief Dik cleared his throat and spoke aloud for the benefit of those whose mindspeak was minimal or nonexistent, although he also continued to beam his message silently. Milo had explained how unusual and valuable this flexibility was, had explained it on the day he had discovered to his pleased surprise that, with training, Bettylou would one day be capable of speaking orally and mindspeaking at one and the same time.

Smiling broadly, Chief Dik said, "Kindred, this child was captured of the Dirtmen by Tim in the very raid we are here to celebrate. Although born of Dirt and reared to it"—he patted Bettylou's belly lightly with his multilated hand—"any man or woman or cat or horse can easily see that she most assuredly is fertile. She has broad hips and heavy teats, nor is her face at all ill to look upon; moreover, she has mindspeak."

At this last, there was an appreciable murmur from the assembly. Few Dirtmen of any description or type seemed to have even a trace of telepathic abilities; indeed, a third or more of born Kindred never owned enough mindspeak to benefit them or their clans.

Djahn Staiklee, Tim's father, arose and demanded, "But do we know anything of the sire of the babe she carries, Dik?"

The short man just shrugged. "Uncle Milo says that he was the paramount chief of this particular batch of Dirtmen, Djahn. It's about four days' ride northeast, if you'd care to go and inquire into his Dirtman pedigree." He grinned mischievously.

"But what matter such trivialities, say I. The chit's babe will be reared with us, by us, to be one of us. I have no sure knowledge who my own sire was . . . nor do I particularly care, for I *do* know for certain who my mother was. This girl's child will feel the same way."

But Staiklee was not quite mollified. "She's a bit long in the tooth. What's her age? Eighteen winters? Seventeen, anyway."

"Not quite fifteen winters, the way we reckon time, Djahn," replied Chief Dik. "Yes, she's big of bone and tall, but just think of the weight of bow such a woman will be able to draw. Eh? But for the rest of it, Uncle Milo assures me she's both healthy and intelligent. She's already gone far in learning our ways, the ways of the Kindred of Cat and Horse, and she'll learn more . . . quickly.

"Now, young Tim here, my sister's son, would have this girl to wife, which demonstrates his good judgment of womanflesh, I aver. I, Dik Krooguh, as chief, am for declaring them wed this night and her your clanswoman by marriage. Are there any serious objections or questions? And when I say 'serious' I mean just that, too, no more nit-picking about the lineage of sires or other nonsensical questions . . . Yes, Brother Chief. You have an objecton to my nephew wedding his captive?''

"I'd not call it an objection, Brother Chief, not yet, at least," the grizzled man replied, shaking his head. "I'd just like to know what's wrong with her. When she rode into camp, she was bald as a baby's arse and her scalp was terribly discolored; that discoloration has faded now and she's sprouted at least a fuzz of hair on her head, but I want to know what brought about her original condition.

"And this is not nit-picking, Dik Krooguh. Just remember: Disease it was killed the ancestors of the Sacred Ancestors and disease has put paid to more Kindred than war or raidings or any other cause I can just now think of. If I'm to keep company with Clan Krooguh, me and mine, I'd be damned certain that they keep their camp and their bloodlines free of disease.

"No, Chief Dik. let the girl speak for herself. She looks bright enough, and you say she mindspeaks. I'd hear her words and thoughts in this matter."

But Bettylou could not speak, could not even form a thought-beaming, so confused was her mind with a jumble of old litany—Tainted Seed, Scarlet Women, Sinfulness, the Ancient and Deceitful Wickednesses of Womankind. How to make these new, strange people understand . . .?

However, she did not need to speak at all, for Milo arose from his place and said, "Kindred, the girl is not in any way or manner diseased. Her own folk kept her scalp shaved smooth and dyed it with root juices."

"But why, Uncle Milo?" queried the questioner, scratching at his own scalp beneath his thinning hair. "Admitted, these various breeds of Dirtmen harbor some exceedingly peculiar customs and practices that would gag a buzzard, but this batch must all be moon-mad—at least, that's the opinion of Zak Skaht of Skaht."

Milo nodded grimly. "I have scanned this girl's mind and delved deeply into her memories, Kinsfolk, and I have found that I know of her ilk of old. They practice and live by a fanatic and much perverted form of what was, long ago, when the Sacred Ancestors saw birth in the holy city of Ehlai, the principal religion of this land. These folk call themselves the Chosen of God, though I doubt me that any sane god would willingly own them as his. Nor is the pack we raided all of them—there are possibly a full dozen groups scattered along the eastern verges of the prairie.

"As among all folk, more of their females usually live to full maturity than do males; but because their singularly senseless religion allows a man but a single wife and forbids the keeping of concubines, their forefathers devised a cruel means of reducing the excess females in each generation, perverting their already adulterated religion still further in order to countenance their cruelty.

"Even the primal form of their religion taught that woman was the font and container of all evil, that she was the real cause of godly man's downfall from the grace of their creator. That religion also taught that woman was inferior to man, and that to serve man in all ways, to bear and to suckle his children, and, throughout the whole of her life, to implore the still-wrathful creator for forgiveness for her inherited part in her ancestress' misdeed were and could be her only functions."

A ripple of comments, both spoken and telepathic, lapped along the irregular lines of seated clansfolk. Consternation that such silly folk adhering to such arrant stupidities could continue to exist at all was voiced along with heated condemnation of such practices.

Milo raised a hand to draw attention back to himself and his words and beamings. "Wait, Kinsfolk, there is more . . . and far worse. The tenets I just recounted were of the old, the archaic religion upon which the current creed was built.

"Now each separate pack of these peculiar Dirtmen lives under the suzerainty of a man called by the title 'Elder'; this is a hereditary office, I have been told, passed down from father to son and so on to grandson and great-grandson. It is one of the functions of this chief to swive each and every girl as soon as she is become nubile, continuing his swivings of them at intervals until they are wedded to some man of the community.

"However, should any of these girls conceive of the Elder, they are degraded, flogged, reviled; their heads are shaven and their scalps are dyed; they are cast out of their families and denied by all of their kin. They are clothed in rags, assigned hard, difficult and lowly chores and fed only such scraps and garbage as they can scavenge.''

The ripple had now become a murmur like that of distant surf. Warriors and matrons and maidens commented that it might be a good thing to scourge the prairie of such bestial and clearly misogynistic half-wits.

Continuing, with louder voice and stronger beamings, Milo said, ''Should the girl miscarry from her ill-treatment, she is flogged again, dragged far, far out on the prairie and left to wander, naked and helpless. For these folks are not as are we; they know not how to find food or even water and can easily die of hunger and thirst in the midst of what we would consider a plentitude of both.

''If she carried to term and delivers a boy-babe, she will be allowed to remain until that babe be weaned, then flogged and cast out onto the prairie. Should she, however, bear a girl-babe, they both will be cast out as soon as possible.''

There was silence for a moment after Milo ceased to speak and transmit his thoughts, then Zak Baikuh of Krooguh shook his head slowly and spoke.

''It's as has been said here, Uncle Milo, this pack of Dirtmen have all clearly lost their wits; not that Dirtmen of any stripe are renowned for wits to begin with, else they'd none of them live out their entire lives in immobile, stinking hovels, all a-wallow in their own filth, as they do.''

''Uncle Milo,'' asked Djahn Staiklee of Krooguh, ''has ever another Kindred clan admitted a woman born of this singular breed of Dirtmen?''

Milo nodded. ''Two that I know of personally, Djahn. One was Clan Grai, and not too many days' ride from this very spot, either. The other was wedded into Clan Tchizuhm and the girl-babe found with her was adopted, of course. I never got to meet the woman, but I did converse with the daughter, who by then was the first wife of a subchief of Clan Maklenuhn. No doubt there have been others, over the years, but widely spread as our clans are and must be, chances that we would hear of such cases are slim.''

Staiklee wrinkled up his forehead and asked, ''Grai? Clan Grai? Wasn't it Clan Grai that was almost wiped out by some strange malady, years agone? Who better than strangers to bring in disease and needless death to our clan?''

Another warrior stood and added, "Yes, Uncle Milo, there are few enough of us Kindred, and our enemies are numerous, savage, and await only our weakening, whatever its cause."

Chief Dik pursed his lips. "Yes, Uncle Milo, I, too, recall something about that which struck Clan Grai, but . . .?''

"That which struck Clan Grai, which all but wiped them out," interjected Milo, "had nothing to do with strangers, happened twenty or more years before they ever found that poor girl and her suckling babe. I don't know what the illness was and I doubt that anyone else will ever know, but it bore some resemblance to one of the killer plagues that almost wiped out all of mankind in the world that once was. Perhaps the clan chanced to camp among, even dug up, artifacts that still harbored seeds of those terrible plagues. But that is all many years past and bears no relation to the matter of this girl, Behtiloo Hansuhn.

"Tim Staiklee of Krooguh lifted her, so he and his clan have first rights, but I rode that raid, too; I led it. She has dwelt in my yurt since the raid, and she and my wives are comfortable together. So be you all warned, if Tim Staiklee of Krooguh does not, *for whatever reason,* take her to wife, I, Chief Milo Morai of Morai, will surely do so.

"Make up your mind, Dik Krooguh. Clan Krooguh's loss will be the gain of Clan Morai! For," he added shrewdly, knowing full well just how Horseclansfolk thought, what they truly valued in their lives, "the one characteristic that all of these adopted Dirtman castoffs seem to share is that they all have proved fine breeders; and as our kinsman here has but just remarked, we Kindred are precious few in these lands.''

And that last was all that was required. Chief Dik Krooguh of Krooguh clasped an arm protectively around the girl, announcing loudly to all, "No, Uncle Milo, she will wed my nephew, Tim Staiklee of Krooguh. The rite will take place immediately. You, Djahn Staiklee, hold your peace! That is a chief's order. You mean well, I know, but I'm thinking that you fret needlessly in this matter.

"Tim, boy, come closer, stand right there. Now, Behtiloo Hansuhn, would you be a woman of the Horseclans?''

Telepathically coached by Ehstrah Morai, Bettylou replied

with a simple head-nod and softly spoken, "Yes, Honored Chief, I would become such."

Chief Dik returned her nod, smiled broadly, briefly took her swollen body into his arms and kissed her on each cheek, then full on the lips. Stepping back, he announced in a loud voice—a voice of such pitch as to rise even above the tumult of battle, as it often had in times past—"Kinsfolk, this woman here beside me is Behtiloo Hansuhn of Krooguh. Although she was not born of the Kindred, still is she your kinswoman. Defame her, and you will feel my whip; offer her injury, and you will feel the edge of Clan Krooguh steel."

Turning back to her, Chief Dik said, almost conversationally, "Behtiloo Hansuhn of Krooguh, you no longer are a war captive. You are a freeborn clanswoman and, until wed, you are as one of my own daughters. My yurt and all things within it are free to your use.

"But Sacred Sun does not like to shine upon women without men or men without women, for such is not natural or proper. Male needs female and female needs male that both may survive in a world which though often warm and comfortable is just as often harsh and pitiless. Also, as neither the bull nor the cow, the ram nor the ewe, can alone increase the herd or the flock, neither, alone, can the clansman or the clanswoman add to the future strength of the clan."

Still lightly holding her with his one arm, the chief laid his other hand on Tim Staiklee of Krooguh's shoulder. "Now, my nephew Tim here would have you as his first wife, which is a position of honor in the clans. Unless you, yourself, will it otherwise, you will never be less until Wind takes you.

"Tim is seventeen or eighteen winters—I forget exactly which and it doesn't matter anyway. He's a good mindspeaker, a proven warrior and a skilled hunter, and he's no novice bedmate—I'll warrant he's sired a few babes of his own already, were the truth known and did anyone care.

"He owns some loot from his raidings, and I'm told that he's an inborn skill at arrow-making and fletching, so even in his dotage he should be a real asset to his family and clan.

"He's not ill-featured, as any can see, he makes regular use of the sweat yurt, shaves his face and usually affects clean clothing.

"Life is rarely easy, child, but it is less hard for two than for one alone, even less hard for many than for few; so I now ask you, Behtiloo Hansuhn of Krooguh: Will you here and now become the first wife of Tim Staiklee of Krooguh?"

"I . . . I w . . . will, Honored Patri . . . Chief," she replied.

For a moment, all things—the figures of Tim, her new husband, the short, stocky chief, the folk gathered around, the outlines of the yurts beyond them—seemed to shimmer, then the trodden, dusty ground rushed up at her face and all of the world became a roaring, red-black nothingness, spiraling tightly and ever more tightly around and around with a pressure that would have been unbearable had it lasted a heartbeat longer.

When she again opened her eyes it was to behold the inside of the roof of a yurt, but not the now-familiar Morai yurt. This new yurt appeared somewhat larger, more commodious. Gear and clothing and many other items hung from the roof supports, while some dozen or more of the wood-and-leather chests were arrayed around the circumference of the dwelling. Beyond the sleeping-rug on which she lay, she observed the floor to be covered in nothing more than the withered stubs of brittle dried grass.

Not too far away, she could hear raucous voices raised in song and the sound of harps and drums and some wailing instruments she never before heard. When she made to prop herself up on her elbows, a brisk but not unkindly voice spoke from the shadows.

"Stay there, girl." said the deep-pitched female voice. "Don't try to get up yet—you're weaker than you think. You were ill treated and malnourished for far too long, and then that Ehstrah tried to work you to death today. Who can wonder that you fainted?

"That half-wit husband of mine won't come near to you, won't allow any of the rest to. But despite his obsessions, he damned well knows better than to gainsay *me*. Ill you certainly are, but not a bit diseased or my name isn't Lainuh Krooguh.

"My husband's concubine is skilled at brewing herbal teas, and that is what I have set her to. When she brings it, you drink it, all of it, for all it's bitter as gall; then, when you waken, tomorrow, we'll see to putting you to rights, else you'll run the risk of dying along with your babe at the birthing.

"I must now get back to the celebration, but the slave, Dahnah, will watch over you in my absence. Goodnight, my newest daughter-in-law. Drink all the tea, now."

Bettylou's second awakening was to a bustle of activity all around her, with men and women and children rolling up sleeping-rugs and carrying them out of the yurt, then returning to lift down hanging items, pack and bear out chests and trunks and otherwise strip the dwelling down to the grass-stubble floor, Finally, Tim Krooguh came to squat by her side. When he had slipped one arm beneath her shoulders and the other under her knees, he stood up easily and bore her outside, while the woman who had brewed the medicinal tea for her rolled the rug and followed him, replacing it outside that Tim might once more stretch Bettylou upon it.

"T . . . Tim . . .?" she quavered, and he turned back to her, smiling.

"Yes, wife?"

"What is happening? Is there something wrong? Have I . . . did I bring trouble to you too?"

He laughed lightly. "Now how could you possibly bring on trouble, silly? No, Mother has just decided that the yurt has been in one spot for long enough. This happens at least once every moon, sometimes twice. You'll get used to it."

A nude woman strode over to the two of them, the ever-present wind tugging at her still-dripping black hair. For all that Bettylou was certain she must be at least as old as the girl's own mother, the body looked far more youthful, radiant in health, with little sag to the breasts and skin that, where wind and sun had not had their way with it, was even fairer than Bettylou's own.

She came to a stop between Tim and Bettylou and, while squeezing rivulets of water from handsful of her long hair, began to speak in a voice that the girl remembered from the previous night.

"Well, you all woke her up, did you, despite my admonitions? Ah, the more fool I to expect that any of you know what working quietly means. You make more noise than a cattle stampede, I'd swear. I could hear you all thumping and bumping and huffing even while I was inside the sweat yurt!"

"But, Mother," said Tim, "my wife would have been awakened in any case when I bore her out of the yurt."

Lainuh Krooguh sighed. "Did I not clearly recall the birthing of you, Tim, I'd wonder if you truly were my son, at times like this, anyway. What need was there to carry your wife out of the yurt at all? All that was needed was to have lifted the yurt from over her, carried it to the new location I marked out this morning and refurnished it. *Then* you could have come back and fetched Behtiloo here, and she would have had much more sleep. Did no one of you think of so doing the job?" She sighed again, gustily, and shook her damp head, adding resignedly, "No, I suppose not. I thank Sun and Wind I'm here to think for you all."

Turning her piercing blue eyes on the recumbent girl, she spoke again in the brisk but kindly tone of the night before. "So you're awake despite my best efforts. You must be wolf-hungry, and, well as I know my household, it will take them until at least dark to get the yurt moved and decently set up again. So get you up—if you need help in walking, Tim is here; for all else he and his siblings lack, they are all strong as bulls—and we'll stroll over to my brother's yurt for a bit of Chief Krooguh's vaunted hospitality."

Dik Krooguh sat on his sleeping-rug, still wearing most of his feast finery. He looked as if he should have been buried days earlier. His face was gray and stubbled, his eyes were severely bloodshot, and the hands that held a tarnished cup of a medicinal tea were exceedingly tremulous. Moreover, he winced as from a buffet at even the tiniest noises.

Many of the other inhabitants of the yurt still were prone on their own sleeping-rugs, and of the few who were up, most looked little better than the chief, going about their tasks slowly, ineptly and with many a piteous moan.

Bettylou had never seen the like, and she mindspoke the unworded question to Lainuh, who beamed back, "Misuse, last night late, of several gallons of a restorative potion from the far south; it is prepared from a certain plant of the cactus family and is called *taikeelah*. Utilized properly, as the clan supply had been for some years, it is a valuable medicine, but guzzled in quantity as my brother and many of his household did last night, it brings on first gaiety, then deep sleep, then illness such as you see here."

Striding over to where the chief unsteadily sat, heedless of what or on whom her bootheels fell, Lainuh squatted beside her crapulous brother, took the silver cup from his weak grasp and held it firmly to his lips until he had drained it to the dregs. A moment later, he began to gag, and taking his arm, she led him, stumbling, out of the yurt, leaving Bettylou to her own devices in the midst of sleeping or terribly hungover near-strangers.

"Oh, Wind and Sacred Sun, I'm dying, I know I'm dying, but it's taking so long to die." The bubbling, gasping half-moan emanated from a body lying at Bettylou's very feet.

Kneeling, the girl placed a hand on the sufferer's forehead and found it hot, while the breath that wafted up into her face was foul, hot and rank.

She looked around her to find that she was now the only erect occupant of the yurt, the only soul available to give aid or bare comfort to the obviously ill—possibly, deathly ill—man. So she set about it forthwith.

As in the Morai yurt, so in this one; several canvas buckets were hung from the upper framework, and she examined each in turn until she located one that contained water, then searched among the dim clutter until she located a rectangle of cloth and a reasonably clean horn cup.

With the one soaked, then wrung out and the other filled with water, she picked her way among the recumbent bodies back to the side of the ill man. He still moaned weakly, though he had not moved an inch since she had left his side.

He gasped, then groaned when she laid the damp cloth on his fevered brow, his lips moved as if in speech, but no sound issued forth, and she was too preoccupied just then to try a mental probe of his mind with her newfound talent for such.

Kneeling beside her patient, Bettylou propped his head up on the side of her knee and her free hand, then held the horn cup of water to his dry lips, but so maneuvering the vessel that he needs must sip rather than gulp the tepid fluid. When he had drained the cup, she carefully lowered his head and wiped his face with the damp cloth before replacing it on his brow.

". . . too good to me," the man uttered half-audibly. ". . . best slave girl a man ever had. She was right, you know, Dahnah, dammit, she's most always right. Shouldn't have drunk that vile Mehkikuhn concoction last night, not the first jug of it. But, hell, Dik is our chief, after all, and when *he*'s of a mind to imbibe, he will have company.

"Where is herself, Dahnah? I'll bet she's fit to be tied this morning."

The croaking voice was in no way familiar; nonetheless, Bettylou realized from the words spoken that this patient of hers could be none other than her new father-in-law, Djahn Staiklee, he who had voiced so many vehement objections to her marriage into his family.

"I am not your slave woman, Mr. Staiklee," she said finally. "I am Bettylou Hanson, now wife of your son, Tim. Your slave woman, Lainuh, is helping to move your yurt just now; your wife, Lainuh, has taken Chief Dik Krooguh outside to care for his illness."

"I hope he dies this morning!" snarled Staiklee viciously. "And if his hangover is one tenth part as bad as is mine own, he just might. I can now understand why the traders call that damned *taikeelah* stuff 'popskull,' indeed I can.

"And the old bugtit would mix it measure for measure with berry wine and drink it, yes he would, and he would chivvy every one of us into joining him in his suicidal madness, oh yes. I take back my words; I hope he doesn't die this day—a mere death is too good for the likes of him.

"So, herself is caring for him, eh? That's typical, to be expected, that she would ignore me, her own husband, to give her comforts to Dik, instead. Her damned brother has always been of far more importance to our Lainuh than have I or her children or her grandchildren or anyone else, for that matter. Yet she begrudges me my one, single concubine, Dahnah, and will not hear any mention of my buying another. She treats me most unfairly, treats me like a . . . a . . ."

"I treat you a damned sight better than you have ever deserved, Djahn Staiklee!" snapped Lainuh's deep voice from behind Bettylou. "I know that you envy, have always envied, the time I spend with Dik, but I care not how much you pout and natter on that account. Dik is my brother and I love him, and even if I did not love him, even if we two were not so closely related, still is he the chief. He has been and still is a good chief for our clan, but he is aging, is no longer in good health for all of his robust appearance, and I worry about him, as should you and everyone else.

"That is why I so hate to see him unduly sicken himself as he did last night. You folks, the entire pack of you! Had you all refused to drink that stuff with him, had you simply arisen and gone back to your various yurts, he would not have guzzled that *taikeelah,* you know that; such is and has always been his way.

"This morning, outside there, a few minutes ago, the chief of our clan retched up a quantity of bright red blood! He is now in the sweat yurt with Uncle Milo, Ehstrah Morai and a few others. As soon as Behtiloo and I have eaten, I intend to spend the rest of this day and as long else as it takes to heal my brother of the effects of his follies. I'll send Dahnah, shortly, to help you back to our yurt.

"I care not what use you make of yourself as long as I am away tending to Dik. Go hunting, if you wish; lead out a raid; it's of no matter. But you were well advised to stay out of my sight and hearing for at least a week . . . maybe two!"

Staiklee did just that. He left on a hunt the following morning, taking with him his second-eldest son, Djahnee, two of Chief Dik's sons and a few of his own cronies, along with two late-adolescent prairiecats and a sufficient quantity of horses to provide everyone with three mounts.

Nor was his the first or the only such party to embark, for the feasters had consumed a goodly proportion of all of the meat and other foodstuffs in the camp, leaving little more than milk and cheese, butter and herb teas to sustain the folk until more could be brought in.

Chief Milo took a party of young warriors—Tim's eldest brother, Dikee, among them—several veteran prairiecats and a large remuda of horses and mules on a week-long ride that would bring them within raiding distance of a cluster of Dirtman villages to the southeast of the campsite.

"South of here by seven or eight days' ride," he had told the chiefs and subchiefs when he asked for young men to ride the raid with him. "The harvest is just in, and do we want a fresh supply of grain and beans, now is the time to strike and that is the place, for you can rest assured that any new attempt at the place from which Tim Krooguh got his wife so soon after would result in a certain battle with those very peculiar Dirtmen and possible injuries or deaths, even, for some of the raiders."

Chief Skaht shook his head dubiously. "Uncle Milo, no man here doubts your wisdom and war skills, but as I recall, that pack of Dirtmen are tough, some of them really war-trained. We—Clan Skaht, that is—raided them years agone, when I was a younker of some sixteen winters, and though we did drive them out of their place, take loot and burn part of that place, we lost near half our warriors in so doing, and it has taken this many years to again become a sizable clan."

Milo frowned. "Yes, I've been told of that raid and its bitter consequences, years ago, by some of the men who led it. They owned their biggest error was in riding a raid with a friendly but non-Kindred warband, who attacked precipitately and long before all was in readiness for the planned attack. They also held that there just were too many of them for the task, too many to be adequately controlled. Also, they had but one prairiecat, and he was killed early on.

"I, on the other hand, intend to take only the best of the young, but blooded, warriors, enough cats to do the job and enough horses to allow for a speedy escape from the wrath of however many Dirtmen are left when we're done."

"Who will you be wanting for subchiefs?" demanded Chief Skaht, that being his way of announcing that he was dropping his understandable objections of the mounting of the raid.

In deference to his ill health, the council had been held in Chief Dik Krooguh's yurt, and, immediately all the rest had departed, the ailing man shuffled his way over to the tanist yurt to tell his sister of all that had so recently transpired.

At the conclusion of the recountal, Chief Dik said, "He wanted, would have taken, all of my sons and Dikee and Tim, as well. But I said no.

"Our Djahnee has gone riding off hunting with your husband, and that's bad enough. I've had a worrisome foreboding about that since they all left; Djahn is a fine fellow, a tough fighter, a splendid bowman and all that, but any who know him well will also know that he—like every Staiklee man—has a tendency to be reckless on occasion. As if that were not bad enough, he has on more than one hunt done downright dangerous things and gotten some men who tried to emulate him hurt, since few other men own his lightning-fast reflexes. I've already lost two boys I'd chosen to succeed me as chief; I don't like the thought of losing another.

"Worse, I like even less the possibility of the loss of all

your sons and the chaos that that would breed in the Clan Council upon my demise, so I allowed Chief Morai to take only Dikee on his raid. Tim will stay here as surety that come what may, there will be one living legal heir to the chieftaincy of Clan Krooguh.''

CHAPTER VI

Chief Dik Krooguh's looming presentiment was well founded, tragically well founded. The hunting party came back early, fast and with precious little game. There was one fewer rider to return than had gone out, too. Young Djahnee—or his lifeless husk, at least—returned stiff, roped onto the back of his horse.

No one saw Djahn Staiklee's face as he rode into camp, halted before the yurt he called home and dismounted, then commenced the task of untying his eldest son's corpse from the trailing horse could doubt the depth and severity of his grief. So no one attempted oral or telepathic communication until he had freed and lifted down the heavy, awkward burden.

Then, many hands took over the task of bearing the body to the bath area for cleansing. Other men, of both clans, hitched horses to carts, collected axes and mounted other horses before setting out to the nearest wooded area to collect fuel for a pyre.

Bettylou expected the very worst when Staiklee came face to face with his wife, Lainuh, but she was surprised. Cognizant of the sincerity of the man's grief and suffering, the sister of the chief was the very soul of consideration and comfort to the returned hunter, quietly ordering others to unsaddle his mounts and bring in all gear that belonged in her yurt.

When he had been relieved of his gear and outer clothing, had had his riding boots replaced with the felt boots worn in camp, when he had been seated in his accustomed place and had been offered herb tea and milk (both of which he drank) and a bowl of curds (which he refused), he finally told the

63

sad, simple tale of tragedy and death. He opened his mind
that all capable of such might share in his memories.

The scouting cats had spotted a herd of those herbivores
that Horseclansfolk called smaller screwhorns. These creatures,
for all that they stood at most some nine hands at the withers,
could easily outdistance a horse for a long enough time to
lose themselves in the high grasses to the south, so Djahn had
had the best bowmen—himself and young Djahnee included—
dismount and take well-separated paths through the shorter
grasses and brush to attempt to get within certain bow range
of the prized quarry.

That phase of the hunt had been successful. No less than
five of the antelopes had been arrowed, two of them shot by
Djahn Staiklee. It was not until the diminished herd was tiny
with distance that young Djahnee was missed and searched
out.

They found him lying on his back in the grass, already
dead. A smear of blood on his neck and two tiny puncture
wounds just behind the angle of the jaw told the grim story of
snakebite.

The tableau also told the tale of bravery unto death. For the
boy might have been doctored and saved had he cried out, but
that same cry would surely have spooked the antelope herd,
too, and this the stricken lad would not do . . . not even
though he knew full well that his continued silence would
cost him his young life.

Tears streaking her lined cheeks, Lainuh withdrew from
her husband's mind and beamed an urgent call to her brother,
the chief, and to old Djef Krooguh, the clan bard. The chief
must know immediately of the death of his nephew and the
bard must know the full extent of the act of lonely heroism of
the dead boy, that he might compose the verses for the
funeral and add appropriate lines to the Song of Krooguh so
that her son's honorable deeds would be recalled and rever-
enced by the generations that would follow.

That evening, the woodcutters came back with their carts
heaped high, and early the next evening, Djahnee was sent to
Wind—a simple ceremony, followed by cremation of the
body. Tim was often to remark sadly in later years that they
might have better made a larger pyre and waited a few days.

*   *   *

Actually, it was somewhat longer a period—nearly three weeks—before Milo and his raiders returned, all dusty and exhausted, some wounded, but all heavy-laden with assorted loot and wildly exuberant. But not all of them came back from that raid; there were a handful of empty saddles. There was also a litter swung between two mules, and in that litter lay what was left of Dikee Staiklee of Krooguh, barely alive.

When she got her first close look at what the litter bore, Lainuh Krooguh mindspoke Tim, saying, "My son, go at once to your uncle. Tell him to begin with you immediately, for only you now are left to be chief in his stead."

Turning back to Dikee, she tried to enter his thoughts, but found only the confusion of intense pain and semiconsciousness, and she felt even more strongly that his spirit was upon the very edge of taking flight from his tattered, battered husk.

"What happened?" she demanded of no one in particular.

Milo himself answered tiredly, "The Dirtman village is surrounded with a palisade. We had set afire the gate tower and three others and were battering in the gate with a trimmed treetrunk slung between armored horses, all supposedly ready to rush in immediately the gate sundered or fell.

"Then Dikee and certain others—most of them now either wounded or gone to Wind—took it into their heads to scale an undefended section of palisade and try, I suppose, to hack their way through to the gate, to open it from inside.

"By the time we got that gate down and cut our way through to where the group had made their stand, only Dikee was still on his feet and swinging his saber. We arrowed down the three men he was just then fighting—grown men and big, Lainuh, in steel armor—then did what little we could for him, and that was little enough.

"I did not, frankly, expect to arrive back here with his spirit still abiding within his flesh. But the few times he spoke or mindspoke, he vowed that he would not die until he had seen you, his wife and his children once more."

The mother slowly shook her head. "Stubborn and reckless, just like his father. I suppose it's as well for the clan that he won't live to be chief."

Milo laid his grubby hand on her shoulder. "We all grieve with you, sister mine. But Djahnee is a good young man, and he will make a fine chief for—"

She interrupted, "Our Djahnee is gone to Wind, Chief

Milo, Snakebite, while hunting antelope with his father's party almost a moon ago now. Only young Tim is left to us."

"He will make a good, steady, just chief for Clan Krooguh, Lainuh," Milo assured her solemnly. "He's brave enough when push comes to shove, intelligent enough to quickly achieve a measure of wisdom, and he completely lacks that strain of wild recklessness that seems to run through most of the Staiklees. He may well turn out to be the best of all possible successors to Chief Dik. Perhaps that is why Sacred Sun and Wind saw to it that he would be the next chief."

It was decided in a council of chiefs and subchiefs which was convened the next day that the camp should be moved. There were a number of good and compelling reasons for this choice.

Perhaps the most compelling was the fact that the herds of horses, cattle and sheep were perforce moving farther and farther out from the camp perimeters to find sufficient graze; this was dangerous for them and inconvenient for those whose task it was to guard or care for them.

And the camp itself was gradually becoming too spread out as the occupants of each individual yurt sought a fresh location for their dwelling, for all of the fighters to assemble easily in the event of an attack by hostile men.

It were wise, too, that the allied clans seek out some more sheltered spot in which to winter. Their hope was to find a place with a nearby supply of plentiful wood and water, a location with bluffs or high, thick stands of trees to break the force of the wintry winds and retard the buildup of snows too deep for the hoofed ones to scrape away from the grasses beneath.

There was also the possibility that Dirtmen might be on the trail of the raiders Chief Milo of Morai had so successfully led.

"The buggers might feel that they have to fight us again and try to get back the grain and whatnot we lifted off them, are they and their community to survive the winter intact. We came away with some ton or near to it of wheat, plus several hundredweights of dried beans and Wind alone knows how much shelled corn. There were also casks of edible oils, dried or pickled or preserved fruits and vegetables, some smoked meat, spirits of various sorts and a whole other catalog of nonedible loot.

"Because of the limitations imposed upon us by the wounded and dying members of our party and the exceptionally numerous and heavy loads we had to pack, our return trip was both slower and straighter than I would have preferred. So, yes, I agree that we might well show wisdom to move the camp . . . soon and far and with our best speed. Chief Milo of Morai has spoken."

"Cat brothers," beamed old Bloody Fangs, the cat chief, "there is also the fact that during our long sojourn hereabouts, we have killed off or scared away most of the game of any real, meaningful size. Such few as remain are far away or scarce or very, very wary. Milk and curds are fine for you two-legs or for kittens or cubs, but a grown cat wants and needs must have fresh meat every day. So, yes, let us move to an area not hunted out. Thus says Bloody Fangs."

The decision was made and unanimously agreed upon at that meeting. But there was yet another reason for moving the camp, a reason which no one of them would voice in council. They all felt this spot to be unlucky, for no less than nine young men had died while the clans had camped in this spot—six from Clan Krooguh, three from Clan Skaht—and that figure did not even include the old woman who had died in her sleep, the stripling of Clan Skaht who had been tossed and gored to his death by a herd bull, a girl who had inexplicably drowned in a nearby creek and another girl, only a toddler, who had fallen prey to a treecat while foraging in a stretch of forest with others of her clan. So, yes, they all felt deep within them that it was indeed high time to move on to a possibly more salubrious, a luckier place to bide for a while.

Bettylou's first experience of camp-breaking and packing was memorable, to say the least. Preparation, alone for the breaking of camp took something over a full week.

First, the four ponderous wagons and the seemingly numberless profusion of high-wheeled carts—each yurt seemed to have two or even three carts—were manhandled into camp from the space whereon they had been parked since the first pitching of this camp. Knowledgeable men examined the running gear of each conveyance, replacing any questionable axle or spoke or felly, beam, rod, coupling pole, bolster, axletree, hind hound, kingpin, sand board, hub, and so on. Then the bodies of wagons and carts had to receive identical care of scrutiny and, where necessary, repair or replacement.

The wheeled vehicles done to the critical satisfaction of the old men who had supervised every facet of the operations, the men were turned to similar examination of and work upon the yokes and harness for the animals that would draw wagons and carts.

Lainuh had every living soul old enough to reason and walk unaided well organized with assigned tasks, schedules and deadlines for completion or assigned tasks in and about the yurt. Djahn Staiklee and Tim were, of course, with the rest of the men and not available for her assignments, and Dahnah's twelve-year-old son was riding herd guard of nights while undergoing his warrior training of days, and no plea or veiled threat would persuade the subchief in charge to alter the boy's schedule so that he might be free to work for her.

"Lainuh, that boy has less than two years left to become a warrior. And the clan stands in need of warriors just now, as you of all people should know.

"He'll never be better than a middling bowman; he's just not got the coordination for it. But he's a fine horseman and promises to be very strong, and I mean to make a lanceman of him, maybe even teach him the finer points of axework. And both of those take time, time and more time.

"So, no, he's of more and better use to the clan in honing his weapons skills than he could possibly be lugging chests and barrels and the like at your beck."

Lainuh returned to the yurt in a cold rage, and its other occupants wisely avoided her for a while, knowing of long and often painful experience that a thwarted Lainuh was better left strictly alone until she had had a chance to cool down a bit or at least take the razor edge off her anger, take the murder out of her heart.

It was only two days prior to the announced date of departure that the carts were brought to the yurt for packing. There were two smaller carts and one larger, the larger intended to bear the complete yurt and the two smaller anything else that for whatever reason could not be packed on the back of a horse.

Lainuh ranted and raved almost incessantly until the carts' arrival, ceaselessly badgering Djahn Staiklee and Tim whenever they stumbled in, half dead with exhaustion for a meal, a bath and change of clothes or a few hours of sleep.

That is, she did so until the evening when her husband,

pushed beyond endurance by her tirades, dragged her outside by the hair and soundly thrashed her with a leather strap. This gave those in the yurt an entire night of peace and quiet, most welcome, both of them.

The first scouts returned while the packing of the carts and the wagons were commencing. The route agreed upon had been to strike due west for a week, then to bear southwest until a suitable winter campsite was found. The scouts and the cats that had accompanied them had reconnoitered the first leg of the proposed migration and were back to report to the chiefs.

The four scouts and two cats met with the three chiefs in the yurt of Chief Milo, that home now stripped to little more than felt walls, wooden supports and a few carpets.

Djaimz Skaht, a middle-aged nomad who had led the scouting party, announced, "There's no reason why the first fifty or so miles shouldn't be easy, as we'll be trekking roughly parallel to any really big rivers, nor could we find any traces of a recent movement of bodies of men, mounted or otherwise.

"It's a good bit of game on the route we scouted, including a fairly sizable herd of small shaggies we saw on the last day west; they seemed to be heading south or southeast, and had a lot of big screwhorns mixed in with them. There were wolves following that herd, of course."

"And more than wolves, cat-brothers," put in Steelclaws, one of the prairiecats. "We cats found traces of at least one of the great bears and two different kinds of cat—the shaggy cat and the smaller, running cat."

"Shaggy cats? My cat-brother is certain of this?" beamed Milo with clear concern. The so-called "shaggy cats" were no less than the species that long, long ago had been known as African Lions. In the aftermath of the disasters that had nearly extirpated mankind on the face of the earth, many of these and other alien animals then kept in zoos, theme parks and even on private ranches scattered about the North American continent had escaped to freedom and, in the case of lions, at least, had adapted, thrived and multiplied over the intervening centuries. The prides preferred open plains and were mostly found near herds of bison, feral cattle or horses and the native or alien antelopes, trailing after them on their great seasonal migrations to north and south.

They were not of much real danger to an armed and mounted Horseclanner, unless they happened to have hungry designs on the horse. And even then a Horseclan steed could outrun the largest of lions with any sort of a lead on the cat to begin. But mere scent of a lion or two could drive cattle, sheep, even the reasoning horses wild with uncontrolled panic, and more than a few nomads had been killed and maimed in trying to turn the leading beasts of stampedes.

The wolves he discounted; they would be well fed this time of the year and traveling in small, family groups rather than in the huge, murderous, ravenous packs of winter. But the bear could be another question entirely.

He had never heard of lions turning man-eater and -hunter, and though winter wolves would tear apart any creature they could get at—two legs or four—most well-fed wolves had a strong tendency to avoid mankind and his camps. But the huge prairie grizzlies often—too often, for Milo's liking— seemed to relish manflesh and would go far out of their usual ways to get at potential victims, even entering clan camps and tearing through the walls of yurts to come within tooth range of the folk within.

Moreover, they were usually devilishly hard to kill, having immense vitality and continuing to wreak pure havoc even when stippled with so many arrows as to resemble gigantic tailless porcupines.

"Were we trekking due west only," he beamed to the other two chiefs, "I'd say that we should angle a bit to the north and thus avoid any trouble with the predators following that herd. But since we needs must head south after a week or so on the move, I say set out southeast and take our chances with the bear and cats and wolves, while living well off game. At least, Sacred Sun be praised, we're a little too far south here for wolverines or blackfoot beasts."

"Wind be thanked for those favors, at least," nodded Dik Krooguh. "A wolverine it was maimed my hand, you know. We just will have to start beefing up herd guards, day and night on the march—more cats, more maiden-archers and some good lancemen with heavy hunting spears."

"Just so," agreed Chief Skaht, "and more scouts out ahead of us, scouting in depth, no slipshod stuff. Another thing, too, one that no one is going to like, for all it's necessary, all things considered: We'd be wise to start keeping enough horses in camp to mount all our warriors quickly, if push comes to shove, because you all know damned well that no lion- or bear-panicked horse is going to respond to a mindcall. This breed of Kindred horses of ours are smarter than the bulk of their ilk and they can even reason, up to a point, but we'd be foolish to not recognize their limitations and guard against the dire results of a panicky herd on a night of need.''

The cat chief sat up from his crouch and yawned widely agape, carefully curling his long, broad, red-pink tongue away from the winking points of his oversized fangs. ''Cat brothers,'' he beamed, ''as always, you vastly overestimate the reasoning abilities and general intelligence of the horse tribe. Our Kindred race is not all that much more intelligent than many another non-Kindred breed of equine. Most mules, in fact, are far and away the mental superiors of most horses, which is why we prairiecats, if ride we must, would do so on the back of a mule.

''The horse king will be displeased that you insist on keeping so many of his best fighters in camp, but I think you are right, brother chief; all you two-legs are so slow without horses, and when fighting bears or shaggy cats, speed can be the difference between living and not living. Besides, your chosen mounts will be far less likely not to bolt if they know that most of the prairiecats and a whole camp full of armed two-legs are around them to protect them.''

Bettylou would never have believed just how quickly the large yurt could be broken down to its components of felt, canvas, leather and wood and packed upon the largest of the three carts, which was drawn by four, rather than two, horses.

As for the chests, most of them were strapped onto packhorses, while the two smaller carts were used to transport sacks and bags, barrels and kegs and water skins, tripods and kettles and odd-sized or -shaped impedimenta.

The last night on the old campground was slept, what little sleep there was for the adults, under the stars, and with the first light of false dawn, the rugs and coverings of each individual were rolled up tightly, bound into shape, then tucked into odd spaces in the cartloads or strapped behind saddles.

The slow-moving herds had been started on the trail three

days before the scheduled departure of the carts and wagons,
which droving took the services of almost all of the older
children, for numbers of sheep, cattle and a few goats had
been taken in raids on the eastern farming communities while
the clans had camped here and these supernumerary animals
would serve to help to feed both folk and cats in the hard,
cold days of winter-coming when game was scarce or
unobtainable.

Accustomed as she was to farm wagons, Bettylou was still
mightily impressed by the four ponderous wagons each of
which bore the effects of a chief (including the cat chief) and
his immediate family. Each of them cleared almost two cubits
off the level ground, the high-sided bodies riding on wheels
six feet or more in diameter. Like the carts, the bodies were
close-joined and chinked watertight and, she had been in-
formed, could float across rivers just like boats when necessary during treks.

Three of these wagons were each drawn by eight span of
huge, lowing oxen. The other, Chief Milo's, had as motive
power six pairs of brawny mules.

As the Sacred Sun's first rays emerged from the pinkish
eastern haze, whips cracked and the wheels began to turn on
the axles of wagons and carts. Bettylou Hanson turned in the
saddle of her mare to look back at the bare, trampled, dusty
stretch of ground on which the camp had stood and thought of
how much had happened to her there, of how much had
changed, changed for what was assuredly the better.

Farther on, she turned and looked back again, shading her
eyes, wondering if she would ever again see, would ever
again be upon this patch of prairie.

Although she could not then know it, she was to see, to be
upon that patch of prairie again. But it was to be many, many
years later, and the woman who would then look out of those
blue eyes would be changed past anything that the girl,
Bettylou Hanson, could have imagined.

CHAPTER VII

━━━◆━━◆▶━━◆━━

No sooner had a spot been agreed upon for the winter camp, the yurts set up and the most absolutely pressing other necessary things for living done than every nomad not on herd guard set out with sickles and axes to the high-grass areas and the nearest forests to hack down the tough, wiry grasses and fell tree after tree.

An endless parade of carts bore the grasses to central sites within the environs of the camp, where the loads were arranged in thick, high stacks to provide food for the horses when the snows were too deep for the creatures to reach such frozen herbiage as might lie beneath. If it seemed that there would be enough, a small amount of the precious grass hay might even go to the cattle and the sheep. But only a few of these were ever expected to survive a winter this far to the north, in any case; herds would be rebuilt through raiding in the following spring and summer months.

The felled trees were trimmed of branches and dragged to the campsite by spans of oxen, while the larger branches were themselves trimmed, piled onto carts and thus trundled back to add to the growing heaps of wood—wood for fuel, wood for strengthening and insulating the yurts against the coming wind and cold, wood for countless other purposes.

And every day the younger children took carts out to the pasture areas to bring them back loaded with dung—cattle dung, sheep dung and horse dung, plus the droppings of any wild herbivores they chanced across during their trips. This manure was set out carefully to dry on racks made of woven branchlets suspended over a very, very slow and smoky fire and all covered by a makeshift, temporary roof. This structure was situated some three hundred yards from the nearest yurts, in a breezy area and well downwind; nonetheless, her every visit to the latrine pits exposed Bettylou to a stomach-churning reek of the curing dung.

Therefore, she remarked to Ehstrah and Gahbee when they met one morning in the steam yurt, "Whoever thought up that abomination of spread-out dung over on the downstream side of camp knows little about manuring. It should be dumped in a pit and allowed to ferment through the winter, covered in straw."

Ehstrah laughed and shook her head, sending a rain of droplets from her streaming face. "Oh, my dear little fledgling Horseclanswoman! Behtiloo, those cowpats and sheep pellets and horse biscuits aren't for dunging soil; Horseclansfolk don't plant and reap crops, that's for the damned Dirtmen.

"No, we gather and dry out dung for winter cooking fires. Hasn't that damned, conceited, overproud Lainuh taught you anything?"

"But . . . but . . . then what are all those trees being felled for?" questioned Bettylou. "I thought they were for winter fuel."

"They are . . . among other uses," Ehstrah nodded. "But you can be certain that that wood will not be used for cooking in the yurts so long as a single dried cowpat is left to be so used."

"Why?" asked the girl puzzledly. "You and all the others I've seen have been using wood as long . . . well, as long as I've been living with you."

"Yes, that's true, Behtiloo, but you have only lived with us in good weather, warm weather, when the sides are removed from the yurts and the tops often partially rolled up or at least gapped widely, making dissipation of smoke no problem.

"But imagine you how it would be to cook with a wood fire inside a yurt that not only has sides and top firmly closed, save for a peak-hole of the smallest possible size, but has been reinforced with wood and leather and anything else that's available to make it as weather- and air-proof as possible. In a yurt like that, you'll learn quickly to appreciate the true benefits of cooking with dried dung rather than with wood.

"Child, dried dung burns every bit as hot as wood, but it is almost smokeless in the burning. This relative smokelessness makes it far safer, as well, for night-long warmth-fires in a yurt, for more than a few nomads have smothered to death on wintry nights of the smoke from their fires."

"Uncle Milo tells the tale," put in Gahbee, "of nearly an entire clan that died thus, years agone, in a low cave they had walled up with stones and plastered with clay for a winter home."

Bettylou paused, then asked a question that had for long puzzled her. "Why do you and so many of the others call Chief Milo 'Uncle'? And why has he no children or grandchildren or any other blood kin?"

Ehstrah answered, "Behtiloo, Milo is called Uncle because that is what he has always been called. Our parents called him that, their parents called him that and their grandparents and their great-grandparents back to the very beginning of the clans. He, Milo Morai, it was in fact who succored the Sacred Ancestors, led them from the Caves of Death and the waterless lands to the high places and showed them how to live a good, free life. Milo it was who forged first the links between us and the cats and, later, our breed of horses.

"When, long ago, the clans were much smaller and lived all together or, at least, not very far distant one clan from the other, Milo lived with them, guided them, advised them in composing the Couplets of Horseclans Law. Now he travels from area to area, living a year with this clan, the next year with another clan. He and I and Gahbee and Ilsah, we will winter here, then we will move on in the spring and join with another clan for the summer and autumn and winter.

"As to why he has gotten no children of any of us three, well, I—for one—may be just too old to quicken of his seed. But the other two? Well, all that I can say is that his failures are not for lack of trying—heh, heh, at his times, he could put to shame every stallion, bull and ram in all our herds. I'd had two husbands and a full share of other bedmates before I wed Milo, child, and I can honestly say that if nothing else, his tenscore and who knows how many more years of life have rendered him the foremost lover on prairie, plains, deserts and mountains."

"Two hundred years?" exclaimed Bettylou. "That's . . . why it's impossible, just impossible! He looks to be no more than twoscore years at the most. You're joking with me, aren't you, Ehstrah?"

The smile left Ehstrah's lined face. She became serious to

the point of solemnity. "No, I am not joking, child; I am recounting no less than the bald truth about Milo's past deeds and length of life. Although I doubt that anyone besides him knows exactly how old he really is . . . it may be, in fact, that even he doesn't know exactly. At least, each and every time on which I've tried to get a straight answer out of him on that subject, he has either evaded the question completely or given some sort of wildly imprecise answer as 'I'm old as the hills.' or 'Old enough to know better.' "

Despite the hot, billowing clouds of steam, Bettylou shivered involuntarily, felt her nape hairs all a-prickle. Her natal people all firmly believed that the total life span which God had allotted to mankind was threescore and ten years. If any man or woman lived as much as a year beyond that Holy Number, it was assumed to be Devil's Work for certain sure and that man or woman was dragged to the Place of Scourgings and of Death and executed by stoning. If to live a single year over seventy years was symptomatic of the Ancient Evil, how much more so must be a man who was firmly believed to have lived two hundred or more years . . .?

But Ehstrah had been prying at her still-weak mindshield and now she chided, "Enough, Behtiloo, enough! Our Milo is no more evil than are you, than is that babe in your belly. You must try to purge your mind of those terrible, venomous, antihuman tenets to which you had the misfortune to be born and bred.

"Oh, aye, Milo may be devilish at times—devilish, in the sense of that word as used in the Horseclans dialect of the Mehrikan tongue—but then many folk are, both old and young, male and female, human and feline. Furball is devilish, in that sense; so too is your father-in-law, Djahn Staiklee."

Bettylou sighed. "I like him, Ehstrah. But Lainuh says he is suicidally reckless, childish and selfish, unfailingly lazy and seldom gives her and her brother, the chief, the respect due them." She hesitated, then continued, saying, "She drives poor Dahnah, his slave, very hard, almost every day, and waxes most wroth whenever one of us tries to help the woman with whatever chore she has been set at."

Ehstrah's face assumed a grim look and she nodded once, brusquely. "Trying to make his concubine too exhausted for any bedsports, come night; sounds just the way her mind would work.

"You are right to like Djahn Staiklee, Behtiloo. You can honestly respect him, too, for he is none of the things of which Lainuh accuses him . . . at least not to the degree she would have you and the rest of her listeners think he is. Let me tell you the tale of Djahn and Lainuh, child. Some of it I know personally, but much I have learned from others since Milo and I and Gahbee and Ilsah joined these two clans last spring.

"I know Clan Krooguh of old, for although I am a Tchizuhm-born, my first husband was a Krooguh, Chief Dik's younger brother, Gil, in fact. I was living with this clan when first Djahn Staiklee appeared. That was at the big Tribe Camp over a score of years ago, where he bested every man or maiden or matron with his bow and outrode every horserider in that huge aggregation. The two who came closest to besting him were Dik Krooguh at riding and my husband, Gil Krooguh, with the bow, and they three quickly became fast friends.

"Lainuh then was married to a man named Hari, of Clan Rohz, so Dik and Gil got Djahn married to her younger sister, Kahnee. She was a willowy, beautiful girl, that Kahnee Krooguh, but her hips were too narrow for her own good and she died in childbirthing before a year was out. That same winter, our camp was raided by non-Kindred nomads—Mehkikuhns, from the south—and although we did drive them back to whence they came with very heavy losses, we too lost warriors, and one of those wounded unto his eventual death was Hari Rohz, Lainuh's husband.

"Poor Hari's ashes were not cold before Lainuh had set her eyes upon Djahn Staiklee. Chief Zak, Dik's uncle, was a dying man even before he went out to fight half-naked in the midst of a blue norther, so everyone in that three-clan camp knew that Dik would assuredly be Chief Krooguh well before the spring thaw, and so it was not as if Lainuh suffered any dearth of suitors—sons and brothers of chiefs, famous warriors, good providers, all. But she would have none save her dead sister's widower.

"Now Djahn, too, could have had any unmarried, nubile female who happened to take his fancy in all that camp, Behtiloo. He was a well-formed, very handsome young man, a consummate rider and bowman, no mean hand with saber and spear and riata or bola, a valued warrior and hunter.

"He failed to respond to Lainuh's most unsubtle overtures, and this drove her near-mad. She always has been very close to Dik, her brother, and has ever been able to slyly manipulate him, so she set him to win over his friend, Djahn, pointing out that if he just rode off, Clan Krooguh would lose a rare bit of human treasure. And so, between the persuasions of Dik and my Gil and Lainuh herself, Djahn was inveigled to stay on as a permanent member of Clan Krooguh. I think he married Lainuh more as a means of staying around his cronies, Dik and Gil, than for any other reason.

"But the poor man made a bad choice, whatever his real motives, child. Although in the first five years of their marriage, while still I was with Clan Krooguh, I can say that she behaved the good, loving wife, seemed to appreciate the exceptional man, warrior, hunter that now was hers.

"But then my husband, Subchief Gil Krooguh, did not come back from a raid he had led against a settlement of Dirtmen. Chief Dik offered to marry me as his third wife, and I must admit that I considered it . . . . for about ten minutes' time."

Ehstrah smiled. "But I simply was not born to be at the beck and call of a younger woman for the rest of my life, so I married a widower of Clan Morguhn that autumn and went with my new clan to the high plains in the following spring, while Clan Krooguh trekked off due north, following the main herds of game, and I did not again see a Krooguh camp until we arrived here with Milo.

"I have been told or admitted into old friends' memories in regard to all or most of the information that now I am going to impart to you, child."

"Lainuh had two sons by Hari Rohz; they were both mere toddlers when their sire was slain and Lainuh married Djahn Staiklee. Dikee and Djahnee and Tim and another son, Gaib, were all born, one after the other, before I was widowed and married out of Clan Krooguh.

"Lainuh doted on the two Rohz boys and early began to groom the eldest of them, Zak, to someday succeed his uncle, Chief Dik. She succeeded in turning both of those boys into spoiled brats, both dead certain that Sacred Sun rose and set, Wind blew, only for them and their personal pleasures. His arrant insubordination got the eldest Rohz boy killed along with several of his cronies in their first raid. Lainuh could not or, more likely, would not recognize her own culpability in the matter and laid full blame for the boy's death at the feet of her husband, Djahn Staiklee, who had been the senior subchief on that particular raid.

"Then, less than a year later, the one surviving Rohz boy, Hari, insisted on riding up into the mountains with a party of seasoned hunters after wild sheep and elk. As you know by now, Djahn Staiklee is a superlative horseman, possessed of an easygoing courage that seems completely natural and supremely unconscious, and has lightning-fast reflexes—a combination which is the more precious due to its true rarity.

"Anyway, in hot pursuit of a wounded sheep, Djahn Staiklee rode his horse down a very steep, shaley slope up in those mountains. Young Hari Rohz, disobeying orders from his stepfather and all the other hunters, made to follow, then lost his nerve halfway down and tried to turn, whereupon his mount lost its balance and feet, fell head foremost and rolled full-weight upon the boy. The mishap killed the both of them, boy and horse, then and there, outright.

"No one of those returning hunters was at all anxious to be the one to tell Lainuh Krooguh of the death of her second son by Hari Rohz, but all of them finally did, many going so far as to fully open their minds and their memories to her that she might know that the words spoken were nothing less than the full, unembroidered truth and that no one of the hunters was or could be held in any way—legal or moral—responsible for that headstrong boy's death.

"Lainuh apparently heard them all out, delved into every proffered mind's memories . . . then placed full blame upon the undeserving shoulders of Djahn Staiklee, her husband and the stepfather of the dead boy, Hari.

"When, some year or more later, he won the slave girl, Dahnah, while gambling with men of Clan Pahrkuh, and made it abundantly clear to all of his yurt that he meant to keep her as a concubine, Lainuh did her utter damnedest to turn her brother, Chief Dik, against his old crony, Djahn Staiklee, but in that particular instance she failed miserably, which failure to continue to exercise a measure of control over her brother in no way improved her general disposition or her attitude toward Sjahn Staiklee and his new acquisition.

"And so matters still stand, Behtiloo," said Ehstrah, then adding, "Your mother-in-law, Lainuh Krooguh, hates and utterly despises your father-in-law, Djahn Staiklee. She is vindictive and conniving and can be violent, so would likely have murdered him long since—though of course using her wiles and exercising her considerable intelligence to be certain that his demise appeared natural—were it not that, according to clan customs, his death would considerably lower her personal status in the camp and vastly lower it in the yurt, making as that circumstance would the first wife of her eldest living son the mistress of everyone and everything in the household. A woman like Lainuh would be unable to abide such an abrupt descent . . . although I and a goodly number of others would dearly love, would give our very eyeteeth, to see such a thing, see the arrogant and overproud Lainuh humbled once and for all."

Ehstrah stood up and said, "Well, I for one have enough steam for today. You and I, Behtiloo, can go into the other yurt and wash while Gahbee goes out to roll around in the snow, as is her peculiar wont. I watched her once, but never again; it fairly raises the hairs on the neck. Tepid water is more than enough of a sensory shock for me, after the heat in here."

Back in the yurt of Tim's family, Bettylou found that affairs looked tranquil enough. Neither Tim nor Djahn Staiklee was about, of course; Tim spent as much time as he could find or make at the side of his sickly uncle, Chief Dik, absorbing the host of things he would need to know when he became chief. Djahn Staiklee, who could not for long abide inaction, had left before dawn with the best hunters of the clans to sweep wide about the area of the camp and search for signs of predators, raiders or any large game animals.

Even before she got really close to the yurt, Bettylou had caught the reek of mutton. Inside, it was all but overpowering, rising from the bubbling pot of sheep fat which Lainuh and Dahnah were using to soften and dress the cured skin of the big brown bear that Djahn Staiklee had killed during the autumn trek from the summer camp to this winter one.

And suddenly in an eyeblink of time, she was again witnessing the events of that terribly terrifying, terribly exciting day.

Hunters had killed three larger screwhorns—beasts each as big as a draft-ox and otherwise looking very much like domestic cattle, save for their twisting horns and peculiar color—field-dressed them all and brought them back to the night camp on carts to be properly flayed, butchered and apportioned out.

The bear had come in from downwind and, with all the hubbub of unhitching teams, offloading carts and otherwise making to set up a camp, no man or woman or child, no cat or horse or mule or ox had seen or scented the great, furry, hungry ursine until, with a roar, he had tried to hook a maiden of Clan Skaht from where she was standing atop a loaded cart with a swipe of his broad, long-clawed forepaw.

The maiden screamed shrilly, mindcalled a broadbeamed plea for help and leaped from off the safer side of the cart all at once . . . and then the campsite was pure pandemonium for a few moments, while the stubborn bear, still trying to get at his originally chosen meal, vaulted to her former place atop the loaded cart.

This action served to stampede the draft horses still hitched to the cart, and the pair raced out across the darkening prairie, vocalizing their terror, with the bear hanging on for dear life and thunderously roaring out his own concern and displeasure, which roars only pumped larger amounts of adrenaline into the team, and the speed of the rocking, bumping, tooth-jarringly springless cart increased appreciably.

In the wake of the runaway cart came pounding half the folk and all of the cats who had been at the campsite—warriors, maidens, matrons, slaves, everyone who had still been mounted or could quickly get astride a mount—and in their wake came more folk racing on foot, armed with whatever had come easiest to hand at the moment.

The bear's portion of the journey had ended when the much-abused cart lost a wheel and he was pitched rolling and roaring onto the hard ground. The mountainous beast lay for a moment, apparently stunned, while the team raced on, still screaming, finally dragging the cart to pieces. By the time the shaken bruin had regained his feet, he was ringed about by snarling prairiecats and the mounted warriors were close upon him.

Despite the broken bones, the crippling injuries that the huge plains grizzly was later determined to have sustained even before the fight commenced, he did put up a fight, enough of a fight to kill two full-grown prairiecats and maim another, so that finally Chief Milo and a half-dozen others started in to settle the bear with wide-bladed wolf spears.

The cats were dancing about, making mock rushes, then springing back to hold the bear in place. His movements never slowed to less than lightning-fast, for all that he was so quilled with arrows, his fur all tacky with blood and the ground about him splattered thickly with it.

It was while the seven spearmen were positioning themselves for their deadly-dangerous task that Djahn Staiklee rode up on a lathered horse. In a trice, he had strung his bow, nocked, and sped a shaft that flew straight and true the seventy-odd yards to strike the beast's eye and sink deeply into the brain beyond. And the fearsome bear dropped, crumpled bonelessly to the blood-soaked ground he had so well defended.

Lainuh had been working at the bearskin off and on ever since. She had skillfully sewn up each and every hole and tear and puncture from the flesh side with fine sinew, she had painstakingly stretched and cured it and now was hard at work making it supple before she put it to use as her winter bedcovering.

As Bettylou began to shed her outer garments in the warm interior of the yurt, Lainuh looked up and smiled at her, mindspeaking, "You were long at the steam yurt, daughter mine."

Bettylou returned the smile and beamed, "Yes, I met Ehstrah and Gahbee and we . . . talked, for a while."

A frown flitted across Lainuh's face. "Gossip, no doubt. That Ehstrah, she is never happy unless her sharp tongue is employed at the telling of slanderous tales. Who was she maligning this day, daughter?"

Bettylou thought fast and lied glibly, "Oh, some story about a woman in Clan . . . ahh, Morguhn, I think. It all was long ago, she said."

Lainuh wrinkled her brow in puzzlement. "Why would she tell you about such old gossip, I wonder? You're certain that she made no allusions to folk in this camp? To me, perhaps? She owns a completely senseless dislike for me, you know."

"Well," said Bettylou, slowly, feeling her way through these treacherous footings, "she had begun by telling me of Horseclans customs and the reasons for them . . .?"

Lainuh's frown disappeared and she nodded, chuckling. "And so our Ehstrah dredged up a choice bit of slime from her cesspit of a mind to illustrate the point as well as joy her soul in the retelling, I'd assume.

"Well, my dear, here's a bit more education for you. Come and help me with my bearskin, then Dahnah can go down to the end of the camp and fetch back a load of dung for our night fire." She had been smiling, but the smile completely vanished as she turned to the other woman, snarling, "You heard me, you slave slut! Get up and go do my bidding. Take the biggest bag and come back with it brimful, if you know what's good for you! And when you've brought the dung back and stowed it as is proper, as you know I like it, you will begin to grind grain for the day. Now, get about it, damn you!"

The two women worked at the bearskin until midday, scraped it with dull wooden spatulas to remove excess fat, then rolled it, and Lainuh laid it atop her bedding rugs. After instructing the widows of Tim's two dead brothers and seeing them begin preparations for the daily meal, she lit the largest of the fat lamps and took out the cloth and the colored threads and the needles to commence Bettylou's continuing lesson in the art of Horseclans embroidery.

Then another two hours were spent at the task of stretching fresh sheepskins on the frames, defleshing them and giving them an initial treatment with whey.

Djahn Staiklee returned quite early, well before dark, with his saddle over his shoulder and his other hand and arm filled with his weapons. He moved stiffly, looked to be half-frozen and had concern writ deeply on his weathered face.

After dumping saddle and gear, he stalked over to stand by the firepit, stripped off his mittens and flexed his fingers in the heat beating up from the smoldering dungfire.

Lainuh ignored him, did not even look up from her work. At length, Bettylou levered her swollen body to its feet, took a horn cup from the stack and, after pouring it brimful of herb tea, proffered it to the man.

A concerted, hissing gasp of apprehension came from Dahnah and the two widows; all expected a torrent of verbal abuse to spew from Lainuh, but the mistress of the yurt ignored this tableau, too, until Staiklee spoke.

"I thank you, Behtiloo, I thank you kindly." Then he raised his voice a trifle so that all might hear clearly. "It could get bad, very bad, for us and our beasts. A tremendous pack of wolves is roaming out yonder, fivescore, at the least, probably more. We found a deer yard the devils had visited; there were only scraps of hide, broken antlers and a few well-gnawed hooves left of what had been a sizable number of deer.

"When we reported of it all to the chiefs, they decided that we'll bring in as many horses as we can fit inside the stockade tonight and we'll keep watchfires going here and out at the herds, too, all night long.

"Then, tomorrow, as soon as it's light enough to see, every man, maiden, stripling and matron who's well and able will hie to the wooded areas and start felling, trimming and dragging or carting back more trees.

"The stockade will be enlarged or added on to so that we can protect not only the horses, but the cattle and the sheep, too.

"The herd guards are all exempted, of course, as are the ill, the very young or aged and women close to foaling; therefore, this yurt will furnish one man and four women to the work party, at dawn, tomorrow."

"One man and *one* woman!" snapped Lainuh in a voice colder than the icicles festooning the eaves of the yurt. "If you and your stinking, lazy slave slut want to freeze in those damned woods tomorrow, I care not; but *I* am the mistress of this yurt and, as such, I have a day's work to do every day here within it and I need the help of my dear daughters-in-law to aid me in performing my many chores. Moreover, I am the eldest sister of a chief and thus the mother of a chief-to-be— unless you, Djahn Staiklee, manage to get Tim, too, killed before his uncle dies . . . as you got all his brothers and half brothers killed!"

Lainuh's low voice had risen to a contralto shout that filled the yurt and must surely, Bettylou figured, be easily audible well beyond the felt-leather-and-wooden walls. Nansee, the widow of Djahnee, went softly, hurriedly, to comfort her babe, who hung in her harness and wrappings from the roof frame and just now was shrieking, Lainuh's angry shouts having awakened the infant to terror.

Djahn sighed deeply and, ignoring the slanders, said tiredly, "It's not my choice to make, Lainuh. If you want to argue a case, I suggest that you go over and do so with your brother and the others, although I seriously doubt that such argument will do you a scintilla of good this time, for this work is just too important to every man and woman and child and cat and horse in the camp. They have already refused to excuse nursing mothers, so why do you think they'd excuse a hale, healthy woman who just simply feels herself to be too busy, not to mention too exalted, too highborn, to swing an axe?''

"You supercilious, mongrel Tekikuhn!'' hissed Lainuh. "You go too far. We all know just *what* you truly are. What do you think yourself to be? I, at least, am pure Kindred by birth.''

Staiklee threw back his head and laughed. "Pure Kindred, hey? You? Lainuh, it is time, I think, to apprise you of the fact that I knew that yarn of yours to be a wholecloth lie even before I foolishly married you—you, with your airs and laziness and tantrums.

"Dik Krooguh's mother never bore a daughter who chanced to live to maturity, so when one of her husband's concubines bore a baby girl who proved to be of his likeness and of decent mindspeak aptitude, she raised her as her own daughter. Now, my first Krooguh wife—your half sister, Kahnee—was by your sire on his second wife and *was* of pure Kindred stock.

"But your dam, Lainuh, was nothing save a Dirtwoman slave, and that is why most of the camp laughs at your pretensions, either behind your back or to your face. Were your half brother not chief and deeply attached to you for various and sundry reasons, you'd have not a friend in this camp. You are more or less tolerated by so many because of the love and respect that all bear for Dik Krooguh, and that is the only reason.

"Now you do as you will, wife. But I much fear me that if you are so unwise as to not heed the summons to work tomorrow for the common weal, not even Chief Dik's stature in this camp will save you the shunning and overt censure of your peers, your betters and even your inferiors.''

Lainuh leaped to her feet, kicked off her embroidered yurtboots and began quickly to don her heavier outside clothing. "We'll just hear exactly what my brother has to say about this . . . this outrage, Djahn Staiklee! Nor do I think that he'll be one bit happy or amused to hear that you chose to humiliate and degrade his only living sister before her daughters-in-law and your slave. And I'll not be back under this roof until I hear your full, abject and public apology to me and my dear brother, too!''

Djahn just grinned. "That is a promise, I hope. In that
case, *wife*, you had better take your bed rug and coverings,
plus all of your clothes—winter *and* summer—for horses will
sprout horns and oxen will climb trees before you hear me
recant what was only truth."

Squatting, her face working, she began to roll her bed for
easy carrying, but when she made to include the bearskin, he
roughly jerked it from her grasp.

"Give it back, damn you!" she shouted hotly. "It's mine,
mine!"

His reply was cold. "You seem to forget—conveniently
misremember, as is your wont—just who killed that bear and
then skinned it out, woman. By custom as well as by the law
of the Horseclans, I can give this prize to whomever I wish. It
is not automatically yours simply because you chose to lay
claim to it, as you have claimed or made shift to claim
everything of beauty or of value that ever has come into this
yurt."

"But . . . but . . ." she stuttered, too angry for a moment
to talk properly. "But *me* it was who cured that skin, *me* it
was who stitched up the tears of fang and claw, the holes
made by the arrows. It has been long and hard, it has taken
me months of daily work on it. You can't just rob me of it
now!"

He just shrugged, saying, "You cannot be robbed of something you never really owned, Lainuh. And as for the vast
amounts of work you claim to have put into the curing and
repair of this bearskin, I am certain that our son and his new
wife here will thank you in winters yet to come, for I have
decided to give it to them."

Lainuh did not return that night. The four women and
Djahn Staiklee ate the stew and the fried bread, then sat for a
long while around the dungfire, nibbling on hard cheese and
chunks of dried fruit and sipping tea, while Djahn spun tales
of hunting and of his youth on the arid southern plains, where
more than a few of the bands of nomads still were neither
Kindred-born nor even allied with the Horseclans by marriage.

All the while he talked, in the near-darkness, Staiklee's
big, capable hands were busy. First, he fitted a new string to
his powerful hornbow, then rubbed every inch of that string
well with a lump of beeswax. That done, he unstrung the bow
and thoroughly dressed it with sheepsfoot jelly before wiping

off the excess and returning it to its weatherproof case of wood, felt and oiled leather.

Then it was the turn of the arrows. He lit a small fat lamp and dumped out the contents of both quivers, checked each shaft for straightness, tightness of head and horn nock, then subjected the feather flights to a painstaking scrutiny, before replacing them in precise order in the two quivers—one, the larger, for hunting arrows, the other for war arrows.

Having found a couple of places on his saber edge that happened to be less keen than he thought proper, Staiklee took that weapon and a stone and began to carefully hone the blade.

Looking directly at Bettylou, he remarked, "The bruin that once wore that skin I gifted you and Tim, well, he wasn't the first of his breed I came up against, you know.

"Now down Tehksuhs way, we hunt more with packs of dogs than with prairiecats. Of course, the most of our dogs are each as big as or bigger than a full-grown prairiecat, some of them as big as lions, to tell the truth; but they have to be, because the bears up here are just puny little critters compared to the bears we hunt in Tehksuhs. Why, the flayed hide off a Tehksuhs bear would cover the whole top of this yurt and hang partway down the sides.

"And the hides on Tehksuhs bears is so thick and tough you can blunt down the edges of a whole beltful of skinning knives a-trying to skin one of the critters, even if you was able to kill him afore he killed you, that is.

"I recollect an old boar bear that my daddy sent me out to kill when I was about fourteen, fifteen winters. Well, that was a bad-luck hunt from start to finish for me, but a damned good day for the bear."

He paused for a moment to rub a fresh application of sheep fat and spittle into the grain of the hone stone, then went on with his tale. "Anyhow, two days out, my horse turned up lame, and I hadn't brought but the one, so I had to throw my saddle on Brootuhs, the biggest of my tooth-hounds."

"Your pardon, Honored Father," Nansee interjected, "but what is a tooth-hound?"

Djahn nodded, smiling, and answered, "I keep forgetting, you Horseclanners don't hunt with dogs. Well, honey, there are three kinds of hounds that go to make up a pack of hunting dogs. The 'nose-dogs' are the ones that find and follow the scent trail of whatever critter it is you're hunting. The 'leg-dogs' or 'runners' (as some folks call them) don't have much of a nose, but they've got keen eyesight to spot the critter, the speed and stamina to run him to earth and enough ferocity to hold him in place until the tooth-hounds get there.

" 'Tooth-hounds' are bigger, heavier and meaner than the other two kinds of dogs. Their job is to bring the critter to bay and, if necessary, to go in and kill him, rather than let him get away before the hunter gets there."

"But they truly are big enough to saddle and ride?" asked Dikee's widow, Ahlmah.

"Of course they are . . . down Tehksuhs way," replied Djahn Staiklee emphatically.

Bettylou truly liked this man so she kept her own doubts to herself. The Abode of the Righteous had kept many canines—both hounds of several varieties and herding dogs—but she had never seen one, even the biggest of these, that stood much over knee height at its shoulders.

"Anyhow," Staiklee went on, "Brootuhs didn't care too much for the saddle and he was downright upset about the bridle and bit, but I gentled him down some before we'd been many more days on that bruin's trail. And we were many a day on that trail, too. Why, I doubt not that me and all the dogs would have plumb starved to death, if I hadn't been able to kill a couple of middling-size rattlers every day."

This last was just too much for Bettylou to take in continued silence. "Father, please tell me how a couple of rattlesnakes a day could feed you and your entire pack of dogs."

Again, he smiled. "It's all just a matter of size, Behtiloo. All critters seem to get bigger or stronger or smarter down Tehksuhs way; even plants do, too. You've seen these scrubby little smidgens of cactuses on the plains hereabouts? Well, in Tehksuhs, they gets tall as twenty lances end to end would be, that tall and as thick through the middle as Chief Dik's wagon is long, too. And . . ."

"Your pardon, Father," Bettylou interrupted again, "but we were talking of two snakes big enough to provide enough meat to feed you and all your dogs for a whole day."

"Yes," he agreed in a dead-serious tone of voice, "they get every bit that big down in Tehksuhs, honey. Big enough to coil all the way around the outside of this yurt and grab their tails in their mouths, was they of a mind to do such a thing. More than a foot thick in the body Tehksuhs rattlers get, some of them nearer to two feet. That's a powerful lot of meat."

"It certainly is," Bettylou agreed, then asked, "But you give the impression that these plains are very dry, near deserts, so what creatures are there of a size to sustain such huge serpents in such a wasteland?"

Djahn Staiklee regarded her shrewdly for a long moment, then he mindspoke quickly and personally, "Child, you are far more intelligent than you seem outwardly. Tim has more of a prize than I think he realizes yet in you. But let be, here, tonight. This is a long-drawn-out mocking tale I spin; don't question it too closely. I mean but to bring a little merriment into this yurt which has seen so many years with little or none."

While beginning to stroke the stone on the next portion of saber blade he felt due his ministrations, he went on with the story.

"So, anyhow, riding Brootuhs and living on snakemeat and cactus water, we trailed that bear for more than half a moon. We trailed him through country so dry that the creeks and the rivers, even, were none of them running with water but running with coarse gravel and rocks, instead—all grinding away, those stones were, as they flowed along.

"But, then, one day, we heard the leg-hounds give tongue—that's how they let you know they've spotted the critter they're trailing—and the tooth-dogs commenced doubling their pace . . . all except Brootuhs, of course, since he was carrying about twice his own weight or almost that. For you see, I was nought but a younker then, and though I was big for my age, like most men or boys in Tehksuhs, two weeks of hard riding on nothing save snakemeat had fined my body down to just whipcord muscle and sinew over my bones.

"Well, by the time Brootuhs and me got up to where the others had brought that old boar bear to bay, he had killed or near killed most of my pack of dogs. Well, I jumped off old Brootuhs and slipped his bridle so it wouldn't hinder his teeth and jaws. Then I slung my lance over my back and took my bow out of the case to string it.

"At that very second, poor, brave old Brootuhs took it in his head to bore in after that bloody-clawed bruin like a weasel after a swamp rat, and as luck would have it, the very first swipe of that bear's forepaw not only broke the poor dog's back like a rotten stick, but simultaneously snapped every shaft in my arrowcase and flung Brootuhs' body—saddle, gear and all—so hard against a big old boulder that the impact snapped the blade of the sheathed saber I had been carrying slung from the pommel.

"And so there I was, all alone, all of my dogs dead or dying or run off, with only a lance and my dirk against two tons or more of hopping-mad Tehksuhs plains grizzly bear . . . and he had finished off the last dog and was coming for me!"

Staiklee took the last stroke of the stone on his saber blade, meticulously wiped off the cursive length of burnished steel, then sheathed it, yawned mightily and looked on the point of arising from his place in the circle.

"But . . . but what happened, Father Djahn?" demanded Nansee, almost bouncing up and down in her excitement. "How did you kill the bear?"

Staiklee looked surprised at the question. "Oh, I didn't kill that bear, honey. He killed *me!* Ate me, too."

CHAPTER VIII

— · · ——

Tim Krooguh, when he rode back into camp to fetch dry bowstrings for the herd guards, found his wife, along with Nansee and several other Krooguh women who happened to be pregnant or otherwise incapacitated, congregated in the yurt of his uncle, Chief Dik. They and the bigger ones of the swarm of children therein were all engaged in making the murderous wolf baits.

One woman would shave the thinnest possible slivers off one of a pile of bones; another would roll these slivers as tightly as possible without breaking or permanently bending them, always making certain that each end was sharply pointed. Another woman would deftly bind these coils of bone into place with a bit of thread-thin sinew. Then yet another woman dipped them into hot liquid fat and set them aside until they were cooled enough for the children to make each one of them the center of a hand-shaped ball of firmer fat, after which they were taken out and placed in a shaded spot to freeze.

These would be thrown out when wolves were known to be near the herds or prowling about the stockade. The wolves, of course, in their typical canine fashion, would gulp the balls of fat unmasticated, and when body heat and stomach acids had combined to melt the fat and dissolve the restraining bit of sinew, the length of sharp-pointed bone would spring out from its spiral shape, at least lacerating if not puncturing whatever portion of that wolf's gut it happened to be in at the time.

Chief Dik lay snoring under a mound of furs and thick blankets. He had been in severer pain than usual this morning and so had been dosed with a stronger than normal analgesic tea which gave him not only cessation of pain but sound sleep in spite of the uproar that filled the yurt.

Mindspeaking on a tight, personal beaming, Tim asked, "You and Nansee, I see here, but where is Mother? Surely *she* must have found a way to keep from going out to cut trees down."

"Not this time around," Bettylou replied, just as silently and privately. "She threw a fit and went tearing out of our yurt last night, when first your father made mention of the day's work party and the reason for it. But when she got here, your uncle put his foot down . . . hard, boot, spur and all. I suppose that with all the other chiefs here, he felt that to excuse even his sister on such flimsy grounds would demean him and his authority. However he reasoned, he told her flatly that either she went out with the other sound Krooguh women or he would appoint a surrogate to thrash her until she was of a mind to obey the dictates of both her chief and the subchief who was her husband."

"So Mother went out to the forest, then?" remarked Tim. "Will wonders never cease to occur? Oh, but there will be one hellish fit in our yurt when she gets back, you can bet on it. It's glad I am that I'm doing herd duty just now, where I've only wolves and other such beasts to deal with. I warn you, wife, we'll none of us hear the end of Mother's reverses of last night and today until she is with Wind . . . and, knowing her and her stubbornness, probably not even then."

"Possibly not," Bettylou replied to his dire forebodings. "Last night, while she was ranting here after the other chiefs had returned to their own yurts, your uncle limped over to one of the chests, I'm told, and dug through it until he found a device made of iron straps which had long ago been looted from some group of Dirtmen.

"There were several similar things in the Abode of the Righteous, and they were called by the name of 'scolds' bridles.' They are of soft iron and are fitted tightly around the head and jaws by a strong man, then secured with a big lock. While one is in place, the unfortunate wearing it cannot speak, eat or easily drink, since the iron straps prevent the jaws from opening more than fractions of an inch without severe pain.

"Your uncle showed the iron bridle to your mother, explained its purpose and the fitting of it, then told her that he and others would be keeping their ears cocked, and on the very next occasion they chanced to hear her up to another of her screaming tantrums, he would be over with a couple of strong clansmen to fit the bridle to her and would see to it that she wore it until she fainted from hunger, if need be."

"And how did my uncle's wives react to this threat against another clanswoman?" asked Tim.

"I was told all that I have repeated by Dohrah, your uncle's second wife," Bettylou replied. "And she said that all in the yurt were most pleased, being of the concerted opinion that your mother has gotten away with far too much for far too long."

Tim rode back toward the herd with a bagful of the wolf baits, a packet of dry bowstrings and a few lumps of beeswax, a bellyful of warm food and the pleasant thought that things were showing the promise of change for the better in the yurt of his birth. He filed away his uncle's decisions and methods of exacting obedience from an insubordinate relative in his mental "when I am chief" file.

All through the daylight hours, spans of oxen and teams of straining mules dragged back to the campsite the rough-trimmed treetrunks, while the carts made trip after trip after trip piled high with branches.

After sight and smell of the thoroughly hoof-trampled expanse of half-frozen, fecal-laced mud that one night of sheltering a large proportion of the horse herd had made of the area of the camp inside the palisade, the chiefs had made the decision to erect another palisade adjoining the existing one for the horses and another of a different configuration for the pregnant ewes, certain chosen rams and the best of the younger ewes. Only the milk goats would be kept as before in the confines of the human settlement. It would be up to the cattle to fend off the wolves themselves, any of them that got past the roving herd guards.

Throughout the next night, small fires were kept blazing all along the lines which had been traced by Chief Milo and then cleared of snow and ice. Thus, in the morning, when the still-warm ashes were scraped aside, those narrow stretches of ground were not frozen like all the rest of the topsoil for many miles in every direction, so the digging of the trenches to take the palisade timbers went far more quickly and easily than any of the folk had expected or had had any right to expect at this time of year.

Parties with carts were sent back to the wooded areas to seek out and bring back as much thorny or prickly brush as they could find, and when the palisade stakes had been erected, the ground around them thoroughly soaked and given the time to freeze, the children were set to the task of weaving the brush thickly between and around the stakes as high as they could reach easily, at which point adults took over and continued for as long as the supplies of brush held out.

"Not that the brush will stop those gray devils," Chief Milo had remarked, "and the next snow will mean that we'll have to fetch back more brush and raise the height of it again. But at least it might serve to slow the wolves down enough to let someone put an arrow into them before they can get at the horses or the sheep.

"As for the cattle and the rest of the sheep, it might be best to drive them all closer to camp, maybe to where we had the horse herd; the herd guards will have an easier life thus, and in the event that that super-pack strikes at the cattle, we— more of us—will be able to get to the herd to help in killing the wolves or driving them off, and do it in much less time than we could now, with the herds way out there.

"Of course," he confided to the other chiefs gathered in Dik Krooguh's yurt, "if that pack is big enough we could easily, few as we number, lose every head of stock and have a hard fight to keep even our own lives and a few horses. It has happened before, in past years, to other nomads—Kindred and non-Kindred—and some of the smaller, more isolated Dirtman settlements, too, have been wiped out or at least ruined by one of these huge packs during a hard winter.

"Our warriors and striplings and maiden-archers who are not assigned to the herds had better start sleeping in shifts, so that two-thirds of the total numbers of effectives are always available, for those big packs hunt both by day and by night when their bellies are growling, and the only things that will stop them are food, a full blizzard or death."

The Lainuh Krooguh who returned to the Staiklee yurt was a sullen, silent woman who never spoke unless addressed and then only in monosyllables. No one was comfortable in her presence, and she left the yurt only when forced to do so by her natural functions, for she did no work of any kind, only crouched near the firepit, scowling and brooding in utter silence, ignoring all the other occupants of the yurt.

As a consequence, Bettylou was distinctly relieved when she was told by Tim to move their effects to the yurt of Chief Dik, that she might be instructed by the chief's wives in how to properly run the domicile of a clan chief. Dahnah and Nansee, without even being asked, helped her to gather the clothing and gear and sleeping-rugs, and then lug them—slipping and sliding on the uneven footing frozen beneath the thin blanket of fresh snow—over to the Clan Krooguh chief's yurt, then arrange them where and as directed by Dik Krooguh's first wife, Mairee.

When Bettylou had thanked the helpful women and they had departed, she set about the task of unrolling her sleeping-rug and coverings. There was no point in unrolling Tim's, for until the wolf threat abated, he would be at the herders' camp both night and day.

The two thicknesses of carpeting were placed on the ground, with sheepskins atop them, then the two woolen blankets and, finally, the bearskin Djahn Staiklee had gifted. As she unrolled and laid this treasure out, all three of Chief Dik's wives—Mairee, Dohrah and Djohn—came over to stroke and admire the rarity.

"It's not so thick and dense as a winter pelt would've been," remarked Mairee, "but even so, when once it's been properly lined, one entire chest is going to be required to store and transport it. I'll tell old Tchahrlz to start making you that chest; he should line it with cedarwood, which seems to help to keep vermin out, and it ought, really, to be bound and decorated in brass or silver or both together. Perhaps your Tim will luck into some of those metals on one of next year's raids."

"There'll be no need to raid for metals if we camp in one of the ruins, as we did ten years ago," remarked Dohrah. "We must have dug up three or four wagonloads of various metals in those ruins that were called Haiz."

"Yes, and I doubt not that we could've found even more, had the chiefs allowed us to bide in the ruins themselves, not just camp out on the prairie and ride over every day for a few hours," added Djohn.

Mairee shook her head. "You should not criticize the decisions of the chiefs, nor should you doubt the rightness of their judgments, sister. Do not forget just how the ancient folk died who made the settlements that have since become those ruins their homes. Uncle Milo himself has warned over and over again that the seeds of those terrible plagues still sleep here and there in parts of every ruin, dormant, but still no less deadly to the careless or the unwary.

"Remember what those horses in that small feral herd we had to join our Krooguh herd told us, years back? How the entire clan—men, women and children—died, all within a week, after camping among ruins? True, they were not a Kindred clan, but I doubt that those plague seeds discriminate between Kindred and non-Kindred folk. Nor do our chiefs, which is why they would never allow a camp to be established very close to a ruined place of ancient settlement."

With all three of his wives doing duty as matron-archers—one sleeping and two keeping watch at the palisades—Chief Milo took food with Chief Dik that night and, with wolves and wolf packs on the mind of everyone present, he began to talk of wolves, to reminisce of his various encounters with the canny predators over his many, many years of life.

"In the world that existed before this one of ours, you know, in the most of this land, at least, the true wolf was all but extinct. Very few of them were left, and most of those were either not living truly wild and free or were not of pure wolf bloodlines.

"In the immediate aftermath of the deadly calamities that befell that ancient world and its millions of human inhabitants, there were no wolf packs in any of the areas I was able to visit, but rather numerous and highly dangerous hordes of starving dogs—dogs of all shapes and sizes and breeds, all now ownerless, masterless, having little or no fear of mankind and having kept alive so far, since most of them utterly lacked hunting skills, by feeding off dead or dying human cadavers.

"I had some very close brushes with a few of those dog packs, back then, but fortunately very few of those dogs lived long enough to breed more of their kind. As soon as the millions of human corpses were gone and the dogs had to compete with the equally numerous feral felines and the truly wild animals for such food as existed, they lost out and died off in droves; also, those few humans as had lived through the plagues in many cases hunted the dogs for meat and skins to replace worn-out clothing and footwear.

"Some of them survived, of course; we now call them jackals. Others, I am certain, interbred with the coyotes and, I suspect, with the actual wolves. I just don't see any way that an almost extinct species of predator could have sprung back so quickly in so comparatively short a time period unless a good many of the larger dog breeds—those called German shepherd, collie, chow, Malamute, Samoyed, Rottweiler, boxer, Doberman, mastiff, great Dane and several other of the so-called working and coursing breeds—had joined and interbred with the few widely scattered wolves.

"Over the years, I've seen enough to strongly reinforce these beliefs of mine, moreover. I have seen wolves—both living and dead—who possessed dark-purple tongues—an unquestioned mark of the ancient breed of dog called chow. I know that Dik, here, like many another hunter, has run into wolves with long, silky coats, or with the hair tightly curled, like that of a sheep."

The ailing chief nodded his agreement. "Yes, Uncle Milo, and then there are the short-jawed wolves, the ones that some folk call 'round-headed wolves.' I have for long heard it attested that they are not pure wolf."

"Most likely they are not," agreed Milo. "I'd say that such creatures are throwbacks to the dog breeds that the ancients called mastiffs."

"Sacred Sun be thanked for the alliance of Kindred and the cats," said Mairee feelingly. "Were it not for the Wind-sent abilities of the prairiecats, abilities which Wind did not grant to mankind, we never could hope to survive very many of these wolf winters."

Milo smiled. "And yet, it was because of a winter wolf pack that certain Kindred and I first chanced across prairiecats, many years ago and very far west of this place."

"Oh, Uncle Milo, tell us of it, please." The request was almost a chorus from all of those assembled, young and old, and Bettylou's own voice was added to the others.

Milo took out his pipe and bladder of tobacco and began to stuff the one with the contents of the other. "Well, it was some four or five generations back. There were far fewer Kindred then, and we still were mostly confined to the high plains and the western mountains, not being numerous or strong enough to come down to and conquer for ourselves these prairies. As you know—most of you, at least—winters are usually harder, harsher on the high plains, with deeper snows that lie for longer . . . and, as I recall it, this winter of which I now speak was a bad one even for those elevations.

"Although five clans were camping together for the winter, there were fewer people in that camp than in this one. We had slaughtered the last of the cattle for food and were again running perilously low, so two hunting parties went out, all of us resolved not to come back without enough meat to sustain our folk for a while. I led a group of young men from Clan Esmith and Clan Linszee, while a renowned hunter whose name I now forget led a similar group from Clan Aduhmz, Clan Makfee and Clan Djohnz; they set out toward the southeast, we set out in the direction of the southwest.

"The fourth day out, riding through deep snows in territory completely unfamiliar to us, we lucked across a deer yard in a patch of forest. There were four of the bigger, western deer in that yard, and the archers of Clan Esmith dropped them all, only to have one dragged away by some unknown, unseen predator while they were hard at work cleaning the big buck to be certain that the meat would not be tainted.

"Now in our straits, we could not spare the loss of even one of those deer, so it was decided to pack the three carcasses we still had in our possession back to camp along with the most of our party, while I and a smaller party pursued the cat, for such a consummate tracker—one Djim Linszee, he who later in his life was Chief Linszee of Linszee—and I had both determined it must be. And this we did.

"Because of the anticipated terrain in the direction that that feline had taken, we broke down squawwood, built a big fire and left two of our number there in the deer yard with the

horses, going on afoot in pursuit of the thief and our deer.
The way was long, and the canny cat did not make it an easy
trail to follow. Once, in fact, she doubled back and leaped out
of a trailside copse full onto my back and broke my neck.
Had I been as are most Kindred, I would have died then and
there.''

Bettylou glanced around at the faces of the others, lightly
flitted through the surface thoughts of the relaxed, unshielded
minds with her still-new powers, but she could find no one
who doubted a word that Chief Milo had said. She did not
publicly question him as she had questioned Djahn Staiklee,
but she resolved to find him alone somewhere and satisfy
herself as to his supposedly immense age and vaunted ability
to survive death-dealing injuries.

"As it was," Milo continued, "I was some hour recover-
ing from that attack and the attendant injuries and it was
while I was doing so that we all became aware that a huge
pack of wolves was racing upon our trail. Keeping but a few
minutes ahead of those relentless, shaggy pursuers, we sped
on as fast as our legs would bear us, our faces all astream
with sweat despite the frigid air and the tearing bite of the
wind, which had increased in strength through the day. At
length, we found ourselves at the foot of a low plateau and
climbed up it with the pack leaders actually snapping at our
heels, to behold it completely treeless but with a jumble of a
complex of ruined buildings centered upon it a few hundred
yards away from us.

"It was a very near, a frighteningly near thing, but all of us
made it to the ruins, to the top of a crumbling tower of
ancient brickwork. The top of that ruined tower was too high
for any of the wolves to jump, although almost all of them
essayed it at one time or another, so we were safe from them
as long as we did not try to climb down.

"But we were confronted there on our perch by another
and no less deadly menace, for it was clear to any creature
that a blizzard was fast approaching that plateau. And with no
more shelter than that offered us by foot-high walls about the
edges of that tower top, we would have surely frozen to death
in very short order.

"I had not been willing to allow the party to spend their
arrows and darts on the wolves as long as we were in a place

where the beasts could not get at us and were not truly a life threat to us, preferring to save the weapons for a more desperate occasion. Therefore, they had spent their time in throwing loose chunks of bricks at the nearer wolves—killing a couple outright, injuring several others and at least hurting the rest at whom they aimed.

"But they exhausted the supply of brick chunks after a while, and the wolves gradually circled closer and closer to the base of our perch again as no more hurtful missiles flew at them from its apex. There was more brick rubble atop that tower, but it was sunk in a mixture of old brick dust, bird droppings and windblown debris that over the years had become soil; moreover, there was a layer of ice over everything.

"But none of this fazed our Kindred. As soon as one of them had proved that pieces of this brick rubble could be freed for use against the encroaching wolves, they all were at it, prying up the encrusted, frozen brick chunks with their dirks and, with them, causing anew many cases of lupine agony and consternation.

"But here, this recountal could easily take all night, and we sorely need rest, at least, I do. So I will open my memories and you all can enter my mind and see those archaic events as did I and those others—human and cat—with whom I later conversed."

The night spent atop the ruined tower was terrible for Milo and the nomads. Rolling pebbles in their mouths to allay somewhat their raging thirst, they laced their quilted and fur-trimmed hoods tightly and drew the thick woolen blizzard masks up over lips and vulnerable noses. In the very center of the concavity, they huddled together for warmth like so many puppies or kittens, frequently changing position on the hard, uneven surface so that all might have equal time in the warmer centermost spot.

Not that sleep came easily, for in addition to the cold, the wolves were never really silent through the whole of that frigid, blustery night—they barked and howled and snarled and snuffled, they paced around and around the tower, they yelped and whined, wolf after wolf after wolf set himself at the sheer walls of that tower, jumping and falling back merely to jump and again fall back until utterly exhausted. The pack seemed to be driven mad by the scent of so much manflesh and blood so very near to their slavering jaws, yet so unobtainable.

Although it seemed for long and long that dawn would not make an appearance, at last a grudging light dispelled the worst of the darkness, but there was no visible sun and no cessation of the sharp-toothed wind. Milo knew then that were he and his men to survive the coming weather, they assuredly must get off this exposed, wind-lashed pinnacle and into some shelter of some kind. But how?

The gaunt wolves paced the length and the breadth of the plateau. They numbered at least fourscore, probably more— gray wolves and wolves of a dirty, mouse-brown color, yellowish-brown wolves, reddish-brown wolves, several almost white and, here and there, a black wolf. Milo could almost feel pity for the lupines, for they were obviously not far from death by starvation, with rib racks and spinal bumps clearly visible beneath the dull, matted coats.

The pack had lost or forgotten their previous fear of the hurled missiles during the night and now were ranging close about the tower. But the men soon discovered that there were few handy bits of masonry remaining anywhere near to the rim of the tower. Only in the center, where the effects of freezing had been somewhat offset by their combined body heat through the night just past, did there appear to be chunks that could be pried loose without breaking their dirk blades.

With the supply of missiles decreased, Milo awarded such as were available to the four most accurate hurlers—Dik Esmith, the tracker, Djim Linszee, and his two younger brothers, the fiery-haired twins called Bili and Bahb. Milo and the other Horseclansmen set themselves and their dirks to supplying the four, worrying loose more of the bits and pieces of ancient bricks studding the layer of soil that covered the center of the old tower.

Milo thrust his dirk blade under a brick that looked to be almost whole . . . *and felt his steel ring on metal*! He set the others to working upon the same area; slowly, a red-brown ring of pitted, flaking iron was exposed. Shortly thereafter, they had cleared away all of the soil and rubble down to the rusty trapdoor to which the ring was stapled.

One of the Horseclansmen took a grip on the ring and

heaved, vainly. Retrenching, taking his best grip with both grubby hands, half squatting so that he could put the muscles of his legs and back behind the effort, he strained until the throbbing veins bulged from his brows, but the soil-streaked trapdoor never budged an inch from its ages-old setting.

"Wait," counseled Milo. "There may be a bolt or catch of some kind holding it secure."

His dirk blade proved far too wide for the crack between door and metal jamb at the edge closest to the ring; so too was the blade of his skinning knife, and also his boot knife; but when he tried the slender-bladed dagger that he kept sheathed under his shirtsleeve, that blade slipped in easily.

When even with the center of the iron ring, the blade encountered an obstruction. While pushing the dagger against the unseen object, Milo noted that the ring moved a bare fraction of a millimeter or so. Maintaining pressure against the still-unseen obstruction, he gripped the ring in his other hand and twisted it right, then left, then right again. At that last twist the ring creakingly moved half a turn and the obstruction was abruptly gone; he was now able to slide the blade from corner to corner of the doorframe.

He sheathed the little dagger and scuttled backward on his knees, gesturing to the Horseclansman whose efforts had earlier failed to open the door.

"Try it now, Lari."

Obligingly, the man set himself into place again, took his best two-handed grip again and heaved. There was a momentary resistance, then with an unearthly squealing screech that set the nearest wolves to yelping their displeasure, the trapdoor arose amid a shower of rust to disclose the first treads of what looked to Milo like a steel stairway, all covered with dust and cobwebs.

After bouncing his weight experimentally on those two easily visible treads while keeping his hands braced on the shoulders of two Horseclansmen, Milo gingerly began to descend the stairs into the yawning darkness, saber slung across his back and the big dirk ready in his right hand. While the men watched, all huddled about the square opening, Milo gradually disappeared into the waiting blackness, only the ring of his bootsoles telling them that he was still descending. Then, after a short time, even those sounds ceased.

The steel staircase wound down in a tight spiral, and for all that it trembled and crackled under his weight, Milo made it down to the bottom safely. Once there, he mindspoke the men waiting above him.

"The stairs held me, so they'll certainly hold you, one at a time, but don't come down yet. This room seems rather small. See if you can get that trapdoor open wider, then get back from around it so what light there is up there can penetrate to me. It's black as the inside of a cow down here."

The long-unused hinges shrilled like the screams of damned souls in protest, but the wiry nomads put their backs into the job, and presently they got the trapdoor almost flat to the floor of their eyrie, then moved to the edges of that eyrie.

In the increased amount of light, Milo could see that the chamber in which he now stood was indeed small, a bit smaller actually than was the roof above. Every visible surface was thickly covered with dust and hung with better than a century's worth of cobwebs. But he could spot no droppings of any size or description, so apparently no animal or bird had ever gained access to this room.

Staring hard, cudgeling his brain, it took him long moments to remember, to realize what the dust-shrouded object reposing on a shelf at waist level was. It was a gasoline lantern!

"I wonder . . . ?"

Wiping away the dust and cobwebs, he could see that there was little rust on the artifact, it being finished in chrome or stainless steel. Although very dirty, the glass was also intact, and there was even a filament still in place. Lifting it from the shelf, he shook it beside his ear. It sloshed as if almost full, and if that liquid was gasoline . . . ?

He searched for and found the handle of the air-pressure pump and tried it gingerly. The shaft moved smoothly in its tube. Now, if he only had a match.

Milo let his fingers wander the length of the shelf, and near the far end, they encountered a small brass cylinder, all green and bumpy with a verdigris patina.

Not daring to hope, he brought his new find up into the wan light filtering down from above. It required all the not inconsiderable strength of his hands to break the screwtop free.

"Son of a bitch!" he breathed softly. The cylinder was packed with wooden matches, the head of each covered with clear yellow wax.

With the trapdoor closed and bolted and seven bodies gathered in the close quarters, the nomads soon ceased to shiver, and, as soon as their teeth stopped chattering, they all began to do so, exclaiming upon the clear, intensely bright light cast by the ancient lantern.

A lighted exploration of the small chamber disclosed another, larger, but otherwise identical lantern, two lumps of corrosion that once had been flashlights, an assortment of rusty tools—several differing sizes and types of screwdrivers and wrenches, a couple of ball-peen hammers and a half-dozen chisels—a two-gallon brass can of lantern fuel (so marked and almost full!) and, in a rotted leather holster, a rusted and corroded thing that had once been a heavy-caliber revolver.

There was one other find. Set in the concrete floor at the foot of the spiral staircase was another trapdoor, this one a bit larger than the one above—about three feet by two feet.

Milo filled and lit the larger lantern, then set it on the shelf and opened the second trapdoor with no difficulty to disclose more steel stairs, but these looking to be in better condition for all that they still beckoned down into darkness.

He turned to the others saying, "Dik, Djim, you men all stay up here. I'll mindcall if I need you or when I find food or water. Help yourselves to any of those rusty tools as take your fancy, but leave that thing in the corner behind the can alone—it was once a very deadly weapon, and it still might hurt or kill one of you if anyone tinkers with it."

The floor at the bottom of the second flight of stairs was concrete also, but it once had been covered with asphalt tiles, which crunched and powdered under Milo's bootsoles. To his left a few yards was a jumble of tumbled and broken brick and granite blocks all covered with plant roots. Milo guessed that he was now within the main building of the ruin, whereon the tower sat perched.

Behind and to his right, the remnants of rotted wood paneling partially covered what looked like still-sound brick walls. More of the rotted, ruined wood sheets framed the door ahead of him, its brass knob green with verdigris. Although the knob turned stiffly, it did turn. Nonetheless, the door remained firmly closed. Setting the lantern on the stairs, Milo put both hands and his full strength to the tasks of turning and shoving; at last, something popped tinnily and the door gave under his weight.

The air that wafted out of this new darkness bore a hint of dankness and another ghost of a smell that set the hairs on Milo's nape a-prickle. Loosening the dirk in its sheath, he raised the lantern and cautiously stepped through the doorway.

CHAPTER IX

———— ·· ——◆—— ·· ————

There was a scratching at the door of the yurt. Mairee arose and padded over to open the carved wooden door, then push aside the layers of felt and allow an elderly prairiecat and retired cat chief, Bullbane, to enter.

"May Sacred Sun shine good fortune upon all within this yurt." The newcomer mindspoke the ritual greeting.

"And may Wind blow to you all which you desire, Brother Chief," Dik Krooguh beamed in reply, adding, "Will you not join our circle? Uncle Milo had admitted us all into his memories and was enriching us with the tale of how, long ago, the brave race of the prairiecats first allied themselves with us Kindred."

"Wolfkiller? The mother of our race?" said the old cat.

"Yes, it was Uncle Milo found her and her kittens in much danger and . . . But I am certain that Uncle Milo, who actually was there, so long ago, can recall it far better than I could simply repeat things I have had mindspoken to me over my comparatively short lifetime."

Again Milo opened his mindful of memories, and again those gathered with him in the yurt entered that mind to share of those memories. But these memories now were those things he had learned from a nonhuman source, from that great cat who thought of herself then as the Hunter or the Mother and who only later was known to her many descendants as the Wolfkiller.

The Hunter's memories of that first, fateful day were of icy-toothed wind soughing through the snow-laden branches of the overhanging trees, increasing the chill of an already frigid day. Somewhere within the forest, a branch exploded with the sharp crack of a pistol shot.

But the Hunter had then yet to hear a shot of any kind, and so she ignored that sound as she ignored the other natural sounds which neither threatened her nor heralded possible prey. She was just then concentrating her every sense and ability to get as close as she could creep to her browsing quarry before beginning that swift and silent and deadly rush and pounce that would, if done properly, result in her acquisition of nearly her own weight of hot, bloody, nourishing meat.

And she needed meat desperately. Meat to fill the gnawing emptiness of her shrunken belly, meat enough, maybe, to be borne back to her den for the three waiting little cubs to worry, lick at and chew upon.

But the Hunter also knew that she must be very, very close, far closer than usual for a cat of her size and experience, for she now had but three sound legs. Her left foreleg, deep-gored by the same shaggy-bull cow whose widespreading horns and stamping hooves had snuffed out the life of her mate and hunting partner, was healing but slowly in these short days and long, cold nights of deep snows and scant food.

As the manyhorn browser ambled to another young tree and began to strip the bark from its trunk, the Hunter carefully wriggled a few feet closer, her big amber eyes fixed unwaveringly upon her prey, her twitching nostrils seeking for the first, faint scent of alarm or fear. Then suddenly, she stopped, froze into place, even as the heads of all four of the browsers came up and swiveled to face a spot just a few yards to the Hunter's right.

The Hunter saw the muscles of the largest manyhorn browser contract under the skin of his haunches, but before he could essay even his first wild leap away from proximity of the danger he sensed, four thin little black sticks came hissing from the thick concealment of a stand of mountain laurel and all four of the manyhorn browsers collapsed, kicking their razor-edged hooves at empty air, one of them coughing up quantities of frothy pink blood which sank, steaming, into the deep white snow.

A vagrant puff of wind wafted to the Hunter the rare but still-hated scent of two-legs, and her lip curled into a soundless snarl. *They* were trying to rob her of *her* manyhorn browser, trying to steal life itself from her and her helpless cubs; for if she did not have food now, she knew that soon enough she would lack the strength to get food in this frozen world, and her cubs were still too young and immature to hunt for themselves. Outside the den and lacking the protection of her claws and fearsome fangs, those three furry little felines would be the hunted rather than the hunters.

One of the lung-shot manyhorn browsers, this one a hornless doe, struggled to her feet and crossed the deer yard at a stumbling, staggering run. Another of the hissing black sticks sped from out the laurels to *thunnk* solidly into her other side, just behind the shoulder. The stricken doe managed two more steps, then fell again, this time almost under the Hunter's forepaws. The heady scent of the dying deer's hot blood filled the cat's nostrils and set her empty stomach to growling while her tongue unconsciously sought her thin lips.

The Hunter flattened her long-furred body onto the snow-covered ground and moved not a whisker, for she wanted none of those little black sticks flying in her direction; but neither was she willing to make a quick and silent withdrawal, leaving behind so much of the meat she had stalked so long and so laboriously.

She watched four of the two-legs, covered in animal hides and furs, rise up from out the mountain laurel clump that had hidden them. Pulling long, shiny things from someplace at a point just above their hind legs, they went from one to another of the manyhorn browsers, opening the big throat veins and holding hollow, pointless horns to catch the hot red blood, which they then drank off with broad smiles and obvious relish.

The Hunter's keen ears could hear other two-legs and a number of the rather stupid, hornless four-leg grazers that often carried two-legs on their backs proceeding from a short distance downwind. She knew then that if she was to have any half-decent chance of getting clear with one of these dead manyhorn browsers that meant so much to her and her most recent litter, it must assuredly be done immediately.

Those four visible two-legs had stopped drinking browser blood, and now three of them were half carrying, half dragging the largest carcass—an adult buck of twelve points—toward a thick-boled tree at the other side of the yard. The fourth two-leg was shinnying up the bole with one end of a rawhide rope clenched between his flashing white teeth.

She had wormed herself to the uttermost limits of available concealment. Now only a snow-crusted log and a bare body length of open ground lay between her and the dead doe. With careful and deliberate speed, she drew her powerful hind legs beneath her, tensed, then uncoiled like a huge steel spring. In barely a human eyeblink, the great cat was over the log, had reached the side of the doe, sunk her long fangs into its neck, then disappeared with her prize back into the snow-choked brush between the forest trees, her pearl-gray coat with its dark-gray markings blending perfectly with the wintry landscape.

Entirely absorbed in fitting the rawhide rope between the hocks and the tendons of the buck's hind legs, the quartet of men neither saw nor heard the movement of the great furry cat.

A hundred yards uphill, deeper into the thickening forest, the ravenous cat could no longer resist the temptation. Dropping her burden at the base of a tall pine tree, she employed her daggerlike upper canines to rip open the doe's belly, then avidly tore out mouthfuls of hot, tender liver and other choice parts.

From behind a currant bush, a vixen thrust out her wriggling black button of a nose and an inch or so of her slender, rufous-furred jaws. The Hunter rippled a low snarl of warning, whereupon the nose was abruptly whisked back out of sight and the vixen scurried away . . . but not far, for she knew that her turn would come soon or late, and she had the patience to await it.

Her sharpest pangs of hunger temporarily assuaged, the Hunter arose, gripped anew her now somewhat lighter burden and limped on over ice-glazed rocks and between the boles of trees toward her well-hidden den and her hungry kittens.

Once the Hunter was well out of sight among the snow-weighted brush and dark evergreens up the slope, the vixen crept warily from beneath the currant bush and first cleaned up every scrap that she could see or smell of gut or organ, then began to lap at the bloody snow.

The Hunter had been aware that the two-legs were coming after her almost from the moment they had set out on her trail, since the pursuers made nearly as much racket as an equal number of shaggy-bulls would have created in passage through the woods. But she was easily maintaining her lead, despite the lancing agony that her left foreleg was become with the strain of dragging the heavy, stiffening carcass through the wet, breast-deep snow and over the rough ground beneath it.

Only when she neared the high place atop which lay her den did she decide to take action against the pursuing two-legs. Perhaps if she stopped long enough to kill one of them, the rest of the pack would feed upon him, as wolves did, and give her time to cover her trail to the immediate environs of her den.

The Hunter had had but little contact with two-legs—they seldom penetrated the perimeters of her range—but when a two-year-old, she had seen her mother killed by two-legs, pierced through and through with the hateful little black sticks, then pinned to the ground, still snarling and snapping and clawing, by a longer and thicker stick in the forepaws of a two-leg who sat high astride the back of a hornless grazer four-leg. She did not hate two-legs, really, any more than she hated other competitive predators, but she did respect those of the little black sticks, recognized their deadly potential, and so she took great care in the laying of her ambush.

She continued well past the spot she had decided upon, then adroitly broke her trail by the expedient of leaping atop the bole of a fallen tree, now scoured of snow by the wind. Climbing onto the mass of dead roots and frozen earth, she reared to her full length on her hind legs and carefully hung her precious doe over the broad branch of a still-standing tree. Below that branch all the way down, the trunk stood bare of all save slippery bark encased in even slipperier ice, so the carcass should be safe from the depredations of any other predator or scavenger save perhaps a bear or another cat.

But the only bear that shared her range was denned up for the winter a full day's run to the north, while the smaller cats of varying sizes and races hereabouts ran in mortal fear of the Hunter and would never dare to venture so close to her den while she was about.

The soil was thin and studded with many rocks on the slope, and over the years many a tree had fallen to storms or winds or simply the erosion that bared roots. The canny cat now made good use of the raised way provided by these fallen treetrunks to wend her way back toward the ambush point she had earlier chosen without leaving telltale signs of her return passage in the snow.

Arriving at last in the patch of saplings and thick brush, she bellied down and made a swift and silent trip to the opposite side of the copse. There, in what she felt to be the ideal spot, she crouched, motionless as the very rocks frozen beneath the shrouding snow, waiting.

The lead two-leg, slightly crouching, with his gaze locked on her tracks and the broad trail made by dragging the deer, came abreast of the Hunter, then passed her, a long, shiny-tipped stick dangling from one forepaw. Next, one behind the other, came trotting two two-legs, each of them grasping one of the cursive, horn-covered sticks that threw the deadly little black sticks.

All of these she allowed to pass out of sight around the point of the copse, for the very next two-leg was, she could see, bigger than the others, which meant that he was the pack leader, thought the Hunter. He bore neither long stick nor cursive horn-stick and little ones, but rather three of an intermediate size.

Soundless as very death itself, the Hunter hurled herself upon this leader of the two-leg pack, and even as her weight and momentum bore him toward the snowy ground, she thrust her good right forepaw around his head, hooked her wicked claws bone-deep into the flesh over the jaw, then jerked sharply back and to her right.

The Hunter growled deeply in satisfaction at the sound and the feel of the snapping of the neck of the biggest two-leg. Then she spun upon her furry haunches and bounded easily back to become instantly lost to sight among the snow-covered undergrowth of the copse, leaving the remaining two-legs all making loud noises behind her.

Many of the little black sticks flew after her, but only one of them fleshed itself at all, and that one did no more than to split the very tip of her ear before hissing on to rattle among the treetrunks until spent.

Well pleased with both her plan and its execution, the Hunter negotiated the width of the copse and made her way back to where she had cached her doe. Soon she and her three cubs would be feasting upon tasty deer flesh in their warm, safe, comfortable den, while the remaining members of the two-leg pack filled their own bellies with the carcass of their dead leader.

With only the one reliable forepaw, the Hunter found it a

long and difficult and very painful task to maneuver the stiff and weighty deer carcass through the twisting, turning tunnel, but finally she arrived in the spacious den, to the most raucous welcome of her three cubs.

When her belly was stuffed with venison, when the cubs had consumed as much of the meat as they desired and then nursed, the Hunter padded over to the pool that was never dry but ever full of icy water in any season. Her thirst slaked, she padded back, thoroughly washed the sleepy cubs, then curled up with them to sleep.

She was aware, thanks to her keen hearing, that a winter pack of wolves was approaching the high place on which this den of hers was situated, but she harbored no fear of even so many, not while she lay safe in the den. No single wolf, no matter how outsize, could be a match for the Hunter, and the inner portions of the convoluted passage which was the only entry to the den of which she was then aware could be negotiated by no more than a single wolf at a time.

Many winters ago, she and her mother and her littermates— they then being something over a year old—had whiled away a snowy afternoon by taking turns killing wolves as the lupines reached the first turn in the entry tunnel. One by one, they had slain or seriously maimed the marauders, who then were dragged out backward by their packmates, torn apart and eaten. Finally, as darkness approached, the huge pack— their bellies by then partially filled with wolfmeat from their cannibalistic feast—departed the high place to seek easier prey in the forests below.

Aware that among other natural advantages, her sight was far superior to that of the wolves in the almost total darkness prevailing in the tunnel, the great cat anticipated no difficulty in doing the amount of killing necessary to discourage this pack, if matters came to that.

A sudden intensification of the hot, lancing pain in her left foreleg awakened the Hunter, that and a thirst that was raging. Arising, she hobbled unsteadily across the high-ceilinged, airy den to lap avidly at the pool in one corner.

Her thirst sated for the nonce with the water, which, though always crackling-cold, never froze over in even the most bitter of winters, she did not return to the spot whereon the cubs were sleeping, but rather hobbled over to take a sentry post at the inner mouth of the tunnel, for her senses told her that a large number of wolves now were on the high place and were, some of them, milling about and sniffing at the track she had made while dragging the dead doe's carcass.

Lying down there, for she seemed strangely devoid of energy, the big cat instinctively licked at her swollen, throbbing left foreleg, at the inflamed spot where the horn had pierced her, but even the gentle touch of her tongue sent bolts of burning, near-intolerable agony coursing through her body. And, of course, that moment was when she heard the first wolf enter the tunnel.

Even while sleeping, an unsleeping portion of the Hunter's consciousness had been made aware by the feline's senses that the two-leg pack, hotly pursued by the wolf pack, had taken refuge upon the high, smooth-sided, flat-topped place, whereon in better weather full many a cat had sunned itself.

But because she did know that eyrie so well, she knew that there was no danger of the two-legs getting from there to her den. She did not think that the wolves could jump high enough to gain to the top of that place, but if they could and they really wanted to eat the two-legs, they were more than welcome to the smelly creatures. As for her, she had nearly gagged at the foul stench of that two-leg she had killed so easily on the preceding day.

When the claw clicks and shufflings and snufflings told her that the lupine invader was past the first turn of the passage, she entered it herself, putting as little weight as possible upon her strangely huge and very tender left foreleg. They two met at a point between the first turn and the second, in a section too low-ceilinged for either to stand fully erect.

The Hunter was supremely confident, for she knew well that she possessed the deadly advantage here; for with only toothy jaws for weapons, the wolf could but lunge for her throat, whereas, completely discounting her own more than adequate dentition, a single blow from her claw-studded forepaw could smash the life out of that wolf as it had of so many before him. But she reckoned without her disability.

Sensing more than seeing the exact location of the intruder's head, the Hunter lashed out with her sound paw. But this suddenly threw the full and not inconsiderable weight of her head and her forequarters onto the fevered, immensely swollen left foreleg. Squalling with the hideous pain, she stumbled, and so her buffet failed to strike home, the bared claws only raking the wolf's head and mask. Before she could recover, the crushing lupine jaws had closed upon her one good foreleg, the canines stabbing, while the carnassials scissored skin and flesh and muscle, going on to crack bone.

But the wolf did not have time to raise his bloody, tattered head, for the Hunter closed, sank her own long fangs into the sinewy neck and crushed the spine of the would-be invader.

Even as the wolf's jaws relaxed in death, the Hunter slowly backed down the tunnel, dragging her two useless forepaws, growling deep in her throat as the waves of agony washed over her. Weak and growing weaker each moment, she tumbled the two-foot drop from tunnel mouth to den floor.

Two of the cubs, trailed closely by the third, bounced merrily over to her, but a snarled command sent them all scurrying back into a far, dark corner. The Hunter knew that all four of them now were doomed. She might have enough strength remaining to kill with her fangs the very next wolf that emerged from the yawning mouth of that tunnel, perhaps even the second and the third. But there would be another and another and yet another, and at last she would be too weak to deal with the next in the succession of invaders, and that wolf would kill her. And then the pack would be through the undefended tunnel and at the helpless cubs, ripping the soft little bodies to bloody shreds, eating her orphaned young alive.

Deciding to guard the cubs as long as possible, the great maimed cat painfully dragged herself across the den and took her death stand before them.

Milo again opened his own personal memories to the folk and the cat who sat with him in Chief Dik Krooguh's yurt.

The door Milo had finally forced led into a room that was really just an extra-wide stair landing. These stairs were of concrete; one led down and the other had once led upward, but it now was solidly choked with assorted masonry debris and lengths of rusted iron pipe from about halfway up its course. The high-held lantern showed Milo that although there were bits and pieces of the debris on many of the descending stairs, they were mostly clear enough for easy passage.

Along the wall facing the stairs was a bank of metal cabinets, each about five feet high and some foot wide. They looked to him like army wall lockers. His exploration of the cabinets proved them bare of very much that was still in any way usable—a few small brass buckles, a handful of metal buttons, otherwise just rotted cloth and leather, flaking rubber and plastic, one pair of metal-framed sunglasses.

When he opened the last cabinet, he jumped back and cursed at unexpected movement, his hand going to the worn hilt of his big dirk. The hefty brown rat struck the floor running and scuttled down the steps, only to return up them running at least twice as fast and shrieking rodent terror. The little beast streaked over Milo's booted feet, jumped back into the cabinet and crouched petrified until the man reclosed the door.

Thus warned, Milo descended the stairs slowly and carefully, holding the lantern high for maximum visibility. It was well that he did so, for the bare concrete floor of the room at the foot of those stairs was littered with nearly two dozen sluggishly writhing rattlesnakes!

"Well," thought Milo, relieved, "that answers the food problem for a couple of days, anyway, and when these are gone, there's always that nice fat rat and maybe some of his family, like as not."

But as none of the vipers lay between the foot of the stairs and still another closed door across the room, he left them alone for the moment. This door proved the hardest to open of any he had as yet encountered, but at last he did so, to find himself facing a short stretch of corridor and three more doors—one each to his right and his left, one more straight ahead of him.

The doors to both left and right were secured by massive padlocks. Stenciled in big block letters on the face of the right-hand door was FALLOUT SHELTER—KEEP OUT—THIS MEANS YOU!; the left-hand door bore the message PRIVATE SANCTUM OF STATION DIRECTOR—TRESPASSERS WILL BE BRUTALLY VIOLATED!

The door straight ahead was unmarked, and though it bore no padlock in the hasp and staple provided for such hardware, it was held firmly shut by an iron bar at least two inches thick which bisected it horizontally and was supported by two U-shaped brackets firmly bolted to the masonry.

Since it opened inward, Milo thought that it might well be a portal to the outside. He put an ear to the steel-sheathed door, but could hear nothing. Removing the bar, he swung it open a crack, keeping shoulder and foot braced hard against it, just in case a wolf or three should try to come calling.

But stygian darkness lay beyond this door, too, a damp darkness and an overpowering odor of cat. He closed the door again for long enough to draw his saber, then opened it wide, held the lantern aloft and quickly descended the two steps to the next level, his eyes rapidly scanning the large, high-ceilinged room as far as the lanternlight would extend.

The Hunter tried to raise herself when the two-leg holding in one forepaw a small, very bright sun opened somehow a part of one wall of the den and came in, but she was now become too weak to do any more than growl.

Milo let his saber sag down from the guard position, for the big female cat was clearly as helpless as the cubs bunched behind her supine body. One of her forelegs was grotesquely swollen, obviously infected or deeply abscessed, while the other was torn and bleeding and looked to be broken as well.

There was a flicker of movement to his right, and he spun about just in time to see the slavering jaws and smoldering eyes of a wolf's head emerge from a hole just a little above the floor. In two leaping strides, he crossed the width of the room and his well-honed saber blade swept up, then down, severing the wolf's neck cleanly.

But the headless, blood-spouting body still issued forth from the hole, and as it tumbled to kick and twitch beside its still-grinning head, another, similar head came into view, this one living and snarling fiercely at the man who faced him.

Milo thrust his point between the gaping jaws and through the soft palate. White teeth snapped and splintered on the fine steel and the point grated briefly on bone before he freed it in a death-dealing drawcut, but as the steel came out, the dying wolf came with it, and behind crouched another of the beasts.

The saber split the skull of the third wolf, but even as its blood and brains gushed out, another was pushing the quivering body out of the tunnel and into the den.

"This," thought Milo, "could conceivably go on for hours, as many wolves as there are out there."

But as the fifth wolf was being slowly pushed toward him, Milo suddenly became cognizant of the rectangular regularity of the opening. Man-made! And the men who fashioned it would surely have also fashioned a means of closing it . . . ?

And there that means was! Half-hidden by a camouflage of

dust and dirt and the ever-present cobwebs, a sliding door, set between metal runners on the wall above the opening. But did it still function properly? Or at all?

In the precious moments between butchering wolves, he pulled and tugged and pushed at the door. Setting the lantern down, he drew his dirk with his left hand and used its point to dig bits of debris from around and beneath the door, to dislodge other bits from the grooves of the runners. Clenching the blade of the dirk between his teeth, he hung his full weight from the doorhandle . . . and it *moved*!

Then there was another wolf, this one a huge, coal-black beast. He killed it, chuckling to himself and thinking, "The Chinese used to say that you should never be cruel to a black dog that appeared at your door. Well, hell, I wasn't cruel to that bastard; I gave him a cleaner, quicker death than he and his pack would have given me."

The black wolf had been both bigger and in far better flesh than most of his packmates, so it took the wolf behind a few seconds longer than usual to push the jerking body out of the tunnel, and that few seconds' respite made all the difference.

With all of Milo's one hundred and eighty pounds of weight suspended from it, the ancient steel door inched downward, then, screeching like a banshee, picked up speed. Finally, impelled by a last, powerful thrust of Milo's arms, it slammed shut and latched itself in the very face of the next wolf, which yelped its startled surprise.

Stepping back and carefully wiping off the blood-slimed blade of his saber on the pelt of a dead wolf, Milo mindcalled, "Dik, Djim, the rest of you, take up the lantern and carry it as you saw me carry this one. Be very careful that you don't drop it or strike it against something. Come down the metal steps one by one—they're too old and rusty to bear too much weight at once. Proceed through the opened door and down a flight of stone stairs, but be careful where you step at the bottom of those, for rattlesnakes are denned there.

"Those who have a taste for snakemeat can kill them, but any who'd rather have fresh wolf chops need only join me here and skin and gut and butcher their choice of ten or twelve of the bastards, all fresh-killed.

"Oh, and there's water here too, somewhere; I can smell it."

Then, suddenly, an intensely powerful mindspeak blanked

out any reply the Horseclansmen might have beamed. "What are you, two-legs? You bear a small sun in your paws, you slay many, many wolves to protect cubs not your own, you can somehow open den walls and close them, and you can speak the language of cats, which is a something other two-legs cannot do. *Who are you? What* are you?"

The Hunter felt that she no longer could trust the witness of her own eyes. At times they seemed to be clouded with a dark, almost opaque mist; at other times she seemed to be seeing the images of three of four or even more identical two-legs and as many of the little, intensely bright suns. But none of these images stayed constant, they shifted about, changing not only in numbers but in consistency as well.

Therefore, when first she sensed the two-leg, sun-bearing wolfkiller's mind projecting that silent means of communication used only by cats and a few other of the more intelligent four-legs, she thought that others of her perceptions had suddenly gone as skewed as her visual perception. But at length she beamed a question . . . *and he answered her*!

Milo just stood and stared at the injured cat for a long moment, deeply shaken by the experience of having an animal actually communicate with him telepathically. Then, moving deliberately and slowly, he laid down his saber beside the lantern and took a few steps in the cat's direction, extending an empty hand in the ages-old, instinctual gesture of promised friendship.

"You are badly hurt, sister," he beamed. "Will you bite me if I try to help you?"

The sight of him abruptly faded again into the dark mist, but still his message came clearly into her mind and she said, "Help this mother? Why would you want to help this mother? This Hunter killed one of your pack last sun. Two-legs do not ever help cats, they slay cats, just as you slew those wolves there."

He replied, "Wolves are the enemies of us both, sister, foes of both cats and men. Besides, the other men and I are hungry."

"You would eat *wolf flesh*?" The repugnance in her thoughtbeam was crystal-clear.

He moved his head up and down twice for some unknown reason and beamed, "Hunger can make any meat taste good, sister."

All of the Hunter's life had been hard, and she could grasp the universal truth stated by this remarkable two-leg. Perhaps, then, he was truthful about wishing to aid her. "If the mother allows you to come close, what will you do, two-leg?"

"The bleeding of your torn paw must be stopped, sister, the wounds cleaned out and packed with healing herbs, then wrapped up in cloth . . . uhh, something like very soft skins . . . then the broken bones must be pulled straight and tied in place to heal. All of this will hurt, sister, and you must promise not to bite us in your pain."

"Us?"

"Yes, sister, one of my brothers must help me. He is most skilled in caring for wounds and injuries."

To himself, Milo thanked his lucky stars that chance had had Fil Linszee with this party. The young man was well on his way to becoming a first-rate horse leech, and was always certain to have a packet of herbs and salves and the like secreted somewhere on his person.

"Does your brother, too, speak the language of cats?" beamed the Hunter. She was feeling very strange, much weaker, so weak in fact that it was now all that she could do to keep her big head up and frame the thoughts she beamed.

She half-sensed an answer from the two-leg, but it was very unclear. Suddenly, nothing was clear for her—not sight, not hearing, not touch, not mental perception. The dark mists closed in, thicker and darker. A great waterfall seemed to be roaring about her. Then there was nothing.

CHAPTER X

As it chanced, Fil Linszee was the first Horseclansman to come through the door into the den area. His long spear was in one hand and the writhing, jerking bodies of a brace of headless rattlesnakes were in the other. But at sight of the cat, he dropped the snakes and grasped his spear in both hands, bringing the point to low guard.

But Milo waved the spear away, saying, "You'll not need a spear, Fil, not with any luck. Believe it or not, this cat can mindspeak. We two were having quite a conversation before she passed out a few moments back. We . . . that is, you, are going to try to do what is necessary to heal up those forelegs of hers. Do you think that working on a cat will be radically different from working on a horse?"

Fil came further into the den and critically eyed the cat while keeping a safe distance from her, with his spear shaft held cautiously between them. Then, after sucking for a minute on his long lower lip, he said, "Uncle Milo, that cat must weigh over two hundred pounds, for all she's not really well fed. That near foreleg will be tender as a boil just now, and it needs draining, which means that I'm going to have to cut deeply into it, probably in two places. I value my life and a whole skin, Uncle Milo, so I will not touch the cat unless she is well and firmly tied. She's bound to be too strong for even six warriors to hold down for long."

Reflecting that the man was no doubt right in his assessment of the cat's strength, Milo thought hard. The two or three short lengths of rawhide rope that his party had brought along would be of no good to them at all for the monumental task at hand, nor would their seven belts help.

"Maybe," he thought, "behind one of those locked doors . . .?"

A swift succession of short, powerful blows with one end of the iron shaft that had barred the door to the cat's den did not even dent the massive padlock, but did tear the hasp and staple loose, which accomplished Milo's purpose.

Behind the door marked FALLOUT SHELTER, he found a real treasure trove—jerrycans of fuels, boxes of canned goods, several locked footlockers, three long-handled spades, a pickaxe, a grubbing hoe, a chainsaw, a wrecking bar and a sledge-hammer. All of the metal parts of these tools had been well coated with Cosmoline, then with treated paper and looked to have just come from a hardware store.

The room was bricky dry and there was almost no dust, since the door had been thick, tight-fitting and weatherstripped, to boot, with a sill three inches higher than the floor surfaces on either side of it. There was an identical door let into the opposite wall, but Milo postponed exploring whatever lay beyond it, for he had found those things he immediately needed in the very first footlocker he had opened—several coils of strong rope, both manila and nylon, plus an assortment of webbing straps fitted with buckle fasteners.

Bearing the ropes and straps, Milo, Fil, Dik and Djim filed into the den and headed toward the unconscious cat. But suddenly, there arose a fearsome—if somewhat high-pitched—growl and one of the cat's cubs, probably weighing all of twenty-five pounds, stalked purposefully from behind his mother. His fur and his whiskers were all a-bristle, his ears were folded back against his diminutive head and his lips were curled up off his little white teeth. After advancing a few yards, the cub took his stand, his tail swishing his rage and his fierce resolve.

Milo received the silent warning in a beaming almost as powerful as had been that of the mature cat. "Two-legs keep away from the mother or this cat kills!"

The other Horseclansmen had received the thought transmission, as well, and stop they did, all grinning and nodding their honest admiration of such natural courage and reckless daring in the defense of kin.

"Uncle Milo," said Dik soberly, "if that cub had two legs instead of four, I'd feel honored to sponsor him to my chief for adoption into our clan, for it's clear beyond any doubt that he's a Horseclansman born.''

Handing his coils of rope to another, Milo slowly approached the diminutive feline warrior. Squatting at a distance he hoped was out of range of a sudden pounce, he mindspoke the hissing little cat, while at the same time, on another level of his mind, he broadbeamed a thoughtless message of soothing reassurance, having noticed that such worked well with angry or frightened horses or mules.

"How is my young brother called?''

The cub did not alter his position or his mien of overt menace one whit and he eyed Milo with distrust. When he at last deigned to answer, it was with open hostility.

"This cat is called Killer of Two-legs. He is not the brother of you or any other two-leg. Keep away from the mother or you all will die under his claws and fangs!''

Dik slapped his thigh and guffawed. "Just listen to him! What a warrior he'll be when he's grown! Facing down four full-grown and armed men, and him but a cub cat.''

Milo spoke aloud, saying, "Don't underestimate him, Dik. He's smaller than his mother, yes, but even so, he's near as big as a grown bobcat and I'll wager he could engrave some meaningful furrows in your hide, if given half a chance.''

Then he added, "But we won't give him that chance . . . I hope. Two of you, take off your jackets and then hand one of them to me, *sllooowwwllyy*, then get some of the lighter rope ready. I could argue all day with this obstinate little bugger, and his mother will likely die soon without help.''

With moving men well to either side distracting the attention of Killer of Two-legs, Milo was able to flip the coat over the cub, and then it was a furious matter of grab and tussle, but finally it was done; the raging, squalling beastlet was securely wrapped in two garments of thick leather and the resultant bundle was lapped about with several yards of rope. When defeat of the feline champion had seemed imminent, the other two cubs had beat a brisk and silent retreat to a far, dark corner of the den.

First Fil cleaned out the ragged wolf bite and packed it with dried herbs, then smeared it with salve; adroitly, he set and splinted the broken bones, using part of his own embroidered shirt when he ran out of prepared bandage cloths. But when he first made to shave the infected offside paw with the razor-keen skinning knife, the huge cat, which had remained inert through all of his previous ministrations, roused to full and savagely furious consciousness. She strained mightily at the ropes and straps pinioning her rear legs and her fearsome jaws, growling between the forcibly clenched teeth and fangs.

Vainly, Milo tried to reach her mind, then gave up and added his strength to that of the others to try to keep her still enough for Fil to do what needed doing.

As well as he could, Fil went on about his shaving off of the long, dense fur. As gently as was possible, his sensitive fingers roved over the grossly swollen paw and leg. After gingerly pressing several spots, he chose one of them and rubbed the discolored skin with a few drops of liquid from a small and ancient metal flask, then tilted the bottle at an angle and dipped the slender blade of a knife into it.

At the first touch of the needle-pointed knife, the huge cat squalled, heaved her heavy body once violently, then lapsed again into unconsciousness.

Fil was blessed with the experience to keep clear, but the overcurious Djim, peering closely, caught full in the face the jet of foul greenish pus that erupted around the blade on its initial cut. Cursing sulfurously, he sprang up and made for the water pool.

A long gash was opened, Fil cutting through to the very bone, then pressing harder and harder upon the leg until only blood and clear serum flowed. Once again, he packed the wound with dried herbs, smeared its gaping edges with salve and bandaged it with more of his shirt and part of Milo's.

After feeling the throat pulse to ascertain that his feline patient still lived, he gathered his gear and trudged wearily toward the pool. By the time he had finished laving himself and his instruments, the straining men had heaved and man-handled the limp body of the cat back to where she had originally been lying and had released the bonds from her hind legs.

Fil Esmith took up a watch over his patient, squatting near her with the thrashing length of a decapitated rattler on the floor before him. He gobbled raw fillets of snakemeat just as fast as his busy knife could skin, clean and slice them off. Across the den from him, the redhaired Linszee twins joked and chortled while they lugged bloody wolf carcasses up to the roof of the tower for skinning whenever the blizzard died down.

In one end of what had been the snake den, Djim Linszee was squatting, cub-sitting. Killer of Two-legs, having hotly refused to tender his parole, had not been released; the furious and frustrated little beast was somehow managing to roll his ropebound leather cocoon over and over, from one side of the narrow room to the other, alternately bawling for maternal aid and beaming threats of dire and deadly retribution upon the flesh of every two-leg he had so far seen.

On the other hand, Djim had gained at least the conditional friendship and partial trust of the two slightly smaller and much less pugnacious female cubs. The fuzzy little creatures were mindspeaking less and less guardedly as they avidly devoured the lavish gifts of fresh snakemeat proffered by Djim.

Milo had found the inner door of the fallout shelter to be only closed, not locked, though every crack in and around it had been meticulously packed with some sort of chemically treated fiber, then double-sealed with wide strips of tape. Sealant removed, the door had opened easily to reveal a virtual efficiency apartment—two double-decker bunks, a chemical toilet, a three-burner petrol range, stainless-steel sink with a chrome pump rather than a faucet and a plethora of cabinets and drawers of varying shapes and sizes built into every available inch of wall space.

After he had gone through the contents of some of the cabinets, a healthy proportion of the dragging weight of worry over their predicament lifted from off Milo's mind. Even if the blizzard, now howling around the ruins in full force, should last for a month and the huge wolf pack should maintain their siege right up until spring, he and his Horse-clansmen would be well fed on the big cans of powdered whole milk and eggs and orange concentrate, the stack upon high stack of freeze-dried foods still sealed in their plastic-lined foil pouches. There were jars of freeze-dried coffee (Milo vainly racked his brain trying to recall the last time he had tasted real coffee; although all of the nomads drank certain bastard brews that they invariably called ''kawfee'') and sugar and honey and jams, tins of tea, even a full case of a Jerez brandy (*año* 1972), plus a wide assortment of condiments, candies, herbs and spices and pickles.

Under one of the lower bunks was a steel chest, padlocked as well as being as thoroughly sealed with tape as the inner door had been. The lock yielded to the iron bar, however. Within, the first thing to catch Milo's eye was a finely tooled leather case some four feet long.

With a shiver of presentiment, he lifted the case onto the bunk and unsnapped its catches, then raised the lid. Nestled into a fitted depression in the liner of impregnated sheepskin lay a scope-sighted sporting rifle, its dark-blue barrel, chrome bolt handle and stock of polished curly maple reflecting back the light of the lantern. Arrayed across the lower edge of the case were twelve brightly colored boxes, each of them labeled "REMINGTON .30-06 Sprgfld. 180 gr. pointed soft point, 20 cartridges."

His hands shaking slightly, Milo took the beautiful weapon from its century-old bed and lifted, then pulled back the silvery bolt handle. The archaic Mauser action slid smoothly open and its ejector sent a glittering brass dummy cartridge clattering across the room. Under a light film of lubricants, the interior surfaces of the rifle gleamed every bit as brightly as did the exterior.

Milo slouched back against the door of the cabinet behind him, a grim smile on his lips. Twelve boxes of cartridges, twenty rounds the box, two hundred and forty rounds, then; even if it required one full box to reorient himself to firearms in general and this magnificent one in particular, that and to get it zeroed in properly, he'd still have far more than enough to seriously deplete the wolf population hereabouts; so now he and his companions were trapped here in these ruins only until the weather improved.

"But what," he mused aloud to himself, "about those cats? Even with that big wolf pack wiped out, she's going to be in a bad way. She won't be able to hunt at all for at least a month, and she and those cubs will be white bones before then. True, the men and I, we can kill and butcher game and leave meat behind for her and the cubs. But how long before they ate it all or it got too ripe to eat?

"What other alternatives are there? Take them back to camp with us whenever we go? Well, for the three cubs, that would be easy of accomplishment, I guess: just strap one each on the backs of three men. But how in the devil are seven men supposed to get a two-hundred-and-some-pound injured cat down a bitch of an almost vertical hillside which also is coated with ice and full of loose rocks?

"Of course, what we really should do is just loll around in here until the big cat is mended, then give her the choice of coming with us or staying here, but if I should keep these men away that long, their clans will think they're all dead and, most likely, move the camp to a luckier place. And that place to which they move would probably be in the opposite direction from that we'd go to look for them, too.

"Now if it only weren't for that damned precipitous hillslope, we could easily fashion a sled or two and . . ."

Fil Linszee's mindcall interrupted his musings.

"Uncle Milo, the big cat is waking up."

When Milo strode into the den, Fil, Bili and Bahb were watching the great groggy beast, made clumsy by her bandaged forepaws, trying to get a hind claw under the strap still securing her jaws.

He moved to her side and sank onto his haunches, laying a hand on her head, because he had long ago learned that some form of physical contact always improved telepathic communication.

Then he mindspoke her, saying, "Sister, wait. I'll take the straps off. But you must promise not to tear off the bits of cloth covering your forepaws with your teeth. Will you promise?"

The blizzard blew for three days, but the howling winds began to slacken during the third night and died with the dawn. That fourth morning brought a full blaze of sun and an unclouded blue sky for its setting.

The fourth morning also brought back the wolves, who had wisely departed the dangerously exposed plateau during the blow. Bili and Bahb Linszee were atop the tower working on the frozen carcasses of the wolves Milo had sabered in the den with their skinning knives. As the vanguards of the pack returned to the plateau, they honored an earlier promise and mindcalled Milo.

Carrying the cased rifle and a folded tarp, Milo climbed back up onto the roof of the ruined tower. He had been classed an expert rifleman in every army in which he could recall serving, and during the long blizzard days and nights he had read and reread the booklet that the Browning Arms

Company had packed with the rifle, then stripped the piece, thoroughly cleaned and relubricated it with other contents of the steel chest, and dry-fired it until he thought that he knew all that he could learn of the weapon without actually putting live rounds through the mirror-bright, chromed bore. He also had completely familiarized himself with the scope and its adjusting knobs, for the optic device would be useful to him long after the last round for the rifle had been expended.

Lacking the sandbags he recalled using to steady the piece for long-range shooting, he utilized the tarp-covered frozen carcass of an unskinned wolf, settled himself in the prone position behind it, opened a box of cartridges and filled the rifle's magazine, then removed the lens covers from the scope. Everything now in readiness to give the wolves a rude and very deadly surprise, he relaxed in place, waiting until a maximum number of the predators had come within range of the rifle.

The pack must have not found much if any game during the days of the blizzard, for soon the most of them were gathered about the foot of the tower, engaged in a snapping, snarling battle royal over the skinned carcasses the Linszee twins tossed off the roof as soon as the pelts were off them. But a few wolves were still sitting or ambling at some distance from the ruins, so Milo set about sighting in the weapon.

Far down, near the distant edge of the plateau, sat two of the wolves, intently observing something in the forest below. Milo centered the cross hairs of the scope on the head of the nearer one and slowly squeezed off the first round. The rifle butt slammed his shoulder with a force and violence he had half forgotten. Below the tower, the wolf-pack members were streaming off in every direction—yelping, howling, barking, tails tucked between their legs, looking back as they ran from that awesome sound with wide and fear-filled eyes. But Milo did not notice the lupine exodus, so intent was he in checking the performance of the rifle, which he calculated had thrown a good ten feet short of his chosen target and well to the left.

The two distant wolves had looked around at the noise, but as they never had been hunted with firearms, they failed to connect that noise with danger or with the small something that had drilled its sizzling way through the frozen crust; they may not even have been aware of that something, since it had arrived somewhat ahead of the noise.

Milo chambered a fresh round, adjusted the scope and then resettled himself behind the weapon, remembering this time to push the butt firmly against his shoulder. The second round whizzed out of the barrel. Through the scope, Milo saw the target animal suddenly duck down, then shake his head and raise his long muzzle skyward, looking around above him.

Three more rounds were fired and three more adjustments of the telescopic sight made, but the sixth fired round sent the distant wolf leaping high into the air, to fall and lie jerking and twitching in the snow for a few moments before becoming very still. The other wolf was still sniffing at its mysteriously stricken packmate when a 180-grain softpoint bullet ended its curiosity forever.

Milo had had the tower top to himself for some time. The two Linszee boys had descended the rickety stairs shaking their ringing heads and wondering how even Uncle Milo could stand those incredibly loud noises.

In a way, Milo felt sorry for the pack of merciless killers he was engaged in extirpating, for they none of them had the faintest notion who or what was killing them. The crashingly loud reports tended to keep them well away from the tower, and that distance simply made it easier to shoot them accurately with the long-range weapon.

He tried hard to make each kill a clean one, and the tremendous shocking power of the mushrooming bullets helped him toward his goal. He never knew how many, or how few, of that pack survived, but those that did were those that, for whatever reasons, were not on the plateau that morning, for he stopped firing only when there were no more targets.

When he finally stood up, his joints crackling and protesting, to survey the slaughter he had here wrought, he felt more than a little sick. Of all of the animals, he had always admired the great cats and the wolves. Sight of the tumbled, furry bodies—scores of them, scattered from side to side and end to end of the plateau—and thought of all the fierce vitality that his skill with the ancient weapon had snuffed out so safely and effortlessly pricked his conscience.

But the Horseclansmen, who had climbed up onto the roof of the ruined tower as soon as they could be reasonably sure that those earsplitting noises had ceased, did not any of them share his anachronistic squeamishness, not when they had gotten a good look at the windfall out there on the plateau.

Whooping, they lowered themselves down the sides of the tower and ran to the nearest dead wolves, skinning knives out. Winter wolf pelts were heavy, warm and valuable. They would become wealthy men at the next tribe council, through trading wolf pelts for cattle, sheep, horses, concubines and inanimate treasures.

By the morning of the fourth day after the blizzard had ended, the deer carcass was become but well-gnawed bones, and the den of rattlesnakes an assortment of curing snakeskins. The cat and her cubs had avidly lapped up every last drop of the three gallons of milk Milo had prepared them from some of the milk powder, so he decided to take Dik and Djim down into the forest below the plateau to seek game more edible than frozen wolves.

However, in the wake of the thorough scouring to which the winter wolf pack had subjected the country roundabout, four hares were all that the hunters had to show for three hours of the endeavor. Then Djim's keen eyes picked out some large beast moving through the thick, snow-weighted brush among the tree boles.

Alerted by the soundless mindspeak, Milo raised the rifle and almost loosed off a deadly bullet before the scope told him precisely what the animal was. Lowering the piece and thumbing the safety back on, he pursed his lips and whistled the horse-call of the clans, whereupon the chestnut broke off her browsing to come trotting out of the scrub.

Milo put out a hand to the mare, but she shied away, going instead to Dik and nuzzling against his chest.

Smiling broadly and patting the shaggy neck of the mare, he said wonderingly, "Why, this is my hunter, Swiftwater, Uncle Milo. But I left her with the other horses, back at that deer yard, days ago."

"Then it's a pure wonder that she's not now wolf shit," commented Djim laconically. "I figure most of those horses we left there are such, long since."

Dik hugged the mare's fine head to him, saying, "Well, she won't have to fear that now. I'll take care of my good girl."

"Then we'll have to set you up in a tent down here in the woods," said Djim bluntly, "because there's no way we're going to get a live horse up onto that plateau, Dik."

Dik set his jaw stubbornly. "I'm not going to leave her down here alone again."

Milo nodded. "No, Dik, you're not. You're going to fork her right now and ride back to the camp. Her fortuitous appearance changes the complexion of things. You've got your bow and your dirk. Djim will give you his arrows and his spear, as well.

"Fil says that the big cat may never recover her full strength in those forepaws. I mean to persuade her to come back to camp with us, her and the kittens."

Neither Horseclansman showed or felt any surprise at Milo's stated intent, for both had "chatted" often with the invalid cat, and Djim was now become not only a frequent companion but a virtual parent to all three of the cubs. To their minds, the four cats were human, anatomical differences notwithstanding.

Milo continued, "Dik, tell the chiefs of all we have found and all we have done here. Tell them to come with a large party and plenty of spare horses. We'll strip that ruin up there of anything and everything we can use; then, too," he grinned, "none of you will want to leave any of your wolfskins or snakehides behind.

"Tell the chiefs that I say to hurry, Dik. If they heed me in this instance, they stand to be chiefs of fairly wealthy clans by the time they leave this winter's camp."

With Dik departed, Milo and Djim continued to hunt, vainly, for a while, but then Djim mindcalled, "Uncle Milo, elk dung, still hot!"

Following the clear trail, the two men shortly came out of the thick woods into more open terrain. Well ahead, among the stumps verging a beaver pond, a solitary bull elk had cleared enough snow from off the frozen ground to give him access to the bunches of sere grass that underlay the white blanket; now, he was grazing.

Raising his head with its wide-spreading, still-unshed rack of deadly tines, the huge beast gazed at the two men without apparent alarm. A brief scan of the elk's surface thoughts told Milo the reason for this unconcern—this particular bull had been hunted by men more than once and he now realized that the long distance separating them was just too far for the hurting-sticks to travel through the air. If the two-legs kept to this distance, he was safe. Should they try to close, he would flee. Meanwhile, he would eat grass. Simple.

A single well-placed shot from the ancient hunting rifle dropped the half-ton animal, but Milo put a second into the head at close range as a precaution, for bull elk could be highly dangerous adversaries. Then he and Djim. taking time only for a few refreshing drafts of hot elk blood, set about the skinning and cleaning and butchering of the kill.

"The Hunter and her brood," thought Milo, "should be very happy with some hundreds of pounds of elkmeat, and that's to the good. I want her in a very damned jolly mood when I broach the subject of her and them leaving here for good with us and living out their lives with the clans.

"I would imagine that the idea of a steady, reliable and effortless—on her part, at least—food supply will appeal to her, so that's one point in favor of my plan. For all of her stubbornness, she's highly intelligent—more intelligent than any dog or pig that I ever came across, and they're supposed to be the most intelligent of four-footed creatures—and if you can convince her that something new or different is for her own or her cubs' welfare, she'll usually do as you say—as witness the fact that she has not pulled off her bandages even once, for all that those healing injuries must itch like pure, furious hell.

"If she's a sport, she's breeding true, for all three of her cubs can mindspeak, can beam every bit as strongly as can she, though not yet as far. When she has recovered her physical strength, she and I will have to travel around and see if we can locate a mate for her, since she avers that there are more of her kind in this neck of the woods."

Secure in the belief of the efficacy of his own powers of persuasion, Milo chuckled to himself on that long-ago, snowy, bitterly-cold day, "Who knows? In time, there may yet be still another Horseclan—a four-footed and furry Horseclan!"

"And so there is," beamed old Bullbane. "The Clan of Cats must be the most numerous of all the Clans of the Kindred, for every two-leg Horseclan has an allied sept of Cats. And there must be many claws-count of Kindred clans."

"Yes, honored cat brother," agreed Milo, "I, too, am certain that the full Clan of Cats is the largest of all the clans. Fourscore are the Kindred Clans, and each sept of the Clan of Cats averages some twelve, plus cubs, so there are well over one thousand prairiecats following the herds with their two-leg brothers and sisters. Nor does that figure include some that still are living wild, apart from the clans.''

''The wild life is a good life for a healthy, sound cat in its prime,'' stated Bullbane silently, ''but illness or serious injury or advanced age in the wild presage naught but a slow, painful death. Far better that a cat live out his life with his two-leg cat kin, secure in the knowledge that his abilities are valued, that his belly will be full as long as the bellies of his kin are full, that he will be protected and fed in illness or if injured, and that he will be vouchsafed a quick, painless death when he feels that the time has come for him to go to Wind.''

CHAPTER XI

Tim stumbled into the yurt a little after the dawning, half frozen, his knitted face mask stiff with ice rime. Dark blood had hardened on his mittens and in splashes up his sleeves, with blotches here and there on his trousers. His exhaustion was too great to allow him to do the normal things, so Mairee and Chief Dik's other two wives made haste to fetch his gear from off the horse, then drape the mount with sheets of felt until it had had time to cool properly.

Bettylou helped her husband out of his wet, filthy clothing and into the lighter garb worn within the warm yurts. When she had seen him with a full bowl of last night's stew, she took his bare icy feet into her lap, under the swell of her belly.

Mairee and the other two came in laden with the gear as well as with two stiff-frozen winter wolfskins, each of them of a creamy, almost-white color.

"White wolves are rare, this far south," remarked Chief Dik. "Skillfully assembled, those two will make a fine, warm, heavy cloak, like my own black wolfcloak."

"There are at least two more of these white ones out there," said Tim, mindspeaking, so that he might continue stuffing his mouth with cold stew unhindered. "And they are huge, a third again as large as the biggest of the other, more normal-sized wolves; they're braver, too, and more ferocious and cunning. This brace let the others go after the cattle and occupy our attention while they sneaked into the herders' yurt and tried to drag out a sleeping stripling—a lad of Clan Skaht. They did kill him, but his shouts alerted those of us who happened to be in that vicinity. I was just riding in off herd guard, so my bow was strung. An arrow was enough for one of them; the other I had to get down and take on my spear, which is why the larger pelt is so ragged in the breast area.''

Shaking his head reprovingly, old Chief Dik said, ''You must learn to exercise caution, Tim. You are the last Krooguh in the direct line of the chieftaincy. Were there not other armed clansfolk about who might have faced that wounded wolf in your stead?''

Bettylou felt her husband stiffen then, but when he spoke aloud his voice was controlled. ''Uncle Dik, even when or if I am a chief, I never will ask or expect another man to fight for me against man or beast. Yes, there were other armed folk about out there, but I was closest and my bow was strung. You are chief and you bear honorable scars of manhood, marks of your bravery in battle and in the hunt. Would you advise me to not win such, then? If so, then choose another for your successor, for I would far liefer be a common clansman who fought and died in honor than a living but cowardly chieftain of the richest clan on all the plains!''

Bettylou expected rage from the older man at Tim's words, but Chief Dik only nodded gravely. ''A good answer, Tim, and though strongly worded, spoken with all due courtesy. You much put me in mind of my own uncle. He was a very good chief, and I harbor no doubt but that you will be every bit as good a leader of our Clan Krooguh. A chief must be courteous and display a level head even when driven to anger; you have shown us here that you possess right many of the needed attributes of the chief you soon will be. You please me mightily, nephew.''

Hwahlis Hansuhn of Krooguh was born a little later that day, and, of course, the wolves made their attack against the camp that following night. Asleep with her newborn boychild, Bettylou did not really notice Tim, Mairee and the two other women arm themselves and leave the yurt.

Chief Dik, so stiff and swollen and painful were his joints this night, could not even arise from his sleeping-rug, much less arm and fight. But still the old man insisted that a spear be left within easy reach of both him and the sleeping young mother, for with wolves all about the camp, anything might chance.

Starving one and all, the gaunt wolves made frantic efforts to thrust their bony bodies through the frozen, thorny brush that blocked the apertures of the horse stockade, and each one of the few that succeeded not only encouraged their packmates to renewed efforts but heightened the panic of the milling equines within that stockade. Nor did lupine successes make any whit easier the efforts of their human opponents.

As long as the furry shapes were outside the stockades or even worming through them, the combination of bright moonlight and vaunted Horseclans archery was certain to cost the attackers most heavily. But once inside the stockades, flitting hither and yon among the legs of the milling horse herd, it were a dangerous waste of precious arrows to try for the intruders, and the only options were either to leave them to the horses themselves with the probability that they would kill or cripple one or more before being themselves killed, or to send a brave man in after the marauder with spear and dirk; neither choice was one pleasant of contemplation to the Horseclansfolk.

But the hard choice was made, twenty times or more was it made during that hellish night by desperate men against equally desperate beasts. Some of the horses were savaged by wolves, some were wounded or killed by arrows. But, too, some spearmen were trampled by terror-stricken horses or were injured or slain by wolves as they tried to avoid those heedless hooves.

The deadly carnage went on and on, the survivors of the pack not making a withdrawal until the first rays of Sacred Sun were streaking the sky away to the east. Only then did the weary men and women sheathe their steel, case their bows and wend their way back to the yurts.

Fresh horrors there awaited them.

Tim could only stand and stare at the huge dog-wolf that lay stiffening beside the firepit, the bared fangs coated in the blood it had coughed up after the spear blade had pierced its chest. The second wolf—this one the smallest—had the look of having been clubbed to death. The third had taken the spear at the confluence of throat and chest and lay in a wide-spread pool of coagulated blood.

The three women who had crowded in behind him were no less dumbstruck by the grim tableau presented by the bloody, well-dead carcasses littering the floor of the home.

Mairee was the first to recover from the shock, saying to Chief Dik, "Well, old one, is this what must be expected every time we leave you alone with sharp toys?"

He regarded her without speaking for a long moment, then he spoke, gravely. "Had it been me alone, Mairee, I would have been in that dog-wolf's belly long since, as I cannot so much as close my right hand around the haft of my spear."

"Then who . . . ?" the chorus began, then all eyes sought out the only other adult human in the yurt, where she now lay in slumber with her day-old infant. "Behtiloo?"

The old chief showed his worn yellow teeth in a smile. "None other! She had but just arisen and hung the babe high—which was fortunate—while she fetched me a sup of water, when that monster forced open the door and entered. She did not even hesitate, but took up the spear that lay by me and, waiting until he rose for her throat, skewered him as neatly as any wolf I've ever seen speared.

"She had dropped the spear and was retching when the bitch wolf came in and made directly for me. I was able to do no more than flip a blanket over the beast, but before it could wriggle free of that binding hindrance, our Behtiloo had lit into it with the iron spit; I could clearly hear those wolf bones crack and crunch under those blows, too.

"The third wolf snarled once before he came in and gave her enough warning to be waiting for him with a spear. She missed the heart thrust, but still she managed to hold him on the blade until he'd lost so much blood as to be weak and helpless."

"And then, Uncle?" demanded Tim.

Chief Dik chuckled. "And then she retched a bit more, but only after she'd secured the door against more uninvited dinner guests. Then she took down her babe and repaired to her sleeping-rug.

"That woman is a rare prize, nephew. See that you always treat her as such."

As the weather became warmer by degrees and the ice of the stream began to thin to nonexistent except along the shallower verges of the waterway, the stockades were breached and the carts and wagons brought in for overhauls or repairs. Harnesses needs must be fabricated anew or at the least altered, for not many oxen had survived the winter just past, and so many more horses and mules would have to be used for draft purposes until replacement oxen could be bought or lifted from the Dirtmen.

A WOMAN OF THE HORSECLANS 137

At the first hint of rising water, the entire camp was struck, packed and moved out onto the prairie, then unpacked and reestablished while the work on harness and conveyances continued. Within a bare week after the move to higher ground, the site of the winter camp was under a yard of roiling brown water and those stockade logs not already washed away downstream were all leaning at drunken angles as the soil packed around their bases eroded swiftly before the force of the water.

All of the clansfolk knew and more or less accepted the fact that the two clans would most likely go in separate directions this spring. Chief Skaht wished to go northwest, where the game would be most abundant through spring and summer and early autumn. Dik Krooguh, on the other hand, intended to head either due south or southeast; there might be less game, but better raiding was there to be had, as well as milder, warmer winters, which last was important to an old man plagued by all of his infirmities. Uncle Milo had not yet seen fit to announce just which clan—if either—he would accompany on this migration.

The prairie near to the stream became soggier and soggier, finally resembling just a single endless morass, cut through at countless points with trickling water, and the clouds of flies and midges made life hellish and all but unbearable for two-legs and four-legs alike. With no announced consensus, the camp was once more struck, packed and moved some two miles further east and it was at that location that they were found by the scouts of clans already on the move.

Bettylou clearly overheard the report that the scout, Ben Krooguh—who, like a fairly large minority of Horseclansfolk, did not mindspeak easily or well with humans or horses, although the powerful minds of the prairiecats seemed to be able to range even marginal mindspeakers—rendered to Chief Dik and Tim.

"The two clans coming up from the south, they're both our Kindred—Clan Makaiuh and Clan Fahrmuh—and they allow as how there's two more Kindred clans traveling a few days back of them, too—Clan Fraizuh and Clan Lehvin. But this bunch coming in from the northeast, they're another bowl of stew entirely, Chief Dik. They're dog-people. Little coyote-sized and -shaped shaggy black dogs herd their cattle, while their scouts ride with war-dogs—beasts bigger than any wolf I hope to ever see, curly-coated and prick-eared, with overlarge feet and long legs. And these dogs of war are fitted out in an armor of boiled leather to protect their throats and chests and necks. The men seem to all be very arrogant and pugnacious, but that might well be simply their fear of us Kindred, their betters.''

"How many warriors do you think, Ben?" asked Tim.

"Between two- and threescore . . . that I could see, Tim. Few of these dog-tribes teach their women to fight or even to draw a bow, of course, so they're not to be counted.''

"Which is not to say that their womenfolk can't fight when push comes to shove, Ben," put in Chief Dik. "Recall, if you will, that Tim's wife, with no weapons training at all and but a few hours after having birthed a babe, speared two grown wolves and beat another to death with an iron spit. You give those dog-tribe women a good reason to fight and they will, ferociously, if not too skillfully.''

No one was aware that Chief Milo had entered the yurt until he spoke, saying, "Which last is a very good reason not to give men or women of this alien tribe any pretext for fighting. There are few enough nomads roaming these lands, and the accursed Dirtmen encroach ever farther out onto the prairie each year; be we to save the grasslands for those who use them in the way Sun and Wind intended they be used, and not see them plowed up and ruined again, nomads must cease to fight each other, but rather must unite to drive the Dirtmen back off the grasslands.

"The dog-people are dog-people only because they have not yet become Kindred, have not yet entered into the bond between two-leg and prairiecat. Otherwise, most non-Kindred nomads are not very dissimilar from Kindred nomads; the two are, at the very least, far more similar to each other than is either to the Dirtmen.

"Let us do as has been done many times before, over the years. Let us meet with the chiefs of these non-Kindred in true peace, determine which way they mean to wander, then wander in company with them, as if they truly were a Kindred clan. By the end of the summer, chances are, they will already be related by a marriage or three.''

Joel and Jonathon Dunlap had been secretly pleased—more than pleased, if truth were known—to leave the Abode of their birth and, in company with some score of other young men, ride the several weeks' journey to the Abode watched over by the Elder Claxton. The party escorted wagons filled with grain and other foodstuffs, weapons (including a few swivel-rifles), two of the infinitely precious, irreplaceable cranklights, and oddments of hardware and harness, as well as the personal effects of the score-and-two of volunteers.

It was not often that young men from the older Abodes of the Righteous emigrated from one established Abode to another; most often, they and an equal number of young women, along with a soupçon of carefully chosen older folk, would set out for virgin territory to establish a new Abode.

But it also was not often that a single Abode would be so hideously afflicted by the heathen raiders of the prairie. The Elder Claxton and his unhappy flock had not even had a bare chance to recover from the devastating effects of a raid that, but for God's Will, would have burned them out when the Hell-spawn raiders returned just before the first snows. They had ambushed an unmounted party of herders and murdered many of those godly men, then driven off the cattle.

Then, an ill-advised, worse-led and too hastily mounted pursuit of the raiders and the lifted herd had resulted in a second ambush, more deaths and woundings and the loss of most of the horses and mules on which the pursuers had been mounted.

Following this debacle, Elder Claxton had sent out men bearing messages both to the original Abode, far to the east, and to some of the second-generation Abodes. The messages told of the raids and of the losses they had engendered in human life, stock and supplies.

"I ask not for charity," his messages ended, "for such is not either needed or desired. This land is good; if it be God's Holy Will, our losses will be replaced of our own efforts. What I do ask of you, my brothers, is young men, for there are many new widows here, as well as girls of marriageable age, while most of the surviving, sound men are either of middle years or not yet mature. Seed grains would, of course, be appreciated if they can be spared, weapons, tools, scrap metals and a wagon or two, if you see fit. Our only remaining cattle are three cows and two heifers; not one single span of draft oxen remains, nor have we a bull. So, send me what God impels you to send along with the young men, but please send the young men—as many as twoscore, total. Are they godly men, untainted by Sin, they will have good lives here on this land.''

So now twenty-two men, ranging in age between sixteen and twenty-seven, were forking horses and mules roundabout the two big wagons and the four spans of oxen that drew each. A young bull, just come into breeding age, plodded on a strong chain tether behind one wagon, occasionally exchanging bawls and lows with the eight cows and heifers being herded along at the rear with the aid of three cow dogs.

For all that the men gave the outward appearance of obeying the man the Elders had designated the leader—dour, ever-serious Enos Penwalt, a twenty-seven-year-old widower whose four children had died the year before from having apparently included the leaves of Dead Men's Bells in a salad they had prepared and eaten—the real leaders of the score of volunteers were Joel and Jonathan Dunlap, and everyone save Enos Penwalt knew that fact.

Enos was a godly man in every nuance of the word. Prayer was on his lips at waking, on beginning or doing or ending his every act during the workday, at the start and finish of each meal, and before composing himself for sleep of nights. Everyone knew that he would someday become a Patriarch. At the same time, no man liked him, for his brand of holiness was of a sort to put the teeth of the more ordinary man edge to edge.

Joel and Jonathan, on the other hand, would never be considered as candidates for Patriarchs, nor would either of them have craved that office. The whipping post was an old acquaintance of both, as were the stocks; they had been preached at and prayed over in public so often that they had lost count, long since. They had been in trouble from their first toddling steps, and, no matter their distinguished lineage (they were nephews of the Elder of their natal Abode), the Patriarchs were delighted to be shut of the terrible twins and, indeed, would probably have conspired to send them away by force had they not conveniently volunteered.

Coming as he did from the original Abode of the Righteous, Enos did not of course know the unsavory, distinctly ungodly reputation of the tall, strapping, red-haired and bright-eyed young men, and so brusque was his manner that no one bothered to enlighten him on the subject.

Jo and Jon—their names for themselves—had always been as alike as two peas in a pod and had always taken full advantage of the fact that usually their own parents and siblings could not tell the one from the other. Moreover, both born leaders, they had quickly become the focal point of the anti-establishment young men of their Abode . . . most of whom had also volunteered, and were every bit as rebellious toward their present appointed leader as they had been toward those who had appointed him to rule over them.

This rebellious faction constituted more than half of the party—twelve, out of twenty-two—and the remainder were not in any way organized to deal with them, coming as they did from no less than three Abodes and therefore not knowing much about each other.

Enos' authority drew its strength from the authority of the Elder and the Patriarchs who had appointed him, but these were authority figures who now were far behind and getting farther in the distance and the past with every turn of the wagon wheels, every plod of the oxes' hooves. What now was there to fear from the ranting old graybeards? No whip they owned could reach this far.

Had Enos been at least companionable or amiable, even bent enough to show himself to be possessed of bare human warmth, he might have stood to retain the status conferred upon him, at least among the older, steadier men of the party. But Enos had never been an outgoing person, had had precious few close human contacts in his natal Abode and had no one to speak in his support when things came to a head in the volunteer group.

Abode-born and -reared to a man, all twenty-one of the other volunteers were keenly aware of the many facets of public piety, and so a communal prayer led by one of their number before and after meals and work had always been an accepted part of life; but these prayers had always been short. Not so with the prayers of Enos Penwalt, however. It mattered not to him that his time-consuming ramblings might be delaying things better done quickly. To him, there was not and could never be anything so important as a good, full-length, all-inclusive prayer. (And he felt that those back at his natal Abode who averred that his children might not have died had he fetched help immediately instead of praying over them until dawn would likely do with praying over themselves!)

In addition to regularly scheduled prayer times, Enos had a maddening habit of suddenly beginning to pray aloud at the top of his squeaky voice at any time of the day or the night, and he seemed at these times to expect every man to drop whatever he might be doing and drop to his knees on the ground until Enos finally wound down. Jo and Jon Dunlap took to calling the outbursts "prayer fits," and soon most of the other men did too—either aloud or under their breaths.

Although good, well-trained draft oxen are much stronger and more docile than are draft horses or mules, they are much more difficult to shoe properly, especially under the make-shift conditions of a small party on the move.

Of a morning, during yoking, it was discovered that the nearside pointer ox of the first wagon had cast the shoe from the inner claw of his off hind foot. To use him the remainder of the journey without that shoe could end in crippling him. The shoe must be replaced, but although there were abundant spare shoes for the horses and mules in the loads on the wagons, someone back at the Abode had forgotten to include any of the quite different ox shoes.

At this disclosure, Enos fell on his knees and began to pray . . . loudly and with fervor. But Jo pulled out and began to set up the odds and ends of farrier equipment with which they had been provided, while Jon raked through the metal scrap and old tools; both had spent fairish amounts of time around the Abode smithy and now were willing to undertake the task of helping God to help them out of the present predicament.

Fortunately, one of the cookfires had not been extinguished. Jo lugged the old anvil, then the tools over to the side of that fire, waved over a brace of his cronies to pile warm charcoal from the smothered fire atop the burning one, then to man the small portable bellows. Enos prayed on.

Meanwhile, Jon had found an implement—a broken hoe—with enough sound metal remaining to be easily refashioned into a fair approximation of the needed ox shoe. Jo examined his brother's find critically, then nodded once and thrust it into the center of the fire, motioning to the two men to start pumping on the bellows.

Turning to the knot of other men, he said, "You boys want to move out anytime soon, spread out in the woods yonder, and find and break down and bring me back all the squawwood you can. Green wood ain't gonna burn nowheres near hot enough for this here job to be done soon."

Still kneeling on the dew-soggy ground, Enos prayed on. Jo Dunlap's hound wandered by, sniffed at the kneeling man's thigh, then lifted leg and rendered a hot, pungent opinion. Enos did not stop or even hesitate; he seemed to not be aware of his canine baptism.

But most of the other men still in camp were. The majority— the rebellious faction—were nearly rolling on the ground in an excess of unholy glee. Even a few of the minority were seen to briefly smile and one was heard to *chuckle*.

"And once again, O Lord God of Israel, Your faithful servant Enos Dunlap beseeches . . . *CLAAANNGG!*

Clang! CLANG, CLANG, CLANG! clangclangclang-clangclang. CLAANNGG!

Jo had begun to rough-shape the iron hoe, aware that could he but establish the proper rhythm, the metal could be redone cold; and he harbored serious doubts that the men in the woods would be able to find enough dry wood to make a real difference. Wood of any sort was not what was really needed, anyway; Jo needed good blue coal or at least hardwood charcoal.

As for Enos, he gave up trying to outshout the metallic clangor finally, and just prayed on to himself, his thin lips moving, but no sound issuing from them.

When he at last had a rough shoe ready for preliminary fitting, Jo had his twin and several other men tie the ox with his head between the front and rear wheels of a wagon. The ox liked not one bit of it and bawled loudly, over and over again.

This last was just too much for Enos. He arose and stamped over to the well-occupied knot of men, his cadaverous face working in frustration.

"All of you, do you hear me? Stop that noise. Stop doing anything and fall to your knees while I pray God for deliverance. Put down that . . . ahh*AAARRRGGGHH*!"

Jon ever after claimed it to have happened by the purest mischance. He and another man, each holding one end of a pole, had placed it forward of the hock and used it to lift the lower leg of the bound ox clear of the ground so that Jo could easily get at it for the first fitting. When Enos Penwalt shouted that everyone should drop everything, he simply let go his end of the pole . . . which then landed with the full weight of the ox's leg propelling it squarely across Enos' broganed foot.

For once, Enos did not pray. The tall, spare man rather rolled on the ground, clutching at his foot and squalling his agony almost loudly enough to drown out the bawlings of the ox.

Within another couple of hours, Jo and his sweating, cursing scratch force had gotten the barely tractable bovine shod. Within that same amount of time, Enos Penwalt's foot had become terribly discolored and immensely swollen, and the twins had discussed camping in place until the swelling had subsided sufficiently for Enos to at least get his shoe back on, but on being convinced by a couple of the older volunteers that there existed considerably more than a possibility that one or more of the bones in Enos' foot were broken, the brothers decided that the sooner a real doctor saw the suffering man, the better.

By rearranging wagonloads, by utilizing some of the led stock as pack animals, a space was made to convey the injured man on a bed of blankets and conifer tips laid on the floorboards of one of the wagons. The track they followed was but infrequently used, rough at the best and overgrown in more places than not; moreover, the wagon was utterly springless, built for strength and wearability, not comfort, but it was the best type of transport they knew how to provide.

"Ever time them wheels turn, it's gonna hurt Enos like blue blazes," Jon opined.

Jo just shrugged. "At least it'll give him suthin' to pray for, brother. And that alone oughta make him happy."

The dog-tribe had not one but rather three chiefs, each the theoretical equal of the others, although the eldest—a short, stocky man of middle years—seemed to do most of the talking for them and the tribe. Clad in gaudy finery, they rode in to meet with Chiefs Morai, Krooguh and Skaht at a meeting ground laid out well away from the clans camp.

For all that few weapons were in evidence to the casual glance, everyone well knew that everyone else was heavily armed, and, consequently, nerves were strung bowstring-tight, while ultimate courtesy was become the order of the day; for everyone there also knew that as often as similar meetings had resulted in friendship and alliance between Kindred and non-Kindred, they had just as often resulted in pitched battles.

The agreement had stipulated that each chief might bring to the meeting, itself, no more than two advisers, athough up to a score of his warriors might await him beyond the confines of the meetingplace. So eighteen nomads sat in the council circle deciding their mutual future, while some sixscore warriors squatted near their horses all around the perimeter, caressing their weapons and eying their counterparts warily, alert for any slightest hint of treachery.

Morai had brought along one warrior each from Skaht and from Krooguh as advisers, Skaht had his brother and another subchief, and Krooguh had with him Djahn and Tim Staiklee of Krooguh.

But all fears of imminent carnage were laid to rest when the dog-tribe spokesman—Kehvin Burk—arose and spoke his mind. "We are from the north, have always been, and the only reason we moved south this spring was in hopes of finding tribes of you cat-people to help us . . . help yourselves, too, for that matter. Problem is these damned farmers. They're moving farther and farther out into the prairies, killing off all the game, burning off the grasses and plowing up the land. You may not have seen too many of the buggers down south, here, but up north, they're becoming thick as flies on a fresh-skinned carcass . . . and, mark my words, your turn will come, and maybe one hell of a lot sooner than you think. These farmers hate and fear all of us herding people, be we cat-people or dog-people, and no mistaking; so it's a pure case of either we hang together now or we hang separate . . . and high, later, but not too much later.

"Now, I've said what I came to say. Let's hear from one of you cat-folk chiefs, say I."

Wearing a broad, very friendly smile, Chief Milo of Morai arose. "Chief Kehvin, you echo my very own sentiments with regard to these abominable Dirtmen, these farmers, these foul despoilers of the prairies and plains . . ."

The conclave went on for all of that day and well into the night, then for several days and nights after. Before it was done, it had been joined by the chiefs of two more Kindred clans—Makaiuh and Fahrmuh—and a firm, mutually agreed-upon decision had been reached.

Milo Morai, Clans Skaht and Fahrmuh would join forces with the dog-tribe and return with them to the north to deal with the Dirtmen there, to try to persuade the agriculturalists that their attempted westward expansions were unhealthy if not downright fatal.

Meanwhile, Clan Makaiuh, the chief of which had not been excessively keen on trekking north this spring anyway, would move back southeast with Clan Krooguh to explore the possiblities of hunting and raiding in that sector.

Once the decisions were made, they were quickly enacted, for the large numbers of stock had all but exhausted the easily available graze. Within days, the clans were on the move.

CHAPTER XII

The spring became summer and that summer became autumn, then winter came once more and Wind sent blizzards howling down from the far north to slay men and women, children and babes, horses and cattle, sheep and goats.

But in the orderly, inevitable progression of the seasons, even the coldest and deadliest of winters at long last became spring again, with rushing streams of snowmelt temporarily turning portions of the prairie into one, vast sogginess before the thirsty roots of the billions of grasses sucked up the moisture and the land was once more covered from horizon to limitless horizon in an endless clothing of shades of rippling green.

And as season followed season, relentlessly, so did year follow year on the prairie as on all of the earth.

The Horseclans roamed the prairies and the high plains, setting up their yurts or tents near to spring or creek or river only for the length of time it took the horses and stock to exhaust the nearby graze and their hunters—human and feline—the game and wild plants that made up much of their normal sustenance. Then the clans would pack up and move on. To north or to south, to east or to west, they moved, wherever the graze and the hunting and, sometimes, the raiding seemed best.

The life was in no way idyllic; far from it, in fact. Folk died in every season and in a multitude of ways, some of them exceedingly painful and protracted. The weak—very young or aged or injured from whatever cause—quickly succumbed to diseases, and there had been occasions when these diseases had extirpated all or most of entire clans of supposedly healthy folk, especially in winter camps, when the clanspeople were perforce packed tooth to jowl and contagions spread with terrifying rapidity.

Spring floodings and the unexpected quagmires drowned folk and stock, while summer brought flashfloods from the terrible storms and, even more fearsome, the lightning-spawned prairie fires which often swept on unchecked for countless miles, consuming all in their paths.

Raiding and warfare claimed lives and caused wounds, but not nearly so many of either as were brought about by the usual mundane occupations of herding and hunting. The stock of the nomad herds were nowhere near as docile, most of them, as were those of the Dirtmen; they had horns and hooves and the strength and will to use both to deadly advantage when angered or frightened.

Hunting injuries and deaths were second most commonplace, killing or maiming both horses and men and, more rarely, the great prairiecats. Due to the universal Horseclansfolk craving for snakemeat, cases of snakebite were fairly common, though few died of it. The majority of hunting casualties were sustained during mounted chases at high speeds over rough ground and resulted from rider or horse and rider falling.

The most dangerous game beasts were plains grizzlies, lions, shaggy-bulls, wild swine and the rare but much-feared monster predator of the far-northern plains called a "blackfoot" by the nomads.

Of this most dangerous list, only wild swine were hunted with any regularity, and then only if there were no Dirtmen nearby who could be raided for domestic swine. Like the wolves and other predators of the plains and prairies, Horseclansfolk left the bears and the lions alone if those beasts, in turn, left them and their stock alone; for these huge carnivores were possessed of formidable strength and always died hard; arrows alone seldom sufficed to deal them death, and going in to finish one at close range with a spear was not an undertaking designed or intended for the inexperienced, the weak of body or the fainthearted.

Fortunately, it was the rare grizzly or lion that forsook the bison, various antelope types and assorted deer species to go after cattle and the men who guarded them. But in the case of the sinister shaggy-bulls, the situation was reversed. The shaggy-bulls seemed to go deliberately out of their way to try to kill men and disrupt herds of cattle. The only good thing that could be said for them was that there were not very many of them even on the high plains where they were most common.

In some ways, they resembled the bison—shaggy coats, colors, thick bodies, the prominent hump over the shoulders—but they ran to far larger sizes than any bison, with adult cows standing up to sixteen hands at the withers and an average adult bull towering as much as four hands higher. Both sexes bore wide-spreading horns, and all were, considering their weights and bulks, amazingly fast and agile in a fight. They were not herd animals, but rather traveled in small groups when not alone.

The long horns of the shaggy-bulls could be fashioned into exceptionally deep-voiced bugles; their hides were the source of the strongest leather known to the nomads, and justly proud was the man who had armor or target made of it. The meat they yielded was choice, and shaggy-bull sinews were selected for the finest hornbows. But the cost of killing one was always high.

Most often, two clans camped and moved on together, and occasionally there were three, very rarely four or more. Every five or six years, as many as twenty-five or thirty clans, they having been notified of time and location by traders or the traveling bards, would gather in conclave for as long as a week, but no more, for so many folk and animals in one place quickly exhausted the supportive capabilities of even the richest area.

Unless visited by natural disaster or by heavy war or hunting losses, the average clan numbered twenty to twenty-five male warriors, fifty to sixty clanswomen-archers (both maiden-archers and matron-archers) and as many as a dozen prairiecats of fighting age. Children, both male and female, over the age of thirteen summers were counted among the warriors or the archers and were considered to be of marriageable age at fourteen, for all that few males wed before eighteen or twenty.

A chief might have three or even four wives, plus a slave concubine or two, but the average clansman had no more than one wife at a time and was considered well-to-do if he could support a second wife or a concubine.

Horseclansfolk loved children and produced as many as

possible, for their life was unremittingly hard and they well knew that half or fewer of their children would survive to an age to sire or bear another generation. All of the children born into a clan were born free, no matter the status of their mothers at their birthings; moreover, all grew up as equals, save only that no son of a concubine could become chief of his birth clan unless his mother first was freed and formally adopted into that clan.

Compared to other times and peoples, the lives of the Horseclansfolk were harsh in the extreme, from birth to death. Perhaps one of each ten babes born into a Kindred clan would survive long enough to see the birth of a grandchild, but it had been ever so, since the time of the Sacred Ancestors; and simply because only the very toughest—physically, mentally, emotionally—ever lived long enough to themselves breed, Horseclansfolk were born with a great tolerance for adversity and privation. To outsiders, the image of the Kindred was of a grim, stoic, humorless, savagely fearsome people; but among themselves, they were anything but products of this mold, being warm-natured, merry, frequently quite emotional.

Of course, outsiders—Dirtmen and traders—never saw the Horseclansfolk at unguarded moments. All that the most of the Dirtmen ever saw was armed warriors, screeching warcries and killing, or driving off stock, burning buildings and crops.

But in a safe camp, Kindred seldom went about armed with anything more lethal than an eating knife, or perhaps an especially prized small weapon worn principally as an ornament. Herders carried riatas of braided rawhide, bolas, bows and arrows, and double-pointed lances (a dull point at one end for prodding cattle, a sharp point at the other). Hunters also carried bows and arrows, bolas, riatas, and usually broad-bladed spears rather than lances. Too, they carried long dirks or hangers, hatchets and an assortment of knives for skinning and butchering; they might also carry a sling and stones for it.

Warriors, on the other hand, were never considered properly accoutered for war or raids without their body armor of leather boiled in wax—all lacquered and decorated with insets of brass and gold and silver—their helmet of the same material or, sometimes, steel, their heavy, cursive saber, and their target of laminated woods and leather. These, along with the double-edged war dirk and an assortment of knives and daggers, plus of course the cased bow and the quivers of war arrows, constituted the basic panoply of the Kindred warrior.

Other weapons were optional and purely of personal choice— light axes, lances, spears, javelins or darts, clubs, staff-slings, bolas, even the humble riata and stockwhip.

On the morning of a late-spring day, two Kindred clans were on the march. Clans Dohluhn and Krooguh were now less than a full day's traveling time from the rendezvous area of which the bards and traders had been telling for more than three years.

Out ahead and on the flanks of the wide-spreading body moved prairiecats and a few young stallions, their keen senses spying out any possible danger or promise of game and mindspeaking their findings back to the jagged line of maiden-archers—all riding with bows strung and an arrow nocked, two more shafts held ready between the fingers of the bow hand—who trailed the foremost cats at distances of a quarter to a half mile.

The chiefs and most of the warriors came next, riding in a line as jagged as the maiden-archers, usually, in clumps of two to four men. They rode fully armed—helmets, armor, targets, bows, sabers and dirks, with lances, spears, light axes, a handful of darts or whatever. But for all their warlike, well-prepared appearance, they rode relaxed, bantering and joking, secure in their knowledge that they would be well warned of any impending danger.

Behind the warriors, formed in a rough extenuated crescent, came the king stallion and his herd. Then the high-wheeled carts and the wagons trundled along, the former drawn by teams of mules or horses, the latter by lowing spans of oxen. The matrons rode beside the draft animals, directing the horses and mules by rein or mindspeak, the oxen by judicious use of ox prod or stockwhip.

Poles and hides and felt strips and the lathing frameworks of tents and yurts, the meager furnishings—carpets, brass lamps, folding tables, chests and the like—spare clothing, bedding, weapons, and personal possessions, nonperishable foodstocks, bales of hides and furs, tools, everything, were packed into or onto the wagons and the carts or onto the loads of pack beasts. Atop the laden wagons and carts rode the very aged, the few ill or infirm, and those children assigned to watch over the prairiecat kittens and cubs tethered here and there to the cargo. (Kittens and cubs not only tired quickly and overheated easily, but were cursed with a distressing and virtually inborn tendency to stray.)

To the rear were the herds—cattle, sheep, a few goats—all herded by a few superannuated warriors and a horde of mounted boys and girls still too young to commence their serious war training. A bit behind the herds, eating dust, rode a widespread rearguard of maiden-archers and a few prairiecats.

Beside one of the chief wagons of Clan Krooguh, the first and principal wife of the chief in all save name ambled along astride a smooth-gaited piebald mare. Having passed her ox prod to* her husband's second wife—Anee Makaiuh of Krooguh— and unlaced the front of her shirt, Behtiloo Hansuhn of Krooguh had lifted her winter-born boychild from the cradle rack affixed to the cantle of her saddle and given him her bright-red left nipple.

On this day, Behtiloo had been Tim's wife and a clanswoman for almost fifteen years, and none save her adoptive kinfolk would have or could have suspected from her appearance, bearing, behavior or demeanor that she was anything save Horseclans-born and -bred. Indeed, Behtiloo herself often experienced some difficulty in recalling how things had been when she was not a Krooguh.

Her exposed skin surfaces were now every bit as weather-darkened as were her husband's, her long, golden hair was done into thick braids and lapped over her crown to bear the weight of her helmet, and she was attired like any other man or woman of the Kindred—the loose, baggy shirt and trousers of richly embroidered homespun, calf-length boots of felt with leather soles and wood-and-leather heels, broad leathern waistbelt supporting a pouch and a couple of knives, with a frog for attachment of the dirk.

Chief Dik Krooguh was so feeble this spring that he could not sit a horse but had to ride in a specially fitted cart, and most people opined that he would never see another spring. But then they had been so opining for more that fifteen years, and he had outlived many a one of the opiners. True, his health had not been good since the first day Behtiloo had seen him, but he had managed to survive all of his wives and concubines, his sister, Lainuh, and all other close kin save Tim, his heir. He had lived longer than any of his old cronies, save only Djahn Staiklee, who upon the demise of his wife, Lainuh, had wed a young, pretty blond woman, Mairee Daioh, when Dahnah had made it clear to him that she would rather remain a concubine than become a Horseclans wife.

The aged chief still sat in clan councils, but every other function of the chieftaincy was carried out by Tim, had been for more than ten years now. Tim it had been who had led the Krooguh warriors who had joined with the warriors of several other Kindred clans in extirpating a savage, treacherous non-Kindred tribe of nomads. This had occurred four years ago, far and far to the northwest of their present location.

At fourteen summers, Hwahlis Hansuhn of Krooguh was already the second-tallest man of his clan (only Djahn Staiklee stood taller) and, with the big bones and rolling muscles of men of his mother's stock, he was an impressive figure of a Horseclans warrior as he rode beside his "father" and chief, Tim, in the warrior line.

The twins, Buhd and Behti, were almost a year younger than Hwahlis, and both were of the small-boned, flat-muscled Kindred stock in appearance, although Buhd was already a bit taller than were most of his peers.

Four of Behtiloo's children by Tim had died at various ages of various causes. Her next-eldest living child was a girl, Ehlee, who at the mature age of six summers was seldom to be found far from her year-younger brother, Shawn. Behtiloo considered herself fortunate in the extreme that so many of her children had so far survived.

For Clan Krooguh stood in dire need of every living soul. Although the united Kindred clans had been eventually and fully victorious in their protracted fight against the northerner nomads, their foemen had fought hard and long and well and the battle losses had been truly staggering. Only a bare score of Krooguh men now flanked Tim and Hwahlis, and nearly half of these men were too young to have taken any part in the costly campaign. The long trek back south had taken three years to accomplish, and with so few veteran hunters left to forage for the clan, each of those three harsh, pitiless winters had cost dearly in terms of young and aged.

They had wintered most lately with Clan Dohluhn, but this Kindred clan, though of normal strength and numbers, had few young men of marriageable age, so Tim was hurrying toward the great Kindred gathering of the clans with the openly avowed purpose of luring young warriors from stronger but poorer clans to the marriage beds of his well-dowered Krooguh maidens.

And well-dowered those maidens would surely be, for the sack of the camps of the northern nomads had vastly enriched each and every clan that had taken part in exterminating those who had dwelt therein. Cattle they had taken, and sheep and goats. Weapons, of course, and horse gear, carts and wagons and harness, furniture of all sorts, metal lamps, fine furs—bales of them—more bales of hides, foodstocks, jewelry and items of adornment, thick carpets and blankets, cookware, hardware, hundreds of yards of cloth as well as existing clothing and cloaks and boots.

In addition to the more mundane items of loot, there had been several yurtlike structures mounted on huge wagons. One side of each wagon could be dropped so that the two halves of the dwelling might be fitted together, and each oversized wagon was drawn by four spans of huge, shaggy-coated, longhorned, but quite docile oxen of a breed unfamiliar to the Kindred. It was decided during the division of loot that one of these curiosities should go to each chief, with the extra one going to Clan Krooguh in recognition of their especially hard fighting and heavy losses.

Behtiloo Hansuhn of Krooguh had been living in one of the wagon-mounted habitations for most of four years now, and she still was not certain that she would not have preferred a simple, honest, everyday yurt. Chief Dik, of course, loved the device, since it kept his bed and swollen joints raised well above the cold and dampness of the ground. But to Behtiloo, it was harder to keep uniformly warm in winter, much more of a bother to get and keep clean inside, and she was always secretly afraid that she or whoever was cooking with the still-unfamiliar metal brazier would burn down the wagon-yurt and everything in it.

It was not the second wagon-yurt in which Behtiloo kept house and lived (that one was occupied by Djahn Staiklee and his new wife, concubine and get) but the larger, more luxurious one, for since the death of the last of his wives, Chief Dik had had Tim, Behtiloo, Anee and their children take over the chief yurt.

In addition to seeking husband/warriors for the clan, Tim had often stated his intention to trade off some of the superfluous loot awarded Clan Krooguh for enough metal to enable Rohluhnd Krooguh, the clan smith, to fashion strong helmets, all of steel and designed in a distinctive pattern developed by the two of them; there was to be a helmet for each of the Krooguh warriors. Tim also yearned for one of the leathern shirts sewn with steel scales, but doubted that the clan could afford so hellishly expensive a purchase, not with so many dowries to be paid.

Behtiloo could count on the fingers of one hand the number of times that the paths of Clan Krooguh and the plains traders had crossed. The mere sight of the long columns of lumbering wagons snaking across the prairies, well guarded by Kindred warriors of many clans who had been hired on for the season, as well as by big steel-clad men on brawny horses from the half-mythical lands far and far to the east, had always been sufficient to give the clansfolk fresh talking-fodder for months after.

Now, Behtiloo could barely wait to tour the dozens of trader booths certain to be erected at the gathering. Tim might have his own ''shopping list'' of husbands and steel armor, but she had her own. First and most important, she wanted steel needles of varying lengths, sizes and shapes, and with them she was in search of the fine, brilliantly colored, fast-dyed threads and yarns with which Horseclans embroidery was done. If she could find them at a decent price, she also intended to buy a few pounds of brass-headed tacks for decorating a certain chest. So much for the professional traders, but for her other desire, she would need to seek out a man or woman of one of the far-southern clans, for only from them could one obtain the all-leather boots that came almost to the knee and were so beautifully tooled and colored and stitched.

With the boychild full of warm milk and sleeping soundly, Behtiloo turned in her saddle and returned the infant to his carrying cradle, secured the straps and thongs, then bade her mare halt while she threw her off leg over the pommel and slid from the saddle. Completely oblivious of the folk moving in carts and wagons, on horseback and afoot all about her, she hitched up her weapons belt, unloosed the drawstring of her trousers and half-squatted long enough to void her bladder, before remounting the mare and taking the ox prod back from Anee.

In addition to more personal purchases, of course, Behtiloo

would be obliged to seek out and bargain for certain items for special purposes within the clan; this came with her function of chatelaine of the chief's yurt. There was need, for one thing, to replenish the supply of alcohol—*taikeelah* or, this far north, probably one of those bastard concoctions that the traders sold under the generic name of hwiskee—a half-dozen twenty-gallon barrels of it, anyway. There were other oddments, as well. Also, Behtiloo had had the joyous surprise of a personal windfall recently, and she had decided to use it to surprise someone else.

Always thrifty, made so by their harsh life, the Kindred had taken everything that had even looked as if it might possibly be of some future use from the camps of their foes. Among the items which had fallen into Behtiloo's hands were some bundles of clothing, most of it bloodstained, having been stripped from the corpses of warriors.

One of these bundles had somehow gotten shoved into the bottom of a chest, and she had excavated it only a few months back, in the depths of the winter just past. It had been while she was picking through the old clothes that she had felt the hard and regular outlines of some dozen items sewn into the quilting of a blood-darkened canvas pourpoint.

Upon removing the stitchings, she had discovered twelve thick, heavy discs of what could only be gold, all the space on both sides covered over in a tracery resembling intertwined vines. As a very young girl, she had seen coinage of gold and silver and copper passed between the Elder and the Patriarchs of the Abode of the Righteous when dealing with traders, so she was dead certain that she now held some variety of coinage, but there was no mark that she could read on it to tell her its true value. She had no slightest trust of any of the traders—none of the nomads (or the Dirtmen, for that matter!) trusted them—and chances were very slim that any of the Kindred clansfolk would know any more about the coins than did she, so she could only hope that Uncle Milo would be there.

He was, looking no whit different than she recalled of him from fifteen years ago. But he did not recall her, not immediately, and she quickly realized that she had been silly or foolish to suppose that he might, so much had time and age and circumstances altered her appearance.

"So you are the woman that that pitiful child became?" he

said wonderingly, at last. "Poor, old Ehstrah—Wind keep her—always said that one day you'd be the very epitome of all the Kindred. Your husband—Tahm, was it?—he became Chief of Krooguh, then?"

She shook her head. "Not yet, Uncle Milo, though he fulfills every function of that office, shoulders every responsibility; no, old Dik Krooguh still clings to life and his title.

"But . . . but, please, Uncle Milo, when did Ehstrah . . . go to Wind? She always was so kind to me, like a mother, she was."

Milo sighed. "Yes, our Ehstrah was indeed a good, a very good woman. It was seven . . . no, eight years ago. I was off on a hunt and she was kicked in the back by a mule. No bones seemed to be broken, though she was winded, of course, and sore, but she went on about her usual tasks. Then, some week or so later, after I was returned from the hunt, she began to piss bloody urine, then pure blood. I suspect that mule's kick damaged her kidneys, but whatever the cause, she continued to lose blood by day and by night, she weakened dramatically, then a flux took her and, weak as she was become, she died of it.

"Gahbee drowned during a river crossing ten years ago. But Ilsah still bides with me. She's my first wife now, though I have taken two others to share the burden with her. You must come and visit our yurt, Behtiloo."

"I will, Uncle Milo, and you must come to the Krooguh chief yurt, too. If old Chief Dik can remember you—for he recalls things and folks seldom anymore, and then only in brief snatches—I know that he'll be mightily pleased to see you. Tim, my husband, will, too; and you must see my son, Hwahlis, and my other children.

"But here and now, I have some strange loot I would like you to look at. I need to know the true value of these pieces, for I mean to buy steel scale shirts for my husband and my eldest son. If possible, I also would like to get enough steel and brass sheets to fashion a score of helmets."

Squatting, facing her in the dust, Milo Morai fingered the twelve discs of ruddy gold, each of them a good two inches in diameter. With his horny fingertips, he traced the weaving, cursive lines standing up from both obverse and reverse of the golden coins.

At length, he asked simply, "Where did you come by these?"

Briefly, she told him.

He nodded once, then said, "The design is not decoration merely, though it serves that purpose too, of course. No, the lines are letters in a very old language called Ahrahbik. This language was in fairly wide use even in the time before this time, and so little has it changed since then that these could well be from that long-ago period. But I think they are newer.

"For one thing, they are not much worn and have not been shaven or clipped at all, as most really ancient coins usually have been. The damage done to that one looks to me like a sword or dirk cut, and the one there that is bent and almost holed, that damage was almost assuredly done by the point of an arrow or small dart point. Sewn into the quilting of a warrior's gambeson, they could easily have been so abused over the years, totally unbeknownst to the erstwhile abusers.

"No, Behtiloo, I am of an opinion that these are coinage of a kingdom that they say lies far to the east of this place, beyond the Great River by moons of traveling. But let us now go to a trader I know of old and see if I'm right."

The head and face of the trader, Flaivin, did not match his beefy, muscular body, nor did his delicate hands with their long, tapering fingers. The head was small and almost completely round, the features sharp and vulpine, the eyes as black and glittery as bits of obsidian. But he seemed friendly enough greeting Milo warmly, like an old and much respected friend.

When he had served small measures of a bittersweet wine in tiny brazen goblets, he leaned back and eyed Milo, saying, "And just what can I do for you this day, Chief Milo?"

Milo smiled. "Put on your moneychanger's hat, friend Flaivin. I've a few pretties for you to look at and value . . . and maybe, to buy."

Flaivin's only movement was a deep sigh. "Oh, my friend, my friend, you'd be better off to rebury your silver and bronze pieces for a while, that or use them to decorate a saddle or the like; when I left Ohyoh country last year, the value of silver was still plummeting, dragging bronze and copper bullion prices down in its wake. So whatever quotation I'd feel safe to give you would likely do nothing but infuriate you."

"Not silver, Flaivin," said Milo in a low tone. *"Gold."*

In a twinkling, or so it seemed to Behtiloo, the tabletop was cleared of bottle and goblets and crowded with various and arcane paraphernalia, all gathered around and about the three broad goldpieces Milo had laid before the trader.

"Reddish." The trader sniffed. "Not pure, then. But the black-skinned bastards seem to like their coinage that color, pure or not.

"These are *ahlf-ryahrs* of the *Kahleefah* of *Zahrtohgah*, friend Milo. I've learned, over the years, to read a little of their snaky script, so I can tell you that these are about seventy years old. They were minted just after the accession of *Kahleef* Moostahfah Itahlit, who only reigned four years before he was poisoned. Rulers seldom last long in that bloody land. Let's see, now . . ."

After weighing and testing the coins, he sat back and said, "Well, friend Milo, each of these three weighs out at an even thousand grains—you see, no metal was lost or removed in the damage to these two—but of course only about eight out of every ten of those grains is gold; there was a heavy addition of copper and a little silver to make up this alloy.

"What were you thinking of trading these for? I could give you the best part of a pipe of a nice little wine for these three . . . ?"

Milo chuckled. "I'll bet you'd like to strike so shrewd a deal, Flaivin. No, two of them for two top-quality scale shirts of steel, as well as enough sheet steel and brass to make up twenty helmets of Horseclans pattern. The other goldpiece for one hundred and fifty gallons of decent-grade hwiskee, plus some oddments of this woman's choosing. Done?"

The trader snorted, most of the friendliness departed from both voice and demeanor. "Chief Milo, to see the goods you desire for such paltry sums would be my utter ruination, as surely you must know. All three of these coins together would not cover the cost and freightage of the amount of steel you demand, especially not decent-quality steel.

"As regards the hwiskee, now, it's devilish costly to carry it so far. We always lose about half of what we start out with in Ohyoh country, what with broken or leaking barrels, thieving wagoners and the like, so that's why we have to set the prices so high, are we to make any profit at all. For two of the goldpieces, or their equivalent in furs or what-have-you, I could let you have a hundred gallons of corn hwiskee, but that's all.''

The haggling went on for some hours, but at length Chief Milo and the trader, Flaivin, reached an amicable agreement. For a total of six of the golden discs, Behtiloo received two steel-on-leather scale shirts and enough loose scales to make another for Buhd Krooguh when his time of warring came, enough sheet steel and brass for thirty helmets, five pounds of brass tacks, two chests of fast-dyed threads and yarns (each chest also containing an assortment of eighteen steel needles), seven twenty-gallon barrels of hwiskee, two twenty-gallon barrels of wine and a bolt of the smoothest, softest, most sensorially pleasing cloth that Behtiloo had ever seen or touched.

As she walked back toward the Krooguh enclave to fetch in strong men and a cart or two to transport her booty, Milo touched the bolt under her arm, saying, ''This is true, first-water silk. I not only cannot imagine where a gaggle of plains traders came by it, I cannot imagine why they wagoned it hundreds of miles to try to sell it to nomads who mostly are dirt-poor. But it arrived here, and you now have it. Use it as cloth, if you wish, but silk makes superlative bowstrings also, and the threads too short for such could always be used in embroidery.

''Now you know the value of those golden discs, so guard them well. Cut a couple of them into four pieces and never show more than one piece at the time would be my advice, especially when you're dealing with traders or the southern Dirtmen. For unlike other metals, gold has the hoary repute of driving men and women mad; to acquire it, they have been known to sacrifice everything they otherwise held dear— possessions, relatives, honor, even life itself. If I did anything right and proper, I pride myself that I was able to breed that particular form of insanity out of the Kindred. To you and all the other clansfolk, gold is but another decorative metal, perhaps more favored only because it is easier to work than copper or silver or brass or the antique metals.

''When you return from your camp, bring your clan smith and have him check every last scale and piece of sheet metal. See that Flaivin's men broach every last barrel, and taste the contents yourself. Make him weigh out that sack of tacks again, too. Go through the sewing chests and see that nothing has been removed or changed about in them. If you find he is trying to cheat or delude you in any way, even the most piddling, remind him of the name Steev Koorhohm and ask if he recalls just how the clans dealt with that trader, years agone. Thought of that incident should drive all ideas of chicanery from his mind.''

"Steev Koorhohm, Uncle Milo?" Behtiloo asked. "I don't understand. Who is Steev Koorhohm?"

Milo smiled grimly. "Steev Koorhohm *was* a plains trader, back before you became a clanswoman. He brought his wagons to the prairies full of diseased slaves and poisonous hwiskee. When two warriors died and more went blind after drinking his goods, a war party rode after his train, took him and brought him back.

"With all the other traders looking on, they bound his yard tightly with wet rawhide, poured water down his throat until his bladder was nigh to bursting, then slit off his eyelids and buried him neck-deep in an anthill. He only lived about a day.''

CHAPTER XIII

Chief Tim of Krooguh died in the fifty-second year of his marriage to Behtiloo, covered with scars and glory. He left children, grandchildren and great-grandchildren behind him, four living wives, three concubines, and one of the largest, strongest, wealthiest Kindred clans resident anywhere on the prairies or plains.

During his thirty-seven years of full tenure, Clan Krooguh had waxed in size, in wealth and in renown. When his husk had been decently sent to Wind, the sixty-three Krooguh warriors gathered and invested the eldest son of their late chief's eldest living daughter.

Even in her grief, Behtiloo Hansuhn of Krooguh felt her old heart swell with fierce pride as she watched her sons, Hwahlis and Buhd, lace and buckle their nephew into Tim's aged, nicked, but brilliantly burnished scale shirt for his formal presentation to the clansfolk at the chief feast.

Later, at that feast, listening while the young clan bard, Bili, sang the Song of Krooguh, Behtiloo's gaze strayed ofen to Chief Sami.

"So like my Tim, he is," she thought. "With his flaming red hair and green eyes, the same snub nose, an almost identical splash of freckles across his face."

She noted that from time to time this new-made chief, her grandson, used gestures that had been peculiar to Tim. But, she reflected to herself, such might easily be expected, since his grandfather had been training him and grooming him for the chieftaincy of his clan for some twenty years or more. And if Sami Krooguh lived and proved as good a chief as his immediate predecessor . . . ?

At Chief Sami's side sat his wife of twenty-two years, Alis

Krooguh of Krooguh, flanked by her eldest living son. Alis and Sami were of an age; they had played together as children, shared together their herding duties and war training, and shared the wonders and pleasures of each other's bodies from puberty.

Every soul in Clan Krooguh had accepted the fact that they two would someday wed long before the day Sami rode back into camp after three years of service as a hired guard for plains traders, married Alis and brought her into his mother's yurt and household.

When, about two years later, his elder brother died of a broken neck while chasing after antelope on horseback, Sami, Alis and their two children had been summoned to live in the household of Chief Tim, that the younger man might begin to learn the art of chieftainship.

Upon Tim's death, which came suddenly and unexpectedly though not in any way violently, Behtiloo began to move her effects to the yurt of her son Hwahlis. But Alis would not even hear of such a thing, for all that she had not tried to stay the departures of the late chief's three younger wives or his concubines when they moved in with grown children and those children's families.

"No, Mother, please stay here with us. This is your home, it has always been your home for as long as I can remember, and . . . and I cannot imagine living here, in your home, without you in it. Father Tim spent twenty years in teaching our Sami to be a proper chief; now you must teach me and watch over me and so see that I behave as becomes the proper wife of a chief. Besides, who but you can so brew the herbs so that children drink the broths without making those terrible faces and rude noises, eh?"

Skilled in compounding herbal tonics, nostrums and remedies Behtiloo Hansuhn of Krooguh assuredly was. She had been for many years, ever since Lainuh Krooguh, Chief Tim's long-dead mother, had first taken her youngest son's captive-wife under her wing and begun to impart her own considerable, in-depth knowledge of the curative properties of wild prairie plants. After Lainuh's death, Behtiloo had learned more from Tim's father's concubine, Dahnah. Then, too, her years of practicing the herbal arts had taught her mightily.

But none of her encyclopedic knowledge availed her in saving the life of Alis Krooguh, who died during the fifth winter after Sami became chief. Sami took Alis's untimely death hard, bitterly hard. He would hear no words of any remarriage from clansmen, subchiefs or even his immediate family, and soon, on the heels of a succession of heated outbursts from the long-grieving man, all the Krooguhs gave up.

All save Behtiloo, that is. She and Sami's daughters-in-law and granddaughters had no trouble among so many willing hands in properly maintaining the chief yurt and household as it always had been, of course; but Behtiloo knew that the very honor of Clan Krooguh lay at stake in this matter. For the chief of so large and wealthy a clan to live without at least one wife would be considered by the other clans odd, to say the least.

She, of all people, knew just how long and hard and how unstintingly her own dear dead Tim had worked in building up the power and image of the clan of his birth. He had devoted much of his life to making the small, insignificant Clan Krooguh large and rich and widely respected by Kindred and non-Kindred alike, and she would not sit idly by and watch her grandson's senselessly prolonged grief undo that work.

She set herself to the task. For two long years, she argued and debated and wheedled with Chief Sami. Then, when she felt the time to be ripe, she exchanged one of the last two of her remaining gold discs for a young, pretty, black-haired, dark-eyed slave girl who had chanced to be part of the merchandise brought west by a train of plains traders.

On the way back to the chief yurt, Behtiloo discovered to her chagrin that the girl spoke no single, recognizable tongue, aside from a few mispronounced words of Trade Mehrikan. At last, almost in desperation, Behtiloo tried to mindspeak.

"What is your name, child? What is your race? What tongue do you speak?"

A rapid-fire spate of foreign words poured from the girl's dark-red lips, but Behtiloo was able to glean their meaning from the mind behind them: "Please, old woman . . . mistress, how can you speak to me without opening your mouth? I don't . . . can't understand how . . . ?"

Again, Behtiloo used telepathy, keeping in mind her own honest bewilderment when, so many years ago, she first had encountered Horseclans mindspeakers. "There is no need to speak aloud, little one. Think what you wish to convey to me, then merely project it. See, like this.''

It quickly became apparent that like Behtiloo herself, the little slave girl had been born with a dormant potential for mindspeak and had needed only instruction in its use. By the time she had had the girl make use of the sweat yurt, wash her body and hair and assume Horseclans garb, Behtiloo was easily engaging in silent conversation with her and had had all of her bitter story, though parts of it had been most difficult for the old nomad woman to credit, on the basis of the prairie life which was all she had ever known.

Leenah Goombahlees had been born far, far to the east, in a great huge place built of stone and brick, tiles and timbers. In this place, people—more people than all of thirty or forty large clans' number—lived out their lives, only leaving, some of them, to till the fields, tend to the flocks and herds and vineyards outside the high, stone walls that surrounded the place, which was called a ''city.''

Then, of a day, a vast host of warriors had marched down from somewhere in the north and camped on the hillsides all around the city. Leenah recalled that time in vague snatches—of her father and her brothers tramping in and out of the house at odd hours, all sheathed in shining steel, with swords and daggers at their belts and spears and axes in their hands; of her eldest brother being brought home, shrieking in agony, to die within hours of the great ragged wound torn in his belly; of a long time when no one had much of anything to eat and it had seemed that every other building was burning.

And then the day of ultimate horrors had come. Her father had run stumbling into the main room of the home, his black eyes blazing, wild, his helmet with all the pretty feathers gone and his armor no longer shiny, but nicked and deeply dented and dull with a profusion of crusty red-brown stains.

Leenah had seen him embrace and kiss her mother, then push her to arm's length, draw his sword and run it deeply into her body below her breasts. Leenah's older sister had screamed then, and turned to run; but her father, in a single, fluid movement, had drawn and thrown a dagger with such force that all of the slim blade had buried itself in her sister's back, and she had fallen, twitching, to the blue-and-white tiles.

Too stunned to run, Leenah had simply stood as her father

turned toward her, raising his bloody sword, his lips moving
but no sound issuing from between them, pure madness shining from his eyes. Then, with an awful clanging and clattering,
his body had fallen face downward at her feet, with the short,
thick shaft of a war dart standing up from the spot where
spine met skull.

Suddenly, too suddenly, the room was filled with strange
bearded foreigners, all garbed in armor and clothing of unfamiliar patterns. . . .

When Behtiloo had tried to prod the girl for more facts
after that point in the tale, she could only arouse an inchoate
confusion of memories of pain and terror and shame, of a sick
and churning disgust. Then the girl had begun to cry, softly,
at first, then with increasing violence.

Once the little slave had cried herself out in Behtiloo's
comforting arms, her mind got around to producing the sad
end to her story.

After a week of rapine, torture, looting and murder, the
victorious besiegers had boated the few hundred survivors of
the intaking of the city across the nearby river and had then
marched them northward to a rendezvous with traders, who
had bought most of the war captives.

Leenah had been but one of some threescore women and
girls bought by men who fed them, gave them clothing to
replace their tattered rags and allowed them to rest for a few
days before loading them onto wagons to begin a westward
trek of many weeks' duration.

All of the captives were used by their new owners from
time to time during the trip, but no other violence was
wrought upon them. They were not beaten, they were fed as
well as the new owners ate, and those who happened to
become ill were treated with solicitude. Finally, the wagons
came down from the mountains they had traversed and rolled
into a riverside town, where the captives and captors boarded
the two biggest boats Leenah had ever seen.

The trip, in toto, had taken months. It had seemed to
Leenah and her fellow slaves that the twisting, turning river
was endless. Moreover, stops were frequent.

At most stops, men would come aboard the boats. They
would be shown the "merchandise," gold or silver coin
would change hands or a few bales and crates would be

winched or carried aboard, and some of the women would go ashore.

After about two months (as near as she could reckon time) on the river, Leenah had become ill, desperately ill. Rightly fearful of possible contagion, her owners had moved her to a small cubicle abovedecks and cared for her as well as they knew how, but she had nonetheless been slow to recover and had still been far from well when the boats were current-borne into an even larger river.

Using their sails, the two boats beat into a small port on the larger river. There the traders, their goods and the score or so of remaining female slaves were transferred to a number of smaller boats—boats propelled by long, heavy oars pulled by the wretched, filthy, sore-covered men chained to them. They traveled against the current of the swift-flowing river for about a week before arriving at the docks below the walls of a bustling town.

After disposing of about half their remaining women, the traders loaded the rest into high-wheeled plains wagons, along with a vast assortment of hard and soft goods and joined with a well-guarded column of similar wagons for the long and hazardous trek westward in search of the nomad clans and the wide-scattered farming settlements along the prairie fringes.

Once the train had reached the territory of the Kindred, the Horseclans, wherein there was greater safety for traders (honest ones, at least) and smaller trains could proceed with fewer guards, the large caravan had split into several smaller ones and headed off in different directions, each group taking two or three of the women slaves.

"Please, mistress," Leenah silently beamed, "why did you buy me? Am I to be your personal maid? To care for you?"

Behtiloo laughed throatily. "Hardly, child Leenah. We Horseclanswomen can care for ourselves in most ways and in most times. No, I bought you to be the concubine to my dear grandson, who is chief of this clan."

Noticing the black eyes in the olive-skinned face cloud, while the surface thoughts of the girl's mind boiled with the old, bitter memories of rapes and sodomies and other enforced degradations, Behtiloo added hastily, "No, little one, do not fear. Our Sami is a tender man, a gentle and a loving man. He has been grieving these last years for the loved wife who was his only wife for above twenty-five years.

"But you will completely replace her, we will see to it, just wait. At first you will replace her in his bed, then in his great heart. I vow to you, my child, as soon as your belly swells with Sami's good seed, I will see you a free woman, formally adopted into Clan Krooguh and honorably wedded to our chief."

And so it came to be. At the wedding feast, Behtiloo foretold that Leenah and her get by Chief Sami would bring newer and greater glory, *thrice* greater glory to Krooguh.

That is why when, four months after the wedding, the new bride was delivered of not one, not two but an unbelievable *three* sons at a single birthing, clansfolk began to treat their chief's grandmother with far and away greater respect than ever before, that awe-tinged respect accorded the proven seer.

A few days after the triple birthing, Behtiloo sat on the steps leading up to the wagon-mounted chief yurt, enjoying the bright, warm rays of Sacred Sun, when a female prairiecat approached and seated herself respectfully some two yards distant.

"Greet the Sun, two-leg female of powers," beamed the cat's strong mindspeak. "Do you guard the den of this first sensible two-leg female in memory, who bears her young in litters?"

Behtiloo smiled and replied, "Yes, cat sister. Do you wish to enter and see her and the babes now?"

Behtiloo and the cat—who was called Blackback and was obviously a recent mother herself, to judge by her heavy and thickened dugs—soon reached the rear area of the yurt. There Leenah reclined while nursing two of her little sons, while Chief Sami—almost bursting with his pride—held the other. The cat immediately bespoke the two women on a narrow, personal beaming.

"It is just as I had thought it would be. You two-legs have but two dugs, so you will never be able to properly nurse all of your litter at once and so one will most assuredly die . . . or all will become weak.

"Now, I bore my litter on the same day you bore yours, female-of-our-chief, but two of mine were born unbreathing, so I have milk and to spare, as well as dugs enough to feed yours and mine together, at the same time.

"I already have broached this matter with the cat chief, Steelclaws, and he says that if his brother, Chief Sami, approves, I may bring my two kittens here to the Clan Krooguh chief yurt and share with you the nursing."

When the matter was put to Sami, he threw back his graying head and laughed uproariously. "Why not, I say, wife? Why not? It's never before been done, so far as I know, in any Kindred clan, certainly not in this one. But then neither has any clanswoman in the memory of the Kindred, right back to and including the Sacred Ancestors, borne a clansman three sons at once. You and I, my dear little Leenah, have already set one all-time precedent. So why should we not set another, hey?"

Then, switching to mindspeak, he beamed gravely, "Cat sister, my yurt will be most honored by the presence of you and your fine cubs. Who was their sire, may I ask?"

"Steelclaws himself," Blackback replied proudly. "My kittens, too, are the get of a chief."

Shortly, Behtiloo and Blackback came back through the camp to the chief yurt, the cat carrying one struggling beastlet in her jaws and Behtiloo cradling the other blind, down-furred kitten in her arms. In months after, it was not at all unusual for visitors to the yurt to see Chief's-wife Leenah nursing a pink-skinned baby boy on one breast and a gray-and-black-furred prairiecat kitten on the other, while beside her lay Blackback on her side, giving suck to the other kitten as well as to two little Krooguhs. Many a cat and human came for the expressed purpose of viewing this most singular sight.

Two years later, at one of the infrequent clan gatherings, all of the Krooguhs walked tall and proud, though none so tall and so proud as Chief Sami. The Krooguh of Krooguh strutted in his fierce pride, and other chiefs were quick to afford an almost reverential deference to this peer of such unmatchable potency of loins that he was capable of siring sons in threes.

So many chiefs and humbler clansfolk flocked to the Krooguh enclave to briefly watch the little triplets wrestling, playing with and making to ride upon the two big-pawed, big-headed sons of Cat Chief Steelclaws and Blackback, each visitor leaving behind a gift of some nature, that Sami had to buy two new carts to carry all the loot away when at long last Clan Krooguh was allowed to quit the gathering.

When leave they finally did, there was not a nubile clans girl or boy of Krooguh remaining unmarried. Further, right many a prepubescent girl or boy or even a babe in arms was by then already promised in marriage to clans anxious to share out among their own folk even a few drops of this suddenly precious Krooguh heritage. As for the triplets themselves, the eldest was promised in marriage to the largest, richest and most powerful of all the Kindred clans, Clan Kambuhl. The second-eldest was pledged to the family of the chiefs of Clan Kabuht, while the third little boy would wed into Clan Esmith, another matrilineal-succession clan.

Nor had old Behtiloo Hansuhn of Krooguh been at all left out of the general hullabaloo following Clan Krooguh's arrival at the gathering. Not only were the live births of the three boys a new, a novel, and a noteworthy occurrence, but that a clanswoman had so accurately forecast their births was purely the stuff of which legends were woven.

All the clan bards and the three or four traveling bards were not content until they had closeted with the grandame, heard her personal history, then retired to compose new songs and new verses to older ones. These were to be the first mentions of Behtiloo Hansuhn of Krooguh in any Kindred histories outside the Song of Krooguh. But they were to be neither the last nor the most glorious.

The triplets remained amazingly similar as they grew from infancy, though they were not and had never been identical. Of them all, only the eldest, Tim, had their father's red hair and green eyes; both Peet and the youngest, Djim, had fair skins and dark-blue eyes, but these were in them coupled with hair as raven's-wing-black as their mother's.

Like all Horseclans children, they were riding almost before they could walk, and they quickly acquired a deadly proficiency with their slings, bolas and light bows, capable of bringing down flying birds and scurrying small game with consistency.

The mindspeak talents of all three were powerful and exceptionally far-ranging. Far-ranging too were their hunting and foraging expeditions, for they seemed utterly fearless; but as they were always accompanied on these expeditions by Kills-elk and Whitepaws—their former "littermates," now grown to mature size and weight, both proven in battle and in the hunt—and sometimes by Blackback, their feline foster mother, as well, no one thought of fearing for their safety away from the clan camp.

In the tenth summer of the triplets' lives, Clan Krooguh chanced to roam farther east than usual and went into camp around a small grove of trees guarding a largish spring from which debouched a rill of sparkling, ice-cold water. As Sacred Sun crested the horizon on the very next morning, Tim and Peet and Djim Krooguh were ahorse, armed for the hunt, and trotting off toward the east with a half-dozen of their two-leg peers, Kills-elk and Whitepaws in search of game and adventure.

Behtiloo watched the party of little boys ride off, quickly passing from view to be lost among the density of the high grasses. She had so watched them many times before, but this time, somewhere deep within her, there was a vague presentiment of danger, deadly danger, and she barely repressed an urge to mindcall them back. All through a day that seemed endless and throughout the long, long night that finally came, that same presentiment gnawed and clawed at her and was, if anything, stronger and more ominous with the next rising of Sacred Sun.

Chief Sami, most of the warriors and many of the maiden-archers were out of camp, along with all the adult and near-adult cats not on herd guard or nursing new litters. As was always done just after choosing and occupying a new campsite, they were routinely sweeping out beyond the herds in hopes of flushing out and dispatching or, at least, driving off any resident predators of sufficient size to harm the stock. And so the camp stood almost empty when what was left of the triplets' hunting party rode their stumbling, heaving, foam-streaked mounts through it to halt before the chief yurt.

Little Peet rode in the lead, with the limp body of Kills-elk draped across the withers before him. A few paces behind his brother, Djim reeled in the saddle to which someone had wisely tied him, his roughly bandaged left arm supported by a rude sling and the cut-off stub of an arrow shaft projecting through the dirty, blood-tacky cloths. Nine little boys had ridden out, only five returned, and two of those died soon after they were lifted from their exhausted, near-foundered mounts.

Immediately, riders and cats were sent racing off in search

of Chief Sami and the camp became a beehive of activity as old men, maidens and matrons looked to weapons, donned war gear and mindcalled favored war horses from the herd. Behtiloo listened with half an ear to Peet's halting recountal, even while her sinewy old hands and her mind were absorbed in seeing to the grievous hurts of Djim and Kills-elk.

Angling a few degrees south of due east from the Clan Krooguh campsite, the mounted party of young hunters had ridden on throughout the early part of the day of their departure, garnering a rabbit or two here, a gamebird there, but nothing larger. While their mounts grazed and rested briefly, the boys had lunched on cheese and jerked venison and the raw fillets of a largish rattlesnake they had chanced across during the morning's ride.

They had ridden on, but with no better luck, through most of the rest of the day. Then, an hour or so before sunset, Whitepaws had flushed out four of the ungulates called by the nomads "lancehorns"—about four feet at the withers, with hair that was white on the back and the flanks, black or a dark brownish on the legs and the belly, bearing tapering horns that stood almost straight up from the head and on large bucks were sometimes almost four feet in length. These lancehorns were fairly common in the better-watered parts of the southern prairies, but were quite rare this far north, and the nine little boys set out in hot pursuit, with the two cats riding on packhorses.

But darkness fell before they came within bow range of the speedy, elusive antelopes, so they made a cold camp near a trickling rill. While the boys ate the last of their cheese and jerky and the horses grazed the lush, bluish-green grasses, the two cats ranged far out in search of something more substantial than a few rabbits the boys had skinned and given them, since they lacked a way to preserve the small carcasses from decay.

Timing themselves by movements of stars and, later, of the risen moon, each boy stood a watch of about an hour over his sleeping comrades, with Peet and Djim taking the first two stints and Tim the last—those being the proven times of most danger, since most attacks took place either shortly after nightfall or at the hour just before the dawning. But that night passed peacefully enough, with Kills-elk padding in just as false dawn was glowing grayly, soberly mindspeaking his presence and intent to the alert Tim Krooguh before exposing his big furry body to the ready bow with its nocked arrow.

While the boys were all yawning, scratching their crotches, rubbing the sleep from their eyes, rolling their sleeping-cloaks, drinking from the rill or relieving themselves, Whitepaws' broadbeam farspeak crashed into all their minds at once.

"Beware, brothers! Dirtmen come from the east, many of these Dirtmen, with bows and spears and long clubs made of wood and metal. They are even now creeping through the tall grasses and soon will they be on three sides of you, brothers."

Horseclans born and bred, the boys wasted no time, moving every bit as quickly and purposefully as would their fathers or older brothers. Mindcalled horses came at the gallop to have saddles slapped upon their backs and speedily cinched, nimble fingers buckled and tied on gear with never a wasted motion. Then riders mounted, strung bows in hands, keen eyes searching the edges of the tall grasses, fifty yards east, for sight of the stalking Dirtmen.

The long arrows fell among the knot of little hunters unseen, coming as they did from the same direction as the blinding rays of the rising sun. They killed three boys outright and wounded three others, one of them Djim Krooguh. Tim's mare reared, screaming in her final agony, then crashed onto her side. The boy pulled leather barely in time and rolled away from the flailing hooves of the dying beast. Another boy fought with mindspeak and reins to control a mount gone mad with pain. Then Kills-elk suddenly went tumbling across the sward, and a second later, there was a crack of thunderlike noise from somewhere within the tall, concealing grasses, while a cloud of dirty-black smoke rose above it.

"*Flee*, brothers, *run!*" Again came Whitepaws' frantic mindspeak. "Run! Run back to the clan camp and fetch back the cats and the warriors, for more Dirtmen now come on horses. They are too many to fight, they . . ."

The cat's mindspeak broke off suddenly, and none of the triplets could again find Whitepaws' mind, range as they might. Between them, Tim and Peet managed somehow to lift the bleeding, dead-weight carcass of Kills-elk onto the withers of Peet's dancing, nervous horse, binding it to the saddle pommel with a length of tough braided hide hurriedly cut from a bola. More bola cords went to bind the three wounded boys into their saddles.

That done, Tim unsnapped his arrow case from the saddle of his dead mare and slung it over his shoulder, then pulled his spear from beneath her. Grasping a handful of mane, he swung astride one of the pack horses that they had not taken the time to saddle, and the six boys rode west at a flat-out run, Tim in the lead, his thick red braids whipping behind him.

They had ridden on for almost a mile when from out a stand of taller grasses on their left ran at least a score of big, tall Dirtmen, with spears, a few long bows and straight-bladed swords, and one with a long, shiny contraption of metal and wood.

"Around them, to the right!" Tim broadbeamed to all the boys. "Fast, brothers, before they can extend enough to block us off!"

Obedient to Tim's command, the knot of riders swerved. Then they were in the clear . . . or so they thought. But another of those horrendous, thunderlike, roaring cracks bellowed behind them and Tim's packhorse mount went down by the nose, sending the boy tumbling over the head of the stricken animal. The arrow case was torn from off his back, but he stoically bore the inevitable bruises and abrasions, refusing to release his grips on either spear or bow or the three arrows between the fingers of his bow hand.

Leaving the wounded in the care of the other unhurt boy, Gil Daiviz of Krooguh, Peet wheeled his clumsy, overburdened horse about to ride back to where his brother was just arising from the ground.

"*NO!*" Tim shouted and mindspoke, both at once, then added in mindspeak only, "No, brother, there are just too many of the bastards for three of us to fight . . . for long, anyway. And your horse has too much of a load already. Tell Father that I died as befits a Krooguh. Now, ride, brother mine, and bring back the clan to avenge my blood and life."

The Dirtmen were now running toward the lone boy and the dead horse, and Peet lingered just long enough to speed a bone-headed hunting arrow which *thunked* into the chest of the big brown-bearded swordsman in the lead. Then the boy reined about and galloped in pursuit of his comrades, his little white teeth set in, drawing red blood from his lower lip, and his unashamed tears flowing freely over his dusty cheeks.

His mind still locked with Tim's, he saw what followed through his brother's eyes. Considering the man with the long thing that he assumed correctly had somehow killed his horse to be his most dangerous opponent, Tim sent his first shaft winging on its goose feathers and took grim pleasure in noting that the tall, gangly man dropped the long thing, a rod that resembled an unfletched arrow and a decorated cow horn, to clutch frantically with both big hands at the short arrow now sunk to its fletchings into his body just below the short ribs.

Tim's second loosing dropped a spearman ten yards away, and his third and last arrow sank into the eye of a smooth-shaven blond man armed with one of the long, straight swords. Then the little boy dropped his now useless bow and crouched with his spear grasped in both small hands for his last stand, breast to breast, hugely outnumbered, but unafraid.

The first Dirtman to reach Tim was fatally overconfident. He stamped in, shouting and swinging a powerful slash with his broad-bladed sword. Tim simply ducked under the hissing steel and used the knife-edged blade of his wolf spear to slash his unarmored opponent's throat. It was all over so fast that the man immediately behind the first had that same bloody spear blade between his ribs before he could even set himself to fight.

Unable to jerk his own spear free, Tim armed himself with the longer, heavier, less well-balanced weapon of his second opponent. He was carefully maneuvering, weighing the unfamiliar spear to locate points of balance and watching the three big Dirtmen warily stalking him, when, with a sudden, intense and unbearable pain all along the left side of his head, all the world became a single, impenetrable blackness.

CHAPTER XIV

When he had had the full story from the open memories of Leenah and Behtiloo (for little Peet, utterly drained, both physically and emotionally, was sunk deep in an exhausted sleep), Chief Sami took only long enough to exchange his boiled-leather hunting armor for his inherited steel scale shirt and his game-wise hunting horse for his big roan stallion, Bonebreaker, king of the Clan Krooguh herd.

Then, summoning all the warriors, maidens and matrons, he gave them a brief rendition of the events—the completely unprovoked sneak attack upon a party of peacefully hunting Krooguh boys by adult Dirtmen. He related the murders from ambush of the first three children to die, told of the two who had suffered grievous wounds and lived barely long enough to get back to camp and of one of his own young sons and a brave cat brother who now lay in the chief yurt, sorely hurt.

Lastly, he spoke with grim pride of the glorious death of little Tim Krooguh, who had slain at least five adult men, then willingly given his own young life that his brothers and his wounded comrades might escape. Speaking, as he was, to Kindred Horseclansfolk, he did not need to stress the inherent baseness of Dirtmen or the depthless evil of men who would coldly slay innocent little children.

Leaving the clan camp guarded by the maidens, the matrons and a few superannuated warriors under the command of his uncle, subchief Buhd Hansuhn of Krooguh, Sami, at the head of seventy-two fully armed warriors and twenty mature prairiecats, shortly rode out on the trail—the very real blood trail—by which the battered party of boys had returned.

They rode out fully prepared for a raid in force or whatever else might befall them: four spare horses for every rider, more horses fitted with the special saddles needed by the prairiecats, packhorses and mules laden with case on case of arrows, bundles of war darts, spare weapons, coils of braided-rawhide rope, pitch and oil for fire arrows, dried herbs and prepared ointments and soft cloths for dressing wounds, many pounds of hard cheese, jerked meat and pemmican, waxed-leather bags of water.

Behtiloo Hansuhn of Krooguh rode behind Chief Sami and beside her eldest son, Hwahlis Hansuhn of Krooguh. Rant and rave and shout as they might, not one of her sons or her grandsons had been able to dissuade her of her intention to ride with the war party. Finally, and as gracefully as the circumstances made possible, Chief Sami had caved in, able to console himself and his pride somewhat by thinking aloud that his grandmother, for all her advanced years, still could pull a heavier bow than could some of his warriors.

Blackback, the prairiecat, had gleaned some useful facts regarding the topography of the route the boys had taken toward the east from the minds of Peet and Kills-elk, and that, combined with her keen senses and those of the other cats, plus the plain splashes of blood here and there, allowed the war party to travel fast and confidently; therefore, it was more than an hour before sunset when they spotted from afar the numerous black specks wheeling in the sky.

That the dead horses had been skinned, their hooves and the larger of their sinews removed, was not upsetting to the Horseclansmen, who were themselves of a thrifty nature. But the savage, depraved, singularly hideous mutilations which had been perpetrated upon the dead flesh of the three little boys was sufficient to drive even the soberest, the most phlegmatic clansman into a true killing rage.

Far back from the scene of the major atrocity, within the tall grasses that had screened the cowardly attack, the cats found the corpse of Whitepaws. Like the horses, he had been skinned; also, his head had been hacked off and all eighteen of his claws had been wrenched out of his paws.

But of brave little Tim, there was no sign, anywhere.

"Come out of there, you accursed heathen spawn!" growled eighteen-year-old Micah Claxton, very brave in the knowledge that the captured pagan boy had been disarmed.

Tall, fair and handsome, in a sullen way, Micah was the

very apple of his grandfather's eye. Possessed of a splendid physique and far stronger than average, he misused that strength to bully younger or weaker men of the Abode of the Righteous, while against those whom he sensed might best him physically, he always invoked the dread power of his doting grandsire, the Elder of the Lord, Elijah Claxton. Micah was universally and most cordially despised by his peers.

"Come out, child of Satan!" he repeated from just outside the doorway of the tiny cell. "The Elder, the blessed Elijah, would see you, would have converse with you and begin to teach you of the glories of God."

Tim had awakened alone in utter darkness. His head had ached abominably, the whole side of it and his face had been caked with dried blood and dirt and there had been a metallic taste in his dry mouth. His first attempt to stand on his feet had been disastrous, so he had explored in the darkness on his hands and knees.

He had discovered that floor and walls were constructed of broad wooden planks, smooth and slightly greasy to the touch of his fingers. Tim had instantly realized that they would take fire quickly and burn nicely, had he only flint and steel, but of course his belt with its pouch and knives was gone from around his waist. The door he finally found was wooden, too, and it seemed to be both solid and heavy, at any rate immovable to his boy's strength.

The furnishings were spartan—a wooden frame strung with strips of hide which supported a canvas bag stuffed full of dried, crackly cornshucks, an empty but foul-smelling wooden bucket and another bucket, this one half full of tepid water. Tim cautiously sniffed the water, gingerly tasted it, then drank down half of it avidly. His raging thirst slaked for the nonce, he wetted the baggy sleeve of his shirt, laved most of the clotted blood from off his face and, working more carefully, from off his head. His fingers told the tale of a long split in his scalp just above his right ear, of that and of a hard, very painful and quite large bump.

After taking stock of his clothing and possessions still remaining, Tim decided that whoever had disarmed him had either been hurried or inexperienced at such a task or both together. Not only had he been left a bone-headed iron pin in his right braid, the small dagger—flat-hilted and guardless but with three inches of razor-sharp steel blade—was still sheathed in place between the layers of felt that made up the leg of his boot.

Squatting against the back wall of his prison, Tim was thinking of how best to make use of his available weapons to the detriment of his captors when the door was opened to admit a blinding burst of sunlight. Then a big man with a loud voice began to yell at him.

Stepping aside, so that his bulk did not block out the daylight, Micah Claxton peered into the tiny windowless cell. The captive child was not on the cot, but was rather squatting or crouching back next to the rear wall, head sunk on his chest, arms hung at his sides. He looked to be smaller than Micah had remembered and utterly helpless, and so, emboldened, he strode in and roughly shook the boy's shoulder.

"Don't you hear me, you piece of filth? Get up and come with me."

And Tim uncoiled like a steel spring! The bone-headed pin was driven its full two inches of length into Micah's belly even as the edge of the boot dagger laid open from temple to chin the handsome face in which Micah had taken such inordinate pride. Screaming like a woman in labor, Micah Claxton stumbled backward out of the cell to slump against the guardrail of the porch, staring stupidly at the blood running from his chin onto the palms of his big hands.

Tim made to follow his victim out the door, but his way was obstructed by two more Dirtmen, who crowded into the cell. One made a grab for the boy's knife hand, but his hand closed around the knife instead, and Tim's reflexive jerk sliced through palm and fingers to grate upon living bone. With a breathless gasp, the farmer backed away, cradling his hurt, bloody hand with the other.

His comrade stamped forward, arms wide, meaning to enfold the little captive in their crushing grasp. But Tim ducked under the sweep of those arms and jammed the blood-tacky dagger up between the man's meaty thighs with all his might.

The second man's deep roars abruptly metamorphosed into a piercing shriek, and he rose onto his very toetips in his vain attempt to raise his suffering body up off the punishing steel. Tim indulged himself, giving the imbedded blade a vicious twist and withdrawing it in a savage drawcut. As the grunting, groaning man slid down the wall, Tim Krooguh once more made for the door and freedom.

Captain-of-dragoons Roger Gorman was a good nine hundred crowflight miles from the country that had given him birth, which—all things duly weighed and considered—could have been deemed a definite plus factor in his continued life and health. He had left his homeland most precipitately and had never returned, for all that his half brother (Roger was the illegitimate outcome of a nobleman's drunken night of dalliance with a taverner's daughter), the Count of Rehdzburk, had offered repeatedly to pay quite handsomely for a sight of Roger's head . . . with or without the body.

Roger Gorman was not a basically evil man, despite the fact that he was rightfully charged with brigandage, highway robbery, maintenance of an illegal armed band, horse theft, cattle rustling, sheep stealing, poaching, arson, extortion, kidnapping, maiming, rape and a goodly number of murders. These were only the major charges. The lesser ones filled two large pages and spilled over onto a third. They included the unlawful display of the arms and devices of the Most Noble House of the Counts of Rehdzburk (Roger always and hotly contended that he had as much inherent right to display those arms as did his half brother, the present Count of Rehdzburk), aiding and abetting a jailbreak, and flight to avoid prosecution. To these latter charges Roger answered that it was a poor sort of a man who would simply ride away and leave good comrades to a harsh and merciless fate, adding that any man who would willingly linger to make the short, sharp acquaintance of a headsman's axe had not the brains of a privy-worm.

Immediately he left the environs of Rehdzburk, he had taken a *nom de guerre* which resembled his real name not even faintly. Under this *nom*, he had served as a Freefighter for a few years, first in the army of the Duke of Eeree when he revolted against the king. When the duke made peace with his sovereign at Harzburk and agreed to honor the warrants of other principalities, Roger thought that a change of scenery might be beneficial to his health and fled to the Duchy of Pitzburk, where another rebellion was arming against Harzburk and the king.

But following a trivial dispute wherein he was forced to

slay a minor nobleman in a fair fight, Roger found the general atmosphere of the ancient City of Steel oppressive and somewhat less than salubrious, and so he rode out into the western mountains to first join, then soon command a jolly group of kindred souls and continue with them in the greenwood the life he had learned to love so in Rehdzburk.

As the long-drawn-out war between Pitzburk and the king wound slowly down, more and more former Freefighters found their way into the ranks of Roger's band, until he was leading a force of over half a thousand seasoned, veteran soldiers. A century earlier, he might have hacked himself out a holding and a patent of nobility with so many good swords to do his bidding, but instead he lost seventy percent of them when his stronghold was surprised and overrun by the strong force sent to crush him by the king and his dukes. Roger and the couple hundred of his men who managed to fight their way out rode west as fast as honest horseflesh could bear them.

They served the Archduke of Kluhmbuhzburk for a while, then his overlord, the King of Ohyoh. But the king proved to be slow in paying due monies and he fought too few wars to deliver any meaningful amounts of loot into his Freefighters' slim purses, so the condotta rode on west again.

In slow, erratic stages, halting here to fight for hire and there to fight for plunder until driven on by armed might, the hundred or so survivors eventually found themselves on the very uttermost fringe of civilization, with the hue and cry raised for them a stretch of a good hundred leagues behind and only the Sea of Grass before them.

Roger and his hard-pressed lieutenants had been on the verge of trying to trade a few of their precious warhorses for the condotta's passage down the Great River to one of the score of little independent kingdoms that lined its eastern bank when they were approached by Dick Gruenberger, a plains trader. In better times or another location, Roger would have spit upon the paltry sum offered per armed and mounted man to ride along with and guard the wagon caravans on the Sea of Grass, but after a brief conference with his starving officers and men, he had accepted.

And so, for five long years, sometime Captain-of-dragoons Roger Gorman and his aging, shrinking force had ridden out from Tradertown each spring beside the huge, high-wheeled wagons, each drawn by as many as a dozen and a half big mules or twelve span of oxen and creaking with their loads. They carried vastly diverse cargoes—bar iron, sheet steel and brass and copper, ingots of copper and alloys of silver, semiprecious gemstones, bolts of various cloths, spools of threads and fine wires, hanks of dyed yarns, steel and brass needles, nails and tacks and other small items of hardware, whiskeys and wines and female slaves, anything and everything that might tickle the fancies of the scattered bands of nomads or the few, isolated communities of farmers.

And each autumn, the wagons rolled back to Tradertown. By then they were packed with bales of hides, bundles of rich, dense furs, intricately worked and profusely decorated leather goods, fine examples of the felter's art, thick blankets and deep carpets, small treasures that the nomads or even the traders themselves had dug out of the various ruined and overgrown cities which the prairie was fast reclaiming for its own, all these plus enamelwork and weapons of Horseclan manufacture. (Horseclan hornbows were unsurpassed, and there was an insatiable market for them in the east, while the blades wrought by Horseclans smiths were unexcelled by any save the very highest grades of Pitzburk steel.)

Long ago, on their very first meeting, Roger had disliked and thoroughly distrusted Dick Gruenberger, and five years as that trader's employee had borne out to him the perspicacity of his initial judgment. Gruenberger and his son shared certain traits in common; both were mean, grasping, unrelievedly avaricious and cruel.

Little as they had originally agreed to pay the men who put their lives on the line to guard the wagons and their contents, father and son still came to the autumn accounting with long faces and even longer lists of their "justifications" for paying far less than that paltry sum.

Consequently, even living communally, the condotta seldom had enough to see it through the winter and so was obliged to draw advances against next season's wages and work for Trader Gruenberger yet another year. Roger had long consoled his dwindling pride with a promise to himself to someday see every last drop of the thin, watery stuff that the Traders Gruenberger—*père et fils*—called life's blood.

Then, this past spring, after some inexplicably delayed but most important shipments had necessitated a very late start of the plains caravan, members of the condotta had discovered that the nineteen slaves chained in the slave wagons were all war captives from the Pitzburk-Ohyoh marches, and despite strict supervision maintained by the four big brutal women Gruenberger was maintaining to make certain that only he, his son, David, and his nephew, Aaron, could get at the women until the train split up farther out on the prairies, Roger could smell an incipient mutiny on the first occasion the traders should try to sell one of the slave women.

For a month of travel, the deadly mash worked and fermented. Then, a day's travel away from the communal farm of a group of strange, stern folk whose fortified dwelling place had always been the last stop before entering into nomad territory, Roger and his fifty-five men had slit the throats of the sleeping teamsters, oxmen and wagoners, cut down the personal bodyguards of the Gruenbergers to a man and freed the slaves. Then, while the men amused themselves with their former employers, in a spirit of fairness, they turned over the disarmed former wardresses to the nineteen women for final disposition. When all of the bodies had been deeply buried, the wagons were driven back and forth over the gravesite a few times, then they proceeded on westward.

The three tall, multistory buildings of stone and timber and homemade brick, interconnected at several levels, would have been laughable as defensive structures anywhere east of the Great River and, no matter their cranklights, few ancient rifles and encircling stockade of half-peeled logs, would quickly have fallen to any determined assault of well-led troops. But here on the Sea of Grass, where the only enemies to be expected were hit-and-run horse-nomads, the structure had proved quite sufficient as a fortress-home to the six generations of farmers it had sheltered, having come through more than one attack by raiders from out on the prairies.

Neither Roger nor his swordsmen had ever felt really comfortable around the grim-faced, hidebound, self-righteous inhabitants of the fortified farm, but Gruenberger had stopped every year to turn a profit in trade. The farmers sometimes paid in hard money—mostly, ancient silver coins—but more usually traded grain and dried beans for such esoteric items as yellow brimstone and pigs of lead, in addition to the more mundane needles, threads, pigs of iron and the occasional bolt of white or black or brown broadcloth, or a new nailheader.

On the other hand, their five seasons on the prairies and plains had bred in Roger and all of his force a liking and a deep admiration and respect for the Horseclansfolk—the sworn and bitter enemies of those who dwelt in the so-called Abode of the Righteous. The customs and the way of life of these nomads made good sense to Roger and appealed to him and the pitiful remnant of his condotta.

It had been their original intention, this decided out of the general parlay held over the gory corpses of Gruenberger and his crew, to continue on westward until they chanced onto a Horseclans clan or two, trade off their late and unlamented employer's goods for livestock and tents, marry into the clans and become themselves Horseclansmen.

"But there," raged Roger to himself, "is another good plan buried in the shit by chancing to be in the wrong fucking place at the wrong fucking time! Damn the wormy, misbegotten guts of that sanctimonious old child-butchering fucker of an Elder Claxton, anyway!"

Roger took a long, thougtful draft of the late Dick Gruenberger's best-quality honey wine from the dead trader's own heavy chased-silver cup, reflecting, "Well, at least I could swear a fucking Sword Oath that me and mine had naught to do with the foul murders of those poor little lads. We've all been brought low, true enough, but we won't never be *that* fucking lowdown! That treacherous volley was loosed long before me and my boys was anywhere near within bow range.

"There was no fucking need to kill them anyhow, not as outnumbered as they were, and a passel of grown men against less than a dozen children, at that. But that pious fucking fool Claxton is so terrified of Horseclansfolk of any size or sex or age that his very ball-less fucking terror and this senseless fucking reaction to it has dropped us all—every man jack—into the shit, nose-deep, by Steel!"

The old soldier grimaced at a particularly unpleasant memory. "And whatall them fucking farmers done to them dead boys' pitiful little corpses . . . the shit-eating bastards! Hell, we didn't do things like that to them Gruenbergers, and everybody knows they plumb deserved such if anybody does.

"When the Horseclansfolks see those bodies, they're sure to go plumb crazy-mad, and I, for one, can't say I blame them one damn bit. Except, where we all are, they're likely to take that mad out on us too, along of the ones what earned it.''

Suddenly, Roger was jolted from his dismal imagery of falling under the dripping sabers of blood-mad Horseclansmen by one of the troopers he had sent to share the guard of the captured nomad boy.

"Cap'n Roger, you better for to come quick. Them fuckin' psalm-shouters is jest set to murder thet pore li'l younker. Guy and his sword is all that's stoppin' the cocksuckers, right now.''

During the course of their shared run up the length of the second-level porch, the trooper shouted out the gist of the tale above the hollow booming thuds of their heavy jackboots on the boards.

Roger suffered only an inconsequential stab in his left forearm during his eyeblink-quick disarming of Tim Krooguh. Then, bouncing the blood-tacky little dagger on one horny palm, he openly mocked the enraged farmers.

"You poor, fucking, God-ridden, ball-less substitutes for men, you! I told you all this morning that this boy is *my* prisoner—*mine*, Captain-of-dragoons Roger Gorman's! Had you heeded me at that time, you'd still have your balls, a good deal more of your blood and''—he grinned derisively at the sobbing, gasping, moaning Micah Claxton, whose blood-slimy jawteeth were clearly visible between the lips of the cheek slash—''your girlish beauty.

"Did you suppose yourselves to be dealing with one of your own browbeaten, dispirited spawn, eh? That boy in there is bred of a hundred generations of fighters, and with nary a hair on his chin yet, he's more a man than any one of you here, who proclaim yourselves as such. I'll wager my horse and sword that he has more fucking sand in his craw than the whole hagridden nest of you fucking religious maniacs!''

"But . . . but how could he have gotten that knife, unless a . . . a demon sent by his father, Satan, brought it to him? He was searched and disarmed, and the door is the only way to enter, and it was solidly locked and barred and guarded by your two men and two of us.'' This speech came from the lips of Jeremiah Herbert, through teeth clenched against the pain of his slashed-to-the-bone hand.

The trooper, Guy, laughed and slapped his thigh in mirth, while Roger snorted disdainfully. "Half-wit fucking amateurs! You had off his belt, and when you found no knives hung down his back or under his sleeves or strapped to his legs or sticking out of his boottops, you figured you'd stripped him of all his weapons, right? Then the more fools, you!"

Roger took the needle tip of the little dagger between callused fingertips and held it up before their eyes, saying, "Did no one of you hopeless fucking shitheads even think of having off that boy's boots and seeing if perchance a flat, slender blade or two might be sewn between the layers of felt? Of course not! Your sole talents lie in the directions of psalm-shouting, plow-pushing, and shit-shoveling, and you'd all be fucking wise to remember that the next time you feel the itch to play at soldiering.

"Now, I'm placing a half-squad to guard this boy, and my orders to them will be to spill out the fucking guts of anybody as tries to get at him without me being with that anybody. Now you sorry fucking pack of arseholes just go tell your fucking Elder that, hear?"

But immediately the bleeding, limping, sobbing, much-chastened farmers were out of earshot, Roger turned to Guy and the other troopers, saying, "We'll post a half-squad up here, right enough. But as soon as it's dark, you two take that boy down and chain him in one of the slave wagons. Make sure he has plenty of water, a slop bucket and some hay balls, and a bedroll. Get him some cooked meat and some cheese and milk, too, if you can. I doubt that he'd know what the bread and greens these people seem to subsist on is for.

"Guy, you're now a sergeant and your sole duty is to care for and guard the nomad boy. Take as many men as you need to guard him round the clock, no less than a half-squad at any time, strung bows and bared steel.

"If this mess gets worse—and I am of the considered opinion that it will, and damned soon, at that—the lad may well be the condotta's safe passage out of it all. And I don't trust this Elder Claxton and his pack of murderous bible-thumpers any further than I could heave a fucking full-grown draft ox."

"But where do you think to ride, Mother?" Hwahlis Hansuhn of Krooguh demanded exasperatedly.

"To the high plains, if necessary. To the lands of frozen earth. To the deserts. Wherever I must ride to find real men. Men who can still recall the old ways, the ancient Horseclans customs passed down to the Kindred from the Sacred Ancestors. Men who still think more of the sacred honor of their clans than they do of their own fleabitten hides," Behtiloo snapped, while she tied the last knots holding the load on her single packhorse.

Activities throughout the clan camp had ground to a virtual standstill. Those of the warriors who had returned with Chief Sami were among the throng of clansfolk watching and listening, all red-faced or staring at the dust, as shamed by her scornful words as by their chief's decision in the matter.

"But, Mother," Hwahlis remonstrated, shaking his graying head, "you were *there*. You *saw* that fence of tall logs. Horses could not pass between them, so we would have to go in on foot, in the face of more than twoscore steel-scale bowmen and Wind alone knows how many Dirtmen. Every single warrior of Clan Krooguh might die without accomplishing—"

"Tell that to the spilled blood of your murdered kin," said Behtiloo coldly. "Your dead father and I once took great pride in you and your brother and in Sami, our grandson. My dear, honorable Tim would have known what had to be done in this instance, and he would have spit upon you and Buhd and Sami for your cravenness."

"Mother," Hwahlis remonstrated with as much patience as he still could exercise, "you know that more than half the warriors and most of the mature cats are still camped about and scouting the environs of Three-House. Two-thirds of the cattle of those Dirtmen now are with or soon will be with our own herds, and some of their sheep and horses, too.

"We've slain or taken every man who ventured out from the place and will continue to do so, since they've refused to trade us Tim for any of their own folk or beasts. So would you have us fire the place and roast your great-grandson alive along with his captors, then?"

Behtiloo paused with one foot in the stirrup, her corded old hands set upon pommel and cantle. "No, creature-I-once-called-my-son, I'd have you all stand up on your hind legs like the men you're supposed to be . . . but you obviously have quite forgotten how to do so."

The old woman spoke not another word, though her blue eyes flashed the cold fire of contempt. Once in the saddle, she mindspoke her mare, the packhorse and the prairiecat, Blackback, and the little group moved slowly the length of the camp, the throng parting before her. She rode west.

CHAPTER XV

———••◆••———

Hot and furious words had flown between Elder Elijah Claxton and Captain-of-dragoons Roger Gorman in the blood-red wake of Tim Krooguh's assaults upon the farmer-guards. The Elder had demanded instant delivery of the Horseclans boy, at the same time announcing his intention of seeing the "Devil's spawn" slowly whipped to death for the edification of his, the Elder's, "flock."

The captain's refusal had been flat, unequivocal and most obscenely worded, whereupon the wild-eyed old man had ordered the assembled farmers to take the boy by force. This very unwise order had resulted in several more wounded farmers and one dead one. It also had resulted in Roger and his men seizing anything they considered a weapon, including the precious, irreplaceable rifles, to forestall any recurrences.

But even with his teeth drawn, Elder Elijah Claxton still growled ferociously, demanding that all of the easterners forthwith quit the Abode of the Chosen of God. That had been just a short time before the Elder was made aware that an unknown—but, presumably quite large—number of Horse-clansmen had already run off most of the pastured cattle and sheep, captured or slain the herdsmen and some hunters who had had the bad luck to be out at the wrong time, and were offering to trade their captives and booty for their little kinsman.

Had Claxton begged, or even politely requested, that the boy be exchanged then and there, Roger would probably have complied, since such would have gone far toward defusing a definitely explosive situation. But on the Elder's arrogant demand that the boy be at once taken out and exchanged for men Roger did not know, did not want to know and cared for about as much as for so many dried-out horse buns, the old soldier's hackles rose and he replied in a firm negative.

He took great pleasure in adding to the refusal a bluntly worded suggestion that the venerable Elder Elijah Claxton publicly perform upon himself a physiologically impossible sexual act. At this, the raging old man ordered his god to strike down Captain Gorman with a bolt of lightning, and, when this event did not immediately occur, he fell on the ground in a raving, foaming-mouthed fit; so Roger had him fettered and thrown into the other slave wagon.

From that day, Roger and his force were in command, easily exercising undisputed control of the besieged Abode, everyone and everything within it. Having learned a bloody lesson at the hands of the hard-faced professional soldiers and bereft of the guidance of their hereditary leader, the sullen farmers did as they were told.

However, on that first day, by the time Roger was ready to take out the boy and, he hoped, have a meeting with the chief, the small knot of mounted Horseclansmen was nowhere to be seen. Nor had any of the farmers he had driven out at swordpoint to find the nomad warriors—not wishing to risk the lives of any of his own troopers or officers—ever yet returned.

Some half a moon after Behtiloo Hansuhn of Krooguh had departed the clan camp, an excited herdboy on a lathered horse came pounding through camp and up to the chief yurt, flung himself from out of his saddle and ran up the steps. Moments later, Chief Sami and his subchiefs were saddling quickly available horses, mindcalling others and bawling for their gear. Mounted and arrayed in their showy best, they all rode out, headed west.

"And so," said Chief Gil Kabuht of Kabuht, his crookedly healed nose affecting his speech adversely, "when we had heard the old lady out, we all agreed that there was naught for it but to ride. My son's second wife is a Krooguh, as you know, and there still are pledges of marriage between our two clans, of course, and blood has always been thicker than water.

"Now, true, Clan Kabuht is not so large and wealthy as is Clan Krooguh, but then Clan Danyuhlz, Clan Esmith and

Clan Morguhn are here, too; they came immediately, they had heard the old lady's tale, so we number near sixscore sabers among us all. Nor will there be a limit on the time we can stay, Brother Sami, for our clans march only two or three days behind us. So treat us here to a good old-fashioned feast of fine fat Dirtman beef and mutton, then let's get busy at putting paid to the former owners of that meat, hey?''

During the very night of that feast, a Kambuhl clansman rode a trembling, heaving, foam-streaked horse into the Krooguh camp to announce that Chief Bili Kambuhl of Kambuhl had been visited by Chief's-widow Behtiloo Hansuhn of Krooguh and was even now on the march with all the warriors of the main clan, plus those of no less than three septs. The messenger, who was every bit as spent as his nearly foundered horse, estimated that Clan Kambuhl would be arrived from the north in two days or less and opined that Chief Bili just might be a wee bit put out should the party start before he and his clansmen came.

"Now how in hell could Grandmother be in two places at the same time?" Chief Sami demanded to know. "How could she appeal to you Kambuhls and to the Danyuhlzes, Kabuhts, Morguhns and the Esmiths separately and all within only a few days?"

The Kambuhl clansman shook his head slowly, tiredly. "I only do the bidding of my chief, Chief Sami. Ask your questions of him; he'll be here soon enough, I'll warrant."

But before even the vanguard of the Kambuhls could appear on the horizon, up from the south, driving their skinny herds before them, came Clans Linszee and Sanderz. Between both clans, they numbered only forty-six warriors; nonetheless, they were true descendants of the Sacred Ancestors and were fairly burning to avenge the blood of murdered Kindred.

Sami Krooguh brought most of his own warriors back to his clan camp for a much-needed rest and continued the encirclement of Three-House with the fresh and eager men of the other clans, all under the nominal command of war-wise Hwahlis Hansuhn of Krooguh, with such other chiefs and subchiefs as happened to be there to assist him.

With so many sabers and bows now behind them, Hwahlis, Buhd and the rest saw that the lines were drawn tighter, though the men of the assembled clans rapidly learned deepest respect for the droning projectiles thrown by the smokelances that could maim or slay a man or a horse at half a mile or more.

By day, the nomad warriors wormed their way in on their bellies, close enough to fire the fields of ripening grain. Twice in the first week after the reinforcement of Clan Krooguh, soot-blackened men on dark-colored horses swept in close enough on moonless or cloudy nights to loose flight after deadly flight of arrows to sweep the tiers of long porches and stockade platforms of the sentinels who manned them.

On other nights, Horseclan drums throbbed and boomed, bagpipes droned and wailed, hunting horns blatted, men shouted at intervals and screeched clan warcries, while the prairiecats raised their hideous, unearthly, yowling screams from sundown until dawn. And at any moment, by day or by night, a single fire arrow could be expected to arc up from some sheltered point to thud into one of the palisade logs, the gates or over the stockade palings and in among the parked wagons.

The length of the shallow valley along the rill was become but a single vast encampment, with the herds spread out for actual miles on either side. And still they came! Clans Daiviz, Kehlee and Rahs arrived together from the southwest, with a total of ninety warriors; Clans Bahrtuhn and Duhgliz with fifty-six; Rohz and Oneel and Higinz between them counted over a hundred more ready blades.

A stray caravan of traders accompanied Clans Kahrtuh and Baikuh, and their pigs of metals were most welcome to the hard-working smiths of the various clans. Soon booths were set up and a note of gaiety was added, though anyone could clearly perceive that this was no ordinary clans gathering, not with the constant comings and goings of fully armed and often mounted warriors, not with forge fires glowing, sending up showers of scintillating sparks by day and by night as well, not with the occasional bearing in of a dead or gravely wounded clansman from the scene of the siege, to the east, at Three-House.

Because the graze was becoming sparse and the game was now nonexistent, the council of chiefs decided to move the huge, sprawling camp closer to their theater of military operations, and over a period of hectic days marked by incredible amounts of unbelievable confusion, this was at last accomplished.

Even as they moved the camp and herds, however, more Kindred clans made their appearance, all claiming to have been fired by the words of old Behtiloo Hansuhn of Krooguh. Some were entire clans with their herds, others were war parties of warriors, maiden-archers, prairiecats and spare horses with pack trains. Another caravan of traders wandered in just in time to replenish the flagging supplies of metals and good eastern-made wines and hwiskee.

And on a day, two lone men rode in from due west. One of them was of advanced years, and a tooled-leather harp case was strapped across his back. The second man was much bigger and looked to be of no more than early middle years; he was armed and accoutered as a Horseclans warrior, and he bestrode a big, handsome red-bay stallion.

As the two men's mounts ambled into the fringes of the camp, a subchief of Clan Kahrtuh recognized the younger, bigger, war-equipped man.

"*Uncle Milo!*" he breathed softly, then he wheeled his mare about and set off for the circle of chief yurts at her best gallop.

Captain-of-dragoons Roger Gorman came running at the first call of the lookout and the sentries on the palisade platforms, buckling on his scale shirt as he ran. There had been the unmistakable signs and sounds of the movements of large numbers of mounted men out yonder, all through the preceding night, and he had been dead certain of and prepared his group for a dawn attack in force.

But when he reached the ground level, no massed formations of mounted clansmen were in sight, though of course any number might still be concealed by the pea-soup-thick ground mist out there. Rather, four horsemen were moving slowly and deliberately in the direction of the palisade's main gate.

"Roger," said Lenny Knapp, his senior lieutenant and oldest living friend, "unless I went blind overnight, that man in the lead there, that be Big Bob Fairbanks, cap'n of Old Homer Potts' caravan guards. And that sure resembles Old Homer hisself, behint him, too. I dunno who them other two is, prob'ly Horseclansmen. Chiefs, by the way they're gussied up and all.''

Thirty yards from the gate, the mounted party drew rein. The scale-shirted man in the lead snapped up the cheekpieces of his open-faced helmet and slid up the nasal. Drawing his long, straight-bladed sword and grasping it by the point, he began to wag it at arm's length over his head.

"*Sword Truce!*" snapped Roger and Lenny together. Then the captain turned and roared at no one in particular, "Bring me my horse, and one for Lieutenant Knapp, at the double, you fuckers! Immediately we're mounted, unbar that main gate and swing it open . . . wide!"

When the two Freefighter captains had exchanged swords, kissed the Sacred Steel and engaged in the other elaborate mutual formalities that inaugurated a binding truce on the field of battle under the terms of the eastern-based Sword Cult, Fairbanks said solemnly, "Roger, Lenny, yawl done got yourse'fs in a shitstorm for sure, this time. Yawl may not know, prob'ly don't, but it's more Horseclans warriors than anybody's ever seed at one time out there." He waved at the mist-shrouded fields. "It's *thousands* of 'em, hear me, from near *thirty* diffrunt clans. They all done come here for to git the bugtits whut kilt them kids. I shore hope to hell it won't you and yourn done thet, Roger."

Captain Roger Gorman shook his head. "No, I had no part in that sorry business, Bob, nor did any of my men; those poor lads were dead before we got to them. That demented old braying ass Elijah Claxton and his prize crew of village idiots killed those boys, then mutilated the bodies, like the savages they are. If Claxton had had his vicious way, he'd have had the one boy we captured tortured to death in public, for amusement, I suppose. But I clapped the old ninny in irons and took over his dungheap yonder."

One of the two Horseclansmen, the older, more flamboyantly attired one, moved his horse forward and spoke without preamble or introduction. "Chief of scale shirts, I have just mindspoken with my son, Tim. He says that you are a brave, decent and honorable warrior, and that you and yours have treated him well, shedding blood to protect him from those who would have harmed him. Release him now and I will spare you your lives."

Roger sighed in relief. "Right gladly, my lord Chief. I'd have made just that trade weeks ago, but none of the riders I sent out to find you and offer it ever came back. But come you all; we are Truce brothers, for the nonce. Let us all ride in and sip some fine honey wine and talk these matters through in comfort."

It was decided that those women and girls of the Chosen not already spoken for by womanless troopers of Roger's force would be divided among the assembled clans, and so too would the babes and children. Because blood cried out for blood, the Elder Elijah Claxton would be executed before the gathered clansfolk, a case of letting the chief take most of the guilt.

The council of chiefs, augmented by the recent arrivals of three more clans, had at first demanded the lives of every male of the Chosen over the age of thirteen, but Chief Morai, Uncle Milo, had talked them around.

The plains trader, Homer Potts, had bid quite good prices—to be paid partly from presently available goods and partly from goods he would bring in next spring—for the men and the bigger boys from the Abode of the Righteous, for while the Horseclansfolk had no use for male slaves, most of the peoples to the east, beyond the Great River, certainly did. If all else failed, Potts knew that he could earn a two- or three-hundred-percent profit from selling the big, strong, healthy farmers to the captains of the river galleys, who were in constant need of fresh oar slaves. And when Milo had the trader detail the lives of such row slaves for the council of chiefs, all agreed that immediate death would be far kinder . . . had any of them felt any degree of kindness toward the wretched murderers of children.

The chiefs had also wanted to burn Three-House to the ground, but again Milo dissuaded them. He had talked long on the matter with the Freefighter officers and the traders. The two plains traders had been quick to comprehend the advantages to them and their ilk of a trade center located at the very edge of the Sea of Grass, rather than weeks away by wagon. With no more danger to be feared from the Horseclans, Roger and his men could dismantle the stockade, build more houses and soon have a new trade town—a convenience for both traders and nomads.

* * *

Before the clans dispersed, Chief Milo Morai sought out the Krooguh clan bard. "The old woman who brought about this unprecedented gathering of our Kindred—sing me of her."

Halfway through the many verses, Uncle Milo slapped his bootleg and exclaimed, "*Yes*! The little pregnant girl that Tim Krooguh, Djahn Staiklee's boy, took. I rode that raid with him and . . . damn! She was lifted from this very place, from Three-House!"

EPILOGUE

For long years after that great gathering, roving riders from Clan Krooguh rode the prairies and the high plains, the deserts of the south and the frozen-earth regions of the far north searching for, if not Behtiloo herself, at least some trace of her, some memory of her recent passing. But at last the search was given up as useless by Clan Krooguh.

But still, it is whispered in the felt yurts and the hair tents of the Horseclans Kindred, *she rides*.

On cloudless nights when the silver moon floats over the lowing herds, when boys and girls yet too young for war training hunch in their saddles and hug themselves for warmth, mindspeaking each other and the prairiecats who help them to guard against wolves and bears and lions, on such still nights, they sometimes see her on the horizon or upon the crest of a ridge—an old clanswoman on her horse, trailed by her faithful prairiecat. Then they straighten in their saddles, forgetting their drowsiness and the cold, and raise their spears in salute to her. To old Behtiloo Hansuhn of Krooguh, accompanied by the prairiecat Blackback, riding still to rouse the Horseclans and remind all Kindred of the value of honor.

ABOUT THE AUTHOR

ROBERT ADAMS lives in Seminole County, Florida. Like the characters in his books, he is partial to fencing and fancy swordplay, hunting and riding, good food and drink. At one time Robert could be found slaving over a hot forge, making a new sword or busily reconstructing a historically accurate military costume, but, unfortunately, he no longer has time for this as he's far too busy writing.

Science Fiction from SIGNET

SIGNET Science Fiction You'll Enjoy

**Buy them at your local
bookstore or use coupon
on next page for ordering.**

More SIGNET Books by Robert A. Heinlein